Praise for

The Red Dog Conspiracy

"This was the first steampunk book that I've read that I actually really loved."

— GABBY'S HONEST BOOK REVIEWS

"... the political intrigue in this story is unrivaled ..."

— TANGO WITH TEXT

"Patricia Loofbourrow has created a world of family intrigue combined with feuding households across the four quadrants of Bridges."

— JUNE LORRAINE ROBERTS, Murder In Common

"This is definitely noir, including the traditional breaking of the narrative timeline. People are doing nasty things for sometimes known, and sometimes not yet uncovered, reasons. It's what makes the world turn for the Families, who are in an uneasy alliance with shifting loyalties, cease fires, and outright aggression."

— MARGARET FISK, Tales To Tide You Over

"... a good read for anyone who likes mystery and suspense mixed with science fiction."

— IVORY MORTON, Beautyful Word

"Do yourself a favor and read this .... You will enjoy."

— GERALD CHAMBERS

For more reviews, visit JacqOfSpades.com

The Ace Of Clubs

Part 3 of the Red Dog Conspiracy

Patricia Loofbourrow

This one is for me.

The Witness

A glittering dome sat on a barren plain. Underneath this vast structure, four mighty rivers traveled to its center, passing hills, fields, forests, and a grand city.

Far in the northeast quadrant amid an expanse of wheat, an enormous stained glass building stood shattered. An army of workers cleared the wreckage around its frame. Nearby, immense hot-air ships rose to, passed through, and descended before the watchful gaze of the Aperture high in the dome's side.

Far in the southeast quadrant, mist covered a country road. A dozen black carriages headed towards the city.

I sat locked inside the third carriage. Pale shapes of trees stood beyond the morning fog.

I understood better now why David Bryce refused to speak.

For a month I had stayed at the Spadros Country House — on doctor's orders. Yet I hadn't spent the past month simply sitting in the sun and walking the gardens. I had put a great deal of thought into the events of this current year, most notably Marja's death.

My husband Tony sat to my right on the bench seat, holding up a newspaper, the breeze ruffling his straight black hair.

Master Blaze Rainbow (who I thought of by the name I knew him first as, Morton) sat on the bench seat across from me, his brown Derby hat in his lap. His fingers drummed on the crown of his hat, then he took out his brass pocket watch and wound it.

Tony's first cousin, Master Ten Hogan (who the men called Sawbuck), sat across from Tony. He appeared stoic and resigned, as if he had some unpleasant and unwanted task ahead.

Between me and Tony: my little white and gray bird, perched inside a white rectangular cage bridging the gap between the bench seats.

I suppose someone thought bringing the bird with us to our Country House would improve my spirits. But I had Tony buy it for me when we married, so I would never forget I lived in a cage.

One of Tony's men rode past the window outside, his pistol in its holster.

My bird chirped in alarm, flitting about as if anxious to be anywhere else.

I lay my hand on the top of the cage, heart pounding. "Shhh. All is well."

Tony smiled at it, his dark blue eyes amused, before turning his newspaper to the next page.

Marja helped raise me. She'd always been kind, especially to my childhood friends Joseph and Josephine Kerr.

Marja treated Josie as her own daughter: bringing her food, finding shoes for her, combing her hair. When Polansky Kerr IV brought his grandchildren to Hart quadrant, Marja accompanied them as their housekeeper.

But something went wrong between them: they sent Marja to work for Josie's uncle in Spadros quadrant. A few weeks later, Marja sent me a note saying "they" planned to kill my mother. Her note never said who or why. The night I went to meet with Marja to learn more, Sawbuck and I found her lying on the sidewalk: shot, dying.

My little bird fluttered around its cage; tiny feathers flew everywhere. I peered at it. "Might we administer a sedative? It seems so agitated."

Tony shook his head. "The doctor said the bird's too small for dosing — an attempt might harm it more than its distress." He glanced out of the window. "We should be home soon."

My bird perched, its tiny chest heaving.

One day I'll fly far from here.

My eyes burned at the sudden memory. I put my arm around

the end of the cage. "All will be well."

Yet we traveled from one prison to another.

I had to learn who killed Marja. I had to get me and my Ma out of Bridges before someone killed us too. Frank Pagliacci and Jack Diamond had to pay for what they did to me, David Bryce, his family, my informants, and Tony.

But locked in that carriage, my captors surrounding it, there seemed no way to achieve any of those things.

The headline on the front page of Tony's paper read:

CORONER'S INQUEST

Zeppelin Explosion Investigation:

Clubbs Refuse Federal Oversight

The headline made perfect sense. I could see no reason to let the Feds into Bridges. This inquest seemed merely a way to placate the city — and the Traveler's Federation — until the Clubb Family disposed of the culprits.

I peered at the newspaper, but with the breeze moving the page, I couldn't read the date. "What day is it?"

"The fifteenth of April," Sawbuck said, in a morose tone.

"Tuesday," Morton said, at the same time.

Tony seemed not to notice my question.

"Mr. Spadros, what news interests you so?"

Tony turned his head towards me slowly, his eyes fixed on the page, then looked at me. "It lists who must appear as witnesses before the inquest." He glanced at the newspaper. "It lists half the city!"

Morton said, "A public examination of gentlemen?"

Tony nodded. "The District Attorney demanded it."

Morton frowned. "It's unseemly."

Tony pursed his lips. "I agree." He peered at the paper. "The affair looks to go on for some time." He shook the paper, folded it to present one page. "This article mentions Dame Anastasia —"

Dame Anastasia Louis had been one of my closest friends amongst the quadrant-folk of Bridges. Now she was dead. Murdered, I suspected, by Frank Pagliacci and his Red Dog Gang.

"— and her swindle of the city, but also, her accomplices."

I leaned forward. "Accomplices?" Perhaps I might learn who gave her the bomb which killed her.

"Well, her 'appraisers'," Tony said. "She coached these men to claim her jewels were worth much more than their actual value in return for a cut of the profits. Every one of them has vanished. Their families are understandably distraught."

Vanished? "This is incredible. How many were there?"

Tony examined the paper. "Over twenty."

I chuckled in spite of myself. "An Oh-one for certain."

Sawbuck snickered.

Tony and Morton stared at us both.

"I don't understand," Tony said.

Of course he wouldn't! "It's something we did in the Pot. When I was a child. A saying." I glanced at Morton, then Tony. "I'm sure it wouldn't interest you."

"Not at all," Morton said. "The Pot's of special interest."

Tony's eyes widened. "Is that so?"

"Indeed," Morton said to Tony, "I've studied it for many years. The Pot was wealthy and beautiful before the Coup." He shook his head. "A pity." He said to me, "What is this 'Oh-one'?"

Sawbuck said, "Mum, that's not something —"

Tony said, "Hush, Ten, let her talk."

Sawbuck frowned, but said nothing.

I stuck out my hand, the index and thumb together, the middle extended, the rest curled under. "Oh-one. You see? It means ..." Absolutely fucked is what it meant, but Sawbuck was right: I probably shouldn't say that in front of fine gentlemen. "... real trouble: everyone for himself. It means run, and no one stop for anyone else, because otherwise we might all die."

Tony blinked. "And have you seen this signal used?"

I chuckled. "Once or twice. Usually there's a meet-up place set beforehand, so you know where to go."

Tony said, "So assuming they're not dead, we might find them, if we find their meet-up."

"It's been over a month," Morton said. "Chances are they've met and gone their separate ways." He frowned. "But if their families haven't heard from them —"

"So they claim," Sawbuck said.

"True," said Morton. "But I'd be surprised if any meet-up hasn't happened already."

Tony sighed. "I hoped we might have something, some witness or evidence to give to the inquest, if only to offer assistance." Tony turned to me. "I hope this doesn't distress you."

I shrugged. The inquest didn't appear to be my concern.

The wind gusted in through the open window; my bird chirped and fluttered around the cage.

I rested my hand on the bars. "Shh, be still."

My mind had gone round and round this past month, yet I had found few answers.

I wanted — no, needed — to get me and Ma out of Bridges. But I couldn't think of how.

I didn't have enough money for one zeppelin ticket, let alone two. Since the explosion, I was constantly watched, so I couldn't take new cases. The Traveler's Federation, outraged over their craft's destruction, had taken over gate and cargo security in the zeppelin station. Everything was being searched, down to the smallest handbag. So there was no longer even a way to be smuggled out.

But if I had the tickets in my hand, I couldn't leave without learning who shot Marja. She was family, and when I found the scoundrel who killed her, he would die.

I had few tangible clues: her note of warning (which I burned) and a scrap of paper in her dying hand which I couldn't read. But she sent the warning from a produce distribution center in Spadros quadrant owned by the Clubb syndicate.

How dare the Clubb Family own a building in Spadros quadrant? Why did Roy Spadros allow it? The idea revolted me.

Morton said, "Was Dame Anastasia as bad a woman as they make her out to be?"

"You would have liked her," I said. "She was old, yet beautiful — with a wicked past."

Morton was in his mid-thirties, and laughed like a man who'd seen more of the world than he liked. "As have we all."

I considered her last letter: *I truly am fond of you, and I wish you well.* "But I'd like to think she meant us no harm."

Tony seemed quite interested in the inquest, and I wondered why. "Who's to appear? Will we be expected to attend?" I didn't particularly want to go — I felt sure it would be in some dank court hall on Market Center — but it seemed best to prepare.

Tony's face turned grim. "You're the key witness."

My bird chirped and fluttered about its cage.

"**I**? For what possible reason?"

Tony folded his newspaper and set it aside. "This is one matter I wished to discuss, since you finally seem to be improving. And since you and Master Rainbow inexplicably appeared at the zeppelin station — in defiance of my father's wishes — as the explosion took place. But up to now, neither of you would speak of it."

Morton grimaced, glancing away.

I feared what Tony might do to Morton to uncover the truth, always feeling relieved when I saw Morton unharmed. "I told you what happened." I'd told Tony that we changed plans at the last minute, going to the zeppelin station to see Anastasia off. A bit unbelievable, given Gardena Diamond's attitude towards the woman, but the best I could come up with.

Tony said, "What I know is you received a letter. In the midst of your trip to the Diamond Women's Club, you insisted on going to the zeppelin station."

"Yet your men forced me to go to Diamond quadrant."

"They took you where I told them to. We had strict orders not to go into Clubb quadrant until the Celebration. My father didn't want the Spadros Family entangled in this."

"So he knew this would happen?"

Tony shook his head. "All we had was rumor. You arrived at the Diamond Women's Club just before one. The attendants at Gate 19 testified you arrived at the gate as the zeppelin left dock, which was half past three. Where were you the rest of the time?"

Morton didn't move.

"We were delayed," I said.

"By what?"

I faced him. "There was a great deal of traffic."

"Traffic," Tony said. "You were in traffic, at one in the afternoon, for two and a half hours? Also, the station guard testified that he greeted you — and a man fitting Master Rainbow's description — at the train station entryway. Yet you tell me the Diamonds brought you by carriage, presumably through the front gate. Which is it?"

Morton and I exchanged an alarmed glance. They had the station guard examined? I recalled the man Morton gave his newspaper to, who directed us to the gate. What reason would they have to question him?

"And so," Tony said, "therein lies the problem. Neither of you will speak. I have need of Master Rainbow — "

Why would Tony have so much need of Morton?

" — so I have not induced him to break his oath — "

Oath? I glanced at Morton, surprised, and he nodded to me.

Very clever, Master Rainbow.

" — and the doctor has been concerned enough about your condition that I haven't pressed you. But the board of inquest will ask the same, and any misspoken word could be used against us. I must learn the truth if I'm to help."

I frowned at him. "Why should I have need of help?"

Tony's eyes widened. "Have you ever been to an inquest? A trial? Court proceedings of any kind?"

"Why, no." No member of the Pot would be brought to trial or stand as witness. We'd either be shot in the street, or deemed unreliable to give evidence in crimes of any magnitude.

"These are serious matters," Tony said. "We'll meet with our attorneys to determine how to answer. But the most important thing is to determine the full truth of the matter." He leaned back. "Then we can decide how to play it. We can't just go in and speak; the words we use might be twisted any number of ways."

"I don't understand."

Sawbuck stirred. "It's open court, mum. The press, the rabble, anyone who wishes to will be present. A stray word, turned into some slogan, and we could have a mob at our door. I don't mean to alarm you — it's just the truth." He lapsed into a glum demeanor, staring out of the window.

"Yes," Tony said, "Ten — as usual — has said it best. So we must plan our course of action before we appear." He leaned against the door frame, closing his eyes.

I felt relieved that he seemed to have forgotten his original line of questioning. Or wasn't willing to speak of it further.

My little bird chirped, but seemed less distraught.

How could I tell Tony what happened? How could I relate my trip with Gardena Diamond to meet her blackmailer without revealing her role in her grandfather's death?

Revealing the contents of Dame Anastasia's letter, why I defied him and his father, disguised myself, and evaded his men, would reveal a great many things: my detective business, Anastasia's relationship with Frank Pagliacci, how I learned about their scam.

If I told Tony that Morton and I rushed to the zeppelin station on the train as the police searched for us with pistols drawn ...

No. How could I tell Tony about any of it? Yet I felt Sawbuck's gaze, and realized there was much **he** hadn't revealed either. For example, that I wasn't in my bed — as Tony believed — the night of Marja's murder.

How long would it be before someone squealed?

I leaned against the carriage wall, heart pounding. The situation was getting out of control.

"I have other ways of learning the truth, Jacqui," Tony said, "but I'd rather hear it from you."

The Return

As we approached Spadros Manor, the courtyard bell rang, the signal for the men guarding the grounds to assemble.

Our butler John Pearson greeted the carriage as we arrived. "Welcome home, mum."

His brown hair seemed a bit thinner than usual, and he looked tired. "Thank you, Pearson."

My lady's maid Amelia rode with her husband Peter and their daughters, and rushed to my side as soon as she alighted. "Here, mum, I'll take you to your room and get you changed." She helped me down the walkway, up the white stone stairs, across our wide porch.

Pearson moved past us to open the door. "It's good to see you improved, mum. I've placed your post in a box on the desk in your study. Would you prefer it brought to your rooms?"

"Yes, thank you."

Tony's — or rather, his father Roy's men assigned to him — gathered near Tony out at the curb.

Pearson bowed as Amelia and I turned towards the sweeping curved stair. Most of the other servants had returned here after our outing last month. They stood lined up in the hall, bowing or curtsying to me as we passed.

Ten year old Pip seemed to have matured in the month we'd been gone, nodding gravely when I smiled at him. Though they'd been apart for almost a month, he didn't so much as glance at his mother Amelia, nor she at him.

Our chef Monsieur, a huge, impeccably dressed man, stood beside Anne, our new Mistress of Kitchens. Then the others ... we had several dozen in all.

The house, a former scientific station turned "manor," was all white — walls, ceilings, and doors — with the floor tiled an ugly pale gray. My bedroom, closets, and bath were the same white and gray, with bedding and cushions of an insipid pale blue.

Nobody had ever cared what I liked or wanted here. Since I couldn't escape, I endured it, as I endured everything else. I took a deep breath and let it out, trying to keep my anger in check as Amelia undressed me.

Having a servant do everything for you might sound glamorous. But this card had two sides; I craved being allowed to do what I wanted without eyes on me night and day.

I stepped out of my petticoats. "Is someone tending to my bird? It seemed distressed."

"Yes, mum," Amelia said, then untied my corset.

I disliked wearing a corset, and always felt relieved when it was removed. Amelia put my black house dress (for mourning a disaster or the death of a friend) over my head just in time: a knock came at the door.

I smiled at Amelia's annoyance. "Come in."

Pearson carried a large box overflowing with mail and set it on the chair closest to him next to my tea-table.

"Where's Honor?" It was my day footman Skip Honor's job to carry and fetch things for us during the day while at home.

"He's tending to something, mum," Pearson said, then left, closing the door behind him.

What could he possibly be tending to?

I let Amelia unlace my boots, pull off my stockings, put on soft black house shoes. I sometimes imagined myself a store mannequin, dressed and undressed, then set to smile and pose.

Every task had a different outfit a "proper lady" wore. My closets overflowed with dresses for every imaginable circumstance. My dressmaker Madame Biltcliffe made my seasonal outfits. But new outfits would appear, sent from Roy and Molly to make sure I was presentable.

It seems sad and silly, looking back on it, but that was my life.

Once dressed, my thick curls were combed out, sprayed with water, and redone into a style suitable for what I wore. Even though I saw nothing wrong with my hair, when I struggled, raged, or protested, it inevitably brought a rebuke — or worse — from Tony's father Roy. I might be lady of the house and married to the Spadros Family heir, but Roy Spadros still ruled here.

I gazed into the mirror. Amelia had braided my hair into an intricate array, weaving in fresh jasmine. "This looks lovely, Amelia, thank you."

She smiled sadly. "It's good to see you looking better, mum." Her nose reddened. "I can't imagine the horrors you saw."

Amelia never mentioned my refusal to speak or the zeppelin disaster until now. "That's very kind of you."

In truth, the zeppelin bombing, the shattering of the station's ancient stained glass-work, even the death and destruction around me in its aftermath, paled in comparison to the deaths of my friends ...

"One day I'll fly far from here. I want to travel the world."

Amelia rushed for a handkerchief. "I'm so sorry, mum, here, you don't want to spoil your makeup." She dropped her hands to her sides, shoulders drooping. "Please forgive me, mum ... I never meant to bring you grief."

Grief. I smiled in spite of how I felt, remembering a bench, an empty street, a little boy, and a long time of weeping for us both.

I longed to see David Bryce again. He needed to know I hadn't abandoned him. I clasped her hand in both of mine, remembering how at peace I felt after I wept that day. "Grief is the only good thing there is, when all is done."

Amelia didn't speak for a bit. "Wise words for one so young."

Amelia had experienced as much grief as I, if not more. I dabbed at my eyes, blew my nose. Then I forced myself to smile for her sake. "Let's tackle Pearson's mountain."

Amelia chuckled at that, then helped me sort it all. Well-wishes on cards from ladies who barely veiled their disdain for me, yet feared the Spadros Family's displeasure if seen to be silent. Copies of the Golden Bridges, a disreputable tabloid. A few notes from friends. I put the notes in my pocket to read later.

I set Amelia to opening the first stack of mail, then, amused, put the newspapers in a pile by my tea-table. Tony forbade anyone to give me a newspaper, read the news aloud, or even leave a paper lying about. I suppose he thought information about the disaster would make my "condition" worse. So most of my information came from servants' whispers.

I wanted news, but I could read old tabloids any time.

Pearson's heavy tread returned. "Luncheon is ready, mum. Would you like it brought to your room?"

"No, I'll come down. Thank you." In spite of our long journey, I felt better. And despite all its faults, it felt good to return home.

The Invitation

Amelia led me down the stairs, then along the bottom part of the "U"-shaped building, then right to the dining room.

Morton sat near the end of the dining room table closest to us, leaning forward, his elbows on the table. Tony sat across from him, holding a letter. The way Tony sat made him look so defeated and alone that I felt ashamed for causing him turmoil.

Our month-long "vacation" at the Country House had contained little rest. Most days, grief consumed my thoughts. Grief for Anastasia, for Marja, and for all the others now lost.

Tony's days were filled with meetings, his men arriving and departing well into the night. His slumber had been much the same as mine, waking in a sweat, or in shouts of alarm, and he would never say why. But he never asked for his husband's prerogative, and for that I felt grateful.

When Tony saw us, he asked Pearson to move luncheon to the veranda.

My little bird seemed happier in its big white wrought iron cage, and it chirped when I came outside. Morton, wearing a brown wool jacket and tan pants, followed at a distance, taking a seat across from Tony, leaving a chair between himself and me.

Our housekeeper Jane Pearson was busily straightening the steaming trays. Her round face was red, a lock of graying blonde hair plastered to its side.

Her daughter Mary began setting the table. "That little thing gave us no end of trouble."

"Oh?" I said.

Jane frowned at Mary. "The missus doesn't need to concern herself with that."

"No, it's fine." I turned to Mary. "What happened?"

Pearson came to the table. "Your bird got loose, mum. Took Honor by surprise and flew off a bit. It took some doing to catch it, but it's back safe, no worries."

I laughed, turning to my bird. "Good for you!"

Mary approached with some trepidation and curtsied. "Pork potato hash, spring peas, mint cake, mum."

"Very good, Mary, thank you."

She curtsied, gave her parents a glance, then brought the filled plates to us. I poured Tony, Morton, and myself some tea.

Tony seemed to relax when I did that, and we began to eat, the servants retreating to a discreet distance.

"I'm glad you feel well enough to join us," Tony said.

"Thank you." I hoped we wouldn't continue our earlier conversation. There was nothing I might add, and the matter might become heated if Tony were to agitate himself on the topic.

Morton said, "Your butler brought you a mountain of post!"

"Yes," I said. "Mostly cards, but I do have some notes yet unopened." I paged through them ... "One from Jon —"

I hadn't seen Jonathan Diamond since Queen's Day dinner two months ago. But he'd sent a note to the Spadros Country House twice a week like clockwork.

"Oh?" Tony said. "I'm surprised he knew to send it here rather than the Country House."

Of course Jon knew what went on in my life. In light of what he'd said in the past, Jon must have spies near the houses surrounding us. But that knowledge was a comfort to me.

"How's he feeling?" Tony said.

"'Much improved,' he says. He'll call when we're 'at home'."

In Bridges, being "at home" simply meant you wanted and were able to receive company; it had nothing to do with whether you were at the house. I returned Jon's note to my pocket and took up the next. "Here's a note from Gardena —"

Tony's jaw tightened, but he said nothing.

At the time, I didn't know what went on between Mr. Anthony Spadros and Miss Gardena Diamond (Jon's sister). But Gardena and Tony had a long history of animosity, particularly on her part, although at times Tony appeared to be in love with her.

Tony blamed Gardena for my presence at the zeppelin station during the explosion, even though I told him going there was my idea. Since then, he became angry whenever her name was mentioned. So I didn't open the letter, but set it hastily aside.

"— and one from Madame Biltcliffe!"

My dear Mrs. Spadros —

Madame Marie Biltcliffe sends her compliments and hopes to have the pleasure of your company for tea on Thursday, April Seventeenth.

This was a novelty. I wondered what it might mean.

"Perhaps Madame would like to make your acquaintance," Tony said, "aside from simply being your dressmaker" ... and it was then I realized I had spoken aloud.

"Of course," I said, cheeks burning. "I'd be happy to take tea with her."

"Only if you feel well enough," Tony said. "There's no obligation for you to do anything whilst in mourning."

I nodded. He had to explain it to me, as ... well, in the Pot, people died every day. If one went about all this ritual every time someone died, nothing would get done.

Madame let me use my visits to her shop as a cover. Tony would believe me to be there when I was actually on a case. Perhaps I'd finally be able to visit David Bryce. "I can send a note if I don't feel well. What will you do with yourself?"

Tony shrugged, his eyes on his plate. "I've been away from the Business far too long. I have more than enough work to do."

I took a sip of tea. "I noticed you also received mail."

Tony gave a bitter snort. "Indeed." He pulled an invitation from his breast pocket: cream stationery edged in gold, the Clubb Family's symbol upon the envelope flap.

Mr. and Mrs. Alexander Clubb present their compliments to Mr. and Mrs. Anthony Spadros and request the honor of their company at the launching of their newest yacht, the *Ace of Clubbs*, on the Twenty-First of April next.

Northwest Quadrant Marina

R. S. V. P.

"This is in six days!" To send a major invitation less than three weeks in advance was exceedingly rude.

"My sincerest apologies, mum," Pearson said. "It was sent a month ago, but here, and never forwarded. In the confusion it was lost until now." He straightened. "I take full responsibility."

I shrugged. It didn't matter. "The *Ace of Clubbs*?" To place the name of a Holy Card on an inanimate object, no matter how grand, bordered on blasphemy. From what I'd seen of the Clubb Family so far, though, I shouldn't have been surprised.

"Indeed," Tony said bitterly. "One of their plots come to hatch at last."

Morton said nothing, focused as he was on his luncheon.

"Will we attend?" I never knew which events we could miss and which were vital. And this invitation seemed to dismay him.

Tony rested his elbows on the table, his head in his hands, murmuring, "What would my grandfather have done?"

He sat like this for a long moment, then straightened, facing me. "Yes, we'll attend. Invitations to these launchings aren't given lightly. All the other Families will be represented, and we can't be seen to slight the Clubbs, not now."

The Departure

My gaze flickered to Morton. Should Tony have said that in front of him? We still didn't know where his loyalties lay.

The day Gardena asked for help with her blackmailer, she told me: *Cesare says the Clubbs are the most dangerous Family in the city, much too dangerous to ally with.*

Gardena's oldest brother was a disagreeable fellow, yet possessed keen insight. What did we know about the Clubbs?

Footsteps headed our way. Inventor Maxim Call, a brown, wiry old man with piercing blue eyes, strode out wearing a dusty tweed jacket, several white-clad Apprentices in his wake.

We immediately rose; the men bowed.

I curtsied low. "Would you like tea, sir?"

Maxim Call considered the matter. "A cup would do." He turned to his Apprentices. "Wait with the carriages." He sat between Tony and Morton, across from me.

I poured his cup, then returned to my seat.

"To what do we owe the honor of your visit, sir?" Tony said.

Inventor Call blew on his tea, then took a sip. "My work's done here. There's nothing more we can do for your Magma Steam Generator. We've searched thoroughly — the controls to it must be in another piling. We've located a piling in Spadros quadrant and are moving to investigate."

Tony's mouth hung open. "You're leaving?"

"Some of my Apprentices will stay in the workshop. I'll have the man in charge introduce himself. But," he wagged a finger, "they'll only stay until their work's completed. I left instructions with your butler as to where we'll be and what we'll need."

Tony paused for a long moment. "There's something you should be aware of."

The Inventor was in the midst of drinking. "Oh?"

"A group called the Red Dogs has attacked several Families, ranging from theft to violence. I've even been assaulted." Tony hesitated. "I can't guarantee your safety should you leave."

"No one would dare attack us!" He chuckled, patting Tony's arm. "I appreciate your concern, dear boy. But I don't order my affairs according to the whims of ruffians. Neither should you." He drained his cup then rose, as did we all. "Good day."

With that, he turned back inside.

"Wait," Tony said. "What about my mechanical computer?"

Inventor Call stopped in the middle of the dining room, then spoke to Tony as if he were a child. "It's a fine idea. Yet how would you operate it without power?" He shook his head. "Finding the controls to the Generators takes precedence over everything. I have a man working on your gadget. But my job lies elsewhere." He rounded the corner and was gone.

Tony sat heavily, shock on his face. "Maxim Call has been in Spadros Manor since I was a boy."

Morton said, "What's wrong with your Steam Generator?"

Tony and I exchanged a glance. If Maxim Call knew about this, the other Inventors did too. But if the public learned Bridges neared standstill because we couldn't fix our own Generators, then the Feds might seize the city, claiming mismanagement.

I didn't know how much Morton knew. Obviously, Tony had such a binding deal with Morton that he trusted him, even though Morton refused to reveal what happened the day of the explosion. Tony had beaten our old Dr. Salmon — who'd been in the Family for generations — for a similar offense.

"He claims it needs repair," Tony said. "But he's got the situation under control."

"That's good to hear," Morton said. "An entirely mechanical city such as this — without power — would be unlivable."

I pictured the rivers stagnant, the streetlights dark, the trains silent, the Aperture unable to open, and I shuddered.

The Fear

The rest of the day, Amelia and I catalogued the notes I received. Jane had ordered thank you cards edged in black (for replying to notes of sympathy). After tea, I spent an hour signing them for Amelia to address and send.

Exhausted, I took dinner in my room, Tony at my side. We ate in silence, but gradually my strength returned. "Do we need to fear this invitation from the Clubbs?"

That sent Tony into a long period of motionless staring at his plate. "I don't know," he said at last. "But I fear it nonetheless."

"At the Grand Ball, didn't they invite us to visit?" Mrs. Clubb invited us to stay a whole week at Clubb Manor. We'd never been invited there before, which is why the comment marked itself so firmly in my mind. But the visit never occurred.

Tony nodded. "Something happened." He drained his glass. "I fear they disliked my answer to Lance on Queen's Day."

"What's it to be named?"

Lance Clubb leaned towards me with a wry smile. "They haven't decided yet. We're considering the Asking Bid."

At the time, it seemed he asked us to declare our allegiances. A test, if you will.

I let out a breath, placed my hand on his. "I didn't know how to answer. Why approach us in front of guests?"

"Why approach us at all? As if I have any say in who the

Family allies with." Tony put down his fork. "My father is still Patriarch, and probably will be long after we're gone."

I chuckled at that.

"But perhaps they have approached my father," Tony said.

This startled me. "They suspect our Family's divided."

"And now they know." Tony shook his head. "Whatever possessed me to name the Harts? My father hates Charles Hart as fiercely as magma hates rock — he wishes nothing less than his utter destruction."

"But why does he hate him? Do you know?"

Tony held my hand in both of his, kissing it with a desperate intensity. "No, and it frightens me." He squeezed his eyes shut. "Did you know he started the Bloody Year?"

Thousands died — long before either of us were born — as Family slaughtered Family. "He did?"

Tony nodded, his eyes still closed. "And he was my age." He peered at me. "Almost exactly. I don't understand anything about him. Yet now I'm sure he feels I oppose him. What might a man like that do when taken by such hate?"

* * *

Later, after the servants undressed us, Tony came to me.

I knew what Tony would do and say; back then, it seemed impossible for him to hide his feelings from me.

"Let's lie down and love each other, as we used to before all this tragedy." He reached up to touch my face, then slid his hand behind my neck and kissed me.

I didn't love Tony, except sometimes as a brother. But his father Roy put a gun to my head before we were married and told me that if Tony learned this, he would kill me.

Tony put his arms around me, sliding them up and down my back as we kissed, his cock hard against the front of my body.

If I thought about it too much it made my skin crawl.

I must not weep. I had to stop the roiling of my stomach.

I can do this, I thought, as I did almost every night.

My mother trained me in her brothel beside the other girls, in everything but the act itself. That had been forbidden me by my mother's patron, who I secretly called the Masked Man because of the dark brown leather mask he wore showing only his eyes.

I was never allowed to touch a man, or even to be in the room when others did, always observing in darkness behind sheer curtains. What fault did the Masked Man find in me to forbid me to take my place with the other women?

Maybe he recognized my inability to put aside my personal wishes and fuck a man I didn't desire.

The thought startled me. Tony said, "What is it?"

Oh, gods, he knows something isn't right. I took a deep breath. "I felt off-balance." I forced myself to giggle. "That's all."

Tony laughed. "Let's lie down then, before we fall over."

We lay down. Tony drew the covers over me, slid his arm under my neck, caressed my face.

My husband was an ordinary-looking man, but the way he gazed at me ... it made me sad. Yes, he was in the Family, but he wasn't evil: he deserved so much better than this pretense.

Perhaps he saw my sadness, because he said, "Your life has been very hard, I see that now. When you spoke about being put in such danger as a small girl ... it troubled me."

I shrugged. "What does it matter? All that is past."

He reached over to smooth my hair. "It matters because it's part of you. We've been in each other's lives ten years, married almost four, yet I never knew this. It makes me wonder what else I don't know." He smiled in a free, relaxed manner, and in that instant he reminded me of the man I loved, Joseph Kerr. "I want to know everything about you, Jacqui. Everything. I love you."

Oh no. The last thing I wanted was for him to start asking questions, especially about my past. My mind raced, searching for something to divert this line of thought.

And I had an idea.

I hated it. It was so dishonest. And I feared what he might say. Would he think I was too forward? Would he rebuke me? Men here were so different than in the Pot; for a woman here even to smile might be improper, depending on the circumstances.

But I had to do something.

I can do this. "Let's talk of that later." I snuggled closer, sliding my trembling hand on his cock. He gasped as I stroked his skin, his body stiffening to my touch.

He closed his eyes, and a deep moan came forth I had never heard him make before. "Oh, Jacqui."

It seemed, at least for a time, that all discussion was forgotten.

* * *

The intersection was grimy, dark, cold. I was small and frightened.

A reeking hand grabbed my arm. I couldn't get away. I couldn't get away! "If she goes, I go with her."

My best friend Air stared at Peedro Sluff in horror. "No!" He ran towards us brandishing a broken bottle. "Leave her alone!"

Peedro's gun rose, and he shot Air.

The light left Air's eyes as they stared into mine. The color left his face, and his little body collapsed into the spray of his own blood.

I stood in the stairwell in Jack's factory. Bodies lay everywhere. Losing balance, I fell forward onto Air's chest. His blood, welling up through his shirt, covered my hands.

Stephen, Herbert, Marja, and Anastasia lay crumpled around me.

Air opened his eyes. "We loved you, Jacqui. Why did you kill us?"

Tony held me. "I'm here, my love. You're safe."

Tony's cousin Blitz Spadros, our night footman, opened the door, candle in hand. "Another dream?

Embarrassment flooded over me. I sobbed, "I'm sorry."

Blitz smiled. "No trouble at all, mum. Good night."

Tony rocked me as I clung to him, and eventually he slept. But I did not.

The Leader

The next morning, Amelia came in with my mail and — finally — the newspaper! To my surprise, the front read:

The Bridges Daily

Editor: Mr. Paul Blackberry

Good for him, I thought. I'd known Mr. Blackberry since I was a small girl, back when he was a photographer. Prior to becoming editor, he'd been one of my informants; his position at the Clubb desk gave him access to all kinds of information.

The Spadros Family murdered the former editor, Mr. Acol Durak, after he let articles supporting Anastasia's fraud and an editorial maligning the Families pass his inspection.

Killing Mr. Durak was so unnecessary, I thought. The man was grieving his wife —

At that instant, I recalled Mr. Blackberry's words: *suicidal, if you ask me.*

And I realized Mr. Durak worked with Dame Anastasia and Frank — and perhaps even allowed Mr. Pike's editorial to pass — in hopes the Families would kill him.

I didn't understand it. Even during my worst days after being sold to the Spadros Family, I never considered taking my own life.

Under Mr. Blackberry's guidance, the paper had changed little. The purpose of the *Bridges Daily* was to promote the views of the Families, rather than to provide any real news. However, it devoted a whole section to the inquest — those scheduled to appear that day and a summary of the previous day's testimony.

The financial news was bleak. Listings for sales of production equipment, buildings, and businesses spanned an entire page. A list of bankruptcy proceedings on the back page left me shocked.

That many speculated on Dame Anastasia's "miracle" gems?

And we had invited her into our home. In their view, we — everyone at my dinner — were suspected collaborators.

* * *

At breakfast, Tony seemed much happier. He went off to tend to the Business after the morning meeting with the staff, and I went to my study.

I wrote to Jon, informing him we arrived safely. Then I opened Gardena's note, which was from her Country House:

> My dear Mrs. Spadros —
>
> I'm so glad to hear you're feeling improved. Jon and I will visit as soon as we can. We both are eager to see you again, and —

Oh, dear, I thought. Tony will **not** be happy to find her here. I wrote in return:

> Dearest Gardena —
>
> Thank you so kindly for your letter. I hope you and your family are well.
>
> I'm afraid Mr. Spadros is in poor humor at present. It might be best if Jon visited alone.
>
> I'm sorry to be the bearer of such bad news. I remain hopeful that in time my husband's disposition will improve.
>
> I'm feeling quite well. I miss seeing you and look forward to visiting together in the future.

The clock struck eleven. I put the pen down, gazing out of the window. Tony blamed Gardena for my being at the station because I told him she brought me there.

But what else could I have said? That I went into Clubb quadrant on my own, uninvited, in direct defiance of orders from Roy Spadros?

Roy hadn't contacted us about any of it. I couldn't imagine Tony's father reacting in any other way than fury.

Since I had little control over this, I lit a cigarette, taking a drag, then poured a glass of bourbon from the bottle I kept on my sideboard. It was well past time to plan my investigations.

It seemed unlikely that the perpetrators of this year's events — robberies, kidnappings, murders, and bombings — plotted and executed these on their own. In my estimation, Frank Pagliacci — while evidently charismatic — was neither skilled nor intelligent enough. Jack Diamond, Jonathan's mad twin brother — though rich and powerful — wasn't sane (by all accounts) for long enough. Thus, this team had a leader yet unseen who directed Frank Pagliacci and Jack Diamond to carry out these crimes.

This man had significant personal power to persuade two such men to do his bidding. He had tremendous means to afford to hire so many men to assist them. He needed remarkable mental skill to plan and implement a conspiracy of this magnitude. And we still didn't know how far the conspiracy went, or even the man's true motivations.

Whoever their leader was, he frightened me.

Three women assisted these men: the rogue Federal Agent Zia Cashout, Dame Anastasia Louis (now dead), and a black-haired woman named Birdie.

What they'd accomplished so far was to take the name and markings of the Red Dogs children's street gang, and frame this gang for the crimes. They then accessed the Hart and Spadros Family funds through forged invoices, in order to do ... what?

If bombing the zeppelin was their goal, there would have been ultimatums, declarations of their intentions, or proclamations of who they were and what they accomplished. Yet no one had said anything of the sort, which suggested the bombing was merely a means to an end.

But what did the murder of hundreds gain them?

I lit another cigarette from the stump of the first, then poured another glass of bourbon.

None of the Families had a motive to bomb the zeppelin, especially on the day of the Celebration. In fact, it was an affront, to the Clubbs in particular.

Could this madness be led by a disgruntled aristocrat? An heir of one of the old families who escaped the Pot before the overthrow of the Kerr Dynasty? That seemed an avenue worth investigating, although I wasn't sure how.

With Anastasia gone, my door to them had closed. Certainly, they were cordial, at least in public. But in the past, whenever I'd called, they'd suddenly be "not at home."

I suppose inviting a Pot rag into your home — especially a "Family pet," as one called me — was too much for these women.

I swirled the bourbon in my glass. Not all of the Red Dogs' purchases using our money had been accounted for. For example, why were they buying black cloth? And what did they buy using the Hart Family's money?

I wrote letters to my contacts, asking who raised accusation against the Harts that they failed to pay. The sort of merchant targeted would reveal much.

But did they just target the Spadros and Hart Families? No, they tried to blackmail Gardena Diamond as well.

Could this be a Clubb plot?

The Clubbs were known as the spy-masters of Bridges. The Spadros Family had dealt in violence these many years; the Clubbs preferred information. Rumor had it you might secure a better price on your zeppelin ticket — or even fly free — should you share a secret they didn't already know.

But would Lance Clubb blackmail the woman he'd just asked to court? If so, why?

The Pain

The clock struck half past eleven. Pearson stood facing away outside the door, hands behind his back. "May I help you, mum?"

I handed him the letters. "Is Master Rainbow here?"

"No, mum, he and Mr. Anthony left together. They aren't expected back until after dinner."

I returned to my study. I'd hoped to get Morton's impressions on the matter, but it would have to wait.

Someone had tried to kill Morton once already by bombing his yacht as he slept. Although Morton disagreed, I felt certain this was the work of Frank Pagliacci and his false Red Dog Gang. Then Birdie shot at Morton outside Vig's saloon. My guess was that Birdie was one of Frank Pagliacci's lovers, who he was using as he used Dame Anastasia, Zia, and who knows how many others.

Morton's encounter with Birdie the night Marja died might have been by chance. Meeting Morton probably surprised her — especially if she believed him dead — her shot being a way to garner favor with Frank by killing Morton for certain.

A female secretary was strange enough, but carrying a gun?

If I could learn this woman's true identity, it might help. Birdie was present moments before Marja died; perhaps she saw the man who killed her.

I had no real information on Birdie other that she was young and pretty (or at least Morton thought so), with black hair. I needed to speak with Morton further about her — if we ever got a chance to speak without others present.

I'd been accompanied by a maid, waiter, footman, or nurse almost every second of every day of the past month up to now, which infuriated me. Perhaps I didn't choose to speak, or have anything to say, but I was no invalid. At times I suspected they knew it, that this intense scrutiny was my punishment for causing them trouble.

Dr. Salmon approved me to return to the Manor as long as I took daily walks in the garden. So after luncheon, I asked Amelia to show me the flowers she put in my hair.

We ambled along the paths. Many of the plants reminded me of Ma's garden.

"You stupid girl! You've ruined everything!"

Ma dragged me by one arm through her garden to the carriage, shoved me inside.

Why did she never contact me? Didn't she care?

Shaking my head to clear it, I followed Amelia to a bush in the far corner. I brought a white blossom to my face, inhaled, the scent bringing back intense happiness and pain.

Oh, Nina.

What did they do to you?

"Mum, what's wrong?"

I shook my head, forcing the terrible image from my mind. "Old memories, Amelia, nothing more."

"Here, mum, let's get you into the shade."

I sat on the grass, closing my eyes, willing back the tears. I couldn't remember her that way. I couldn't.

I was thirteen when I first saw her.

Amelia fanned me. "Here, stretch out for a while. Do you need a drink of water?"

Nina Clubb stepped into the hallway of Spadros Manor, the afternoon sun shining golden through the open doorway on her rosy cheeks. Laughing, she turned to me, her glossy dark brown hair loose like a young girl's, flowing like water straight and heavy past wide hips.

Our eyes met, and I could see nothing else.

"No, Amelia, I'll be fine." Why did I think of Nina Clubb

now, after so many years? "I'm just tired."

I lay gazing at the flowers for some time.

"It's almost time for tea. Would you like it out here?"

"That would be lovely."

Amelia left, returning with Pearson's sons, who carried a tea-table and chairs. Mary appeared a bit later with our tea.

"I'll take dinner in my rooms today," I told Amelia. "And bring some of these flowers for my dresser."

"Yes, mum. Whatever you need."

After Amelia set the vase of jasmine in my room, I lay on my bed, eyes closed.

The aroma of jasmine lay thick in the air ... we lay on our stomachs facing each other on a blanket in the shade of a brilliant summer. Thick straight hair spilled beside round freckled cheeks as her brown eyes met mine. I longed to touch her hair, her face, her lips.

"One day I'll fly far from here," Nina said. The polished wooden beads in her necklace rustled as she moved. "I want to travel the world."

Some day I'd be in a position to avenge Nina, and all the spying in the world wouldn't save Mrs. Clubb.

Tony returned from whatever he was doing well after dinner, climbing into bed. I turned away as he slid his arm under my pillow, molded his body to mine. "I hear you've had a long day." He stroked my hair, kissed it. "Just rest."

I laid my cheek on my pillow, still damp from my tears.

I wished I could rest without nightmares, as I did the night after I rescued David. Yet it was not to happen.

* * *

The next afternoon, Amelia dressed me in my peacock blue dress to visit Madame Biltcliffe's instead of mourning garb. But only after I agreed to wear a long, elderberry-colored shawl to cover it, with a matching hat and veil. "This is most unwise, mum," Amelia said. "It's unseemly to wear bright colors now. And you can't be recognized out and about, it isn't safe."

Somehow she knew I meant to do more than take tea with Madame Biltcliffe. Was I so transparent? "It's our favorite dress." Tony said he liked it because it matched my eyes. "Have you sent Madame Biltcliffe's mourning garb back to her?"

Amelia blinked. "Why, of course, as soon as she sent yours here, just before we left for the Country House."

I smiled. "Good. Thank you."

Amelia stared at me for a moment, then nodded. "Keep this veil with you, mum. It's a good one."

You mean, it's thicker than Madame's, should I go out. I patted her hand. "Don't worry; I'm just going to take tea with Madame."

That day, outriders surrounded the carriage. Outriders had never joined me when I traveled to Madame's shop before. But my old enemy Jack Diamond, a volatile man with a keen hate for my family, had already entered our quadrant more than once despite guards at the bridges and waterfronts.

Madame Biltcliffe's dress shop was on 42nd Street, with a lovely oak storefront and large beveled glass windows behind which stood perfectly coiffed and dressed mannequins.

Today, though, the mannequins stood in odd spacing, as if recently moved and not checked. A hat-pin lay on the floor. The oak chair trimmed in brass which normally held a placard referencing her work for me was missing, and the window hastily cleaned. Bits of eggshell adorned the sidewalk.

Madame, a handsome middle-aged woman with black hair, came outside as the Spadros Family carriage pulled up. Honor came round to help me from the carriage, and I thanked him, as I always do.

Madame approached to greet me. "Welcome, Mrs. Spadros! Come inside." She glanced over my shoulder.

Honor smiled, tipping his hat. For the first time in memory, he was armed. He'd never gone armed before, not even when we went to visit other quadrants.

What was going on here?

"I'm so glad you could visit, my dear." Madame ushered me inside, then locked the door, turning the sign on it to "Closed: entry by appointment only."

As it turned out, Madame Biltcliffe really did want to take tea with me; she had small cakes filled with jelly set out with the usual tea and toast. They were delicious.

"I thought you might need time away from the home and

servants," she said, "but it is pleasant to know you better."

"I appreciate your help."

She waved it off. "It's nothing. Long ago, I needed time to myself, so I have since then always been mindful of ways to help other women." She smiled knowingly. "Perhaps some day I can be of aid in that way as well."

I laughed. *A romance affair?* I felt a stab of longing for Joseph Kerr. But was it fair to encourage his ardor? Was it right to put him in such danger?

If only I had listened to Air, to my Ma ... Joe and I would be together now. None of the past ten years would have happened.

"Your face shows regret," Madame Biltcliffe said. "Never feel sorrow for what is no more." She patted my hand. "Be happy for what is now."

I took a deep breath and let it out, feeling melancholy. "Tell me about yourself, Madame."

"Please, call me Marie."

"Of course."

"Ah, well," Madame said, "there's not much to tell. My husband was a ... you say 'stodgy' ... aristocrat in an equally stodgy town. I took time to myself," she glanced aside with a sad, wistful smile, "yet that didn't last as long as I liked. He discovered my secret, so I came here."

"And he hasn't searched for you?"

She laughed. "Oh, no. His only concern was that there be no scandal. I much prefer this town, and last I heard he has declared me dead and married a woman half his age." She smiled. "I'm sure we are both happier."

"So do you enjoy your life here?"

"Why yes. I enjoy my work, I meet many fine women, and from time to time I enjoy the company of those who intrigue me." She smiled.

At her smile, I blushed: her secret had nothing whatsoever to do with men. "I had no idea." Indeed, I had no inclination, at least, not for Madame. She was beautiful, but as old as my Ma. I suppose up to then I had thought of her more as a mother.

"Ah. I see," she said, then smiled. "Never fear, ma cherie, we shall remain as dear friends."

I felt relieved. "That would make me quite happy; you've done me a great service over the years." Then I felt chagrined. "I'm sorry it's taken so long to know each other." I paused, considering. "If I meet anyone who might wish to meet you, in whatever capacity, I'll speak to you of it at once."

Madame Biltcliffe gave me a soft smile. "I'm sure that would be lovely." She gazed to the side for a few moments as she sipped her tea. "I suppose you'll want to borrow my dress."

"I'm astonished: everyone knows my mind today." I wasn't sure this was a good thing. Perhaps I had been at ease for so long I no longer knew how to keep my plans from my face.

Madame Biltcliffe chuckled. "I only recall your concern for the boy ... the one whose mother was here last time. And it's probably safer to wear mourning. But if you wish instead to converse further, or have more tea, or return home, it's of no consequence."

I checked the clock: half past five. Should I leave so soon? "If it wouldn't offend ..." I couldn't see what harm it might do, and I might be of help to David and his mother. "I believe I might make a short trip to Bryce Fabrics after all."

Madame called out, "Tenni!"

Tenni, a girl of seventeen, came in at once. "Yes, Madame?"

"Clear these plates, then inform the servants of Mrs. Spadros that we will do some preliminary fittings for her Summer gown."

Tenni curtsied, the reddish-brown curls peeking out from under her shop maid's cap bouncing as she left with the tray.

Tenni and I looked similar from behind — the same hair, height, form, and light brown skin — so I often used her as a decoy when leaving Madame's shop to go on my cases.

When Tenni returned, I put on Madame's mourning dress, adding my dark purple scarf, hat, and veil. Then Tenni put on my blue dress and fixed her hair. Once Tenni and Madame went into my private dressing room by way of the front room (so my men might believe I was still there), I left using Madame's back entry.

This was my first time behind Madame's shop at this time of day. The alleyway was busier than usual, with men coming and going, deliveries being made and picked up. The men seemed familiar, although I didn't recall them being here before.

The streets were the same: unusually crowded, but by no one who seemed out of the ordinary. And no one followed me.

After David Bryce's kidnapping, men in brown began following me everywhere, often on orders from Frank Pagliacci. But few of these men wore brown (the color was going out of fashion as spring approached), and the ones who did walked past, paying me no mind whatsoever.

In the taxi-carriage, I took a jasmine-flower from my handbag.

"I want to travel the world," said Nina.

"I do too."

"We could take zeppelins to the seashore, then hire ourselves onto a steamship bound for Europe."

I gasped at the idea. "Could we really go round the world?"

"Why not?" Nina put her plump freckled arm up as men do when they wrestle. "Let's make a pact on it."

Overwhelmed, I cradled her face in my hands and kissed her. A brief hesitation, then her arm went round my shoulders as she kissed me.

In that brief instant, I was happy as I'd never been before: she loved me too.

Madame had taken an awful risk to speak as she did. She worked with women of high standing every day; with one word I was in position to ruin her should matters have turned badly.

"Girls!" Mrs. Clubb pulled me and Nina apart. "This is not the way to behave! It's time for Jacqui to go home."

I only saw Nina once more. To this day, I wish I hadn't.

At the time, I thought: What did they do to her? Was what happened to her because of me?

The Excursion

The taxi-carriage deposited me on a lonely, windblown street in front of a peeling white storefront.

Acevedo Spadros II brought young Molly Hogan here to run a new grocery at the start of their own romance affair. I imagined times long past, when the streets raged with Family warfare.

As I entered, the hinges squealed; a bell rang. Rows of low shelves displayed dusty out-of-date fabrics. The peeling gray-green paint did little to make the cold room appear any better. Across the room, a rickety counter stood in front of a doorway missing its door, the bare wall past it lit by an overcast sky.

A woman with graying brown hair dressed in widow's brown came into view. "May I help you?"

I rushed over. "It's me. Jacqui. How is he?"

Eleanora Bryce sagged. "I'm glad I didn't recognize you." She came around the counter. "Come, it's not safe for you to be here."

I followed Mrs. Bryce through the doorway, surveying their tiny back room. "I hope you're well?"

"I got a good sale the beginning of the month. A pretty young thing, about your age with black hair. She must have had money: she bought all my gray cloth! Said it was for art. To think of it! Spending a whole quarter on art!"

To my left, a boy sat on a bed, curled into a ball, rocking.

David Bryce looked so much like Air that it hurt to see him. Pale skin, dark hair, dark eyes. But David's eyes were lost, empty, as if he had seen things no child should ever see. Arms around his crossed legs, hands pressed upon his thin arms, he stared into nothing, and rocked.

I sat beside him and lifted my veil. "Do you remember me? I brought you home."

His eyes never moved as he continued to rock.

I turned to her. "Has there been any change? Has he spoken?"

Mrs. Bryce drew up the room's lone stool and sat. There used to be three stools; where had the other two gone? A bed was missing, too. "He stopped sucking his thumb. He'll walk to the toilet, and he'll drink broth. I suppose it's an improvement."

"I must know if he speaks. If he identifies who took him —"

Mrs. Bryce sounded numb. "Then what? What if that Diamond man did this to him? I'm a widow, and an outsider at that. Where would I get money for clothes to stand in court, a lawyer or a carriage to get there? And doesn't his Family own the Prison, the courts? I might end up in a cell, or even dead."

I hadn't considered any of this. The Diamond Family held the Prison. Jack Diamond was Keeper of the Prison. Which seemed odd: the man was reportedly both violent and insane. Prison must be a terrible place. "I have some money. Perhaps I could help."

Mrs. Bryce shook her head. "You've done too much already."

It didn't feel that way.

Her voice sounded hollow. "I never liked you as a child — you were too outspoken, too fierce. But Nicholas adored you —"

Grief tore through my chest. Air's real name was Nicholas, and he was Eleanora's eldest son, before I got him killed.

"— and I blamed you for his death, even though you were just a child yourself. I'm sorry."

Air told me not to go. He begged me to go home. He only went because I did, to protect me. And I should never have been there. I should've stayed in bed as Ma asked. She told me not to have anything to do with Peedro Sluff. But I wouldn't listen. "You're right to blame me."

"No, mum, I wasn't." She placed her hand on mine. "You didn't pull the trigger. You were just a little girl. My boy was out at night getting killed and I didn't even know. I was working —"

She was doing what women did in the Pot: selling her body.

"— and I shouldn't have been. Their father was coming for us — he even sent money so I could get Nicky's medicine —"

Shock lanced through me. I went to the corner of Shill and Snow that night because Peedro Sluff told me he'd give me a dollar. I wanted the dollar to get Air his medicine, because he was coughing up blood and the doctor wanted money.

Was everything that happened that night for nothing?

Mrs. Bryce stared at her hands. "But I didn't believe he would bring us out. He'd promised to for so long that I gave up hope. Why would some rich outsider spend all his money on me?" She hung her head. "If anyone other than that wretched Peedro Sluff was to blame, it would be me."

I wondered what she'd say if she knew Peedro was my father.

"You did what we all wanted," Mrs. Bryce said. "The whole city dreams of getting into a Family. You got to the very top. Don't throw it away on account of us. We'll survive." She leaned over to peer in my eyes. "You brought him home. That's all you said you'd do. You don't have to do any more."

You're wrong. I have to. "They did it on my account, Ell."

Mrs. Bryce sat straighter, eyes widening in alarm.

"The scoundrel in brown said so." I gripped David's mattress with both hands, tighter and tighter. "He killed Herbert. He ruined David. He's tried to destroy your family for no other reason but to lure me." Pain lanced through my left ring finger as the nail gave way. "I'm not stopping until I kill him."

The clock tower struck six. I had to leave. I pressed my nail to staunch the spreading wetness, grateful Madame's gloves were black. "What do you need? Can I bring something next time?"

Mrs Bryce shrugged.

I pulled out a dollar, but she held up her hand in front of her as if to push it away. "No, mum — no. That's too much. If I showed up with a whole dollar people'd think I was running Party Time for sure." Her eyes followed it. "Do you have anything smaller?"

I opened my coin purse, giving her all but one of my pennies (I needed that for the taxi), and all my nickels and dimes. It was less than a dollar, but perhaps it would help.

She burst into tears.

"Thank you so much," she sobbed. "I only made the one fabric sale this whole month. I even had to sell the frame around Herbert's portrait for food and rent. I didn't know how I was going to pay Family fees. This is enough for some new fabric."

Our Family was such a burden to these people. Did Tony even know?

David still rocked.

I rested my hand on his shoulder. "It looks bad now, David, but it'll get better. When you want to tell me who did this so I can go kill him, you just tell your Ma. Okay?"

David hesitated, just an instant.

The look in his eyes ...

What had his kidnappers done to him?

But then he began rocking again.

Mrs. Bryce rose. "Stay here. I'll make sure the taxi's ready. You mustn't linger outside."

"Why not? What's going on?"

"People are saying the Families have to go. That even the gangs are better than paying Family fees every month. That they ruined the merchants and blew up the zeppelin."

"What?"

She nodded. "So you don't want to be seen round here."

In more ways than one. She and David might be in danger.

Mrs. Bryce patted my arm. "We'll be fine. You did enough."

On the way to Madame's, I considered Eleanora's words.

Something was very wrong.

Why should anyone blame the Families for the disaster?

But Family fees were resented enough that any reason might make the poor wish to be rid of them. That Thrace Pike dared to produce his editorial in January was all the evidence needed.

Few people paid mind to the true Red Dog gang when they threw rocks at storefronts "to get rid of the Families." And I had considered Thrace Pike's editorial and pamphlet dealt with, especially after he was outed as a Bridger. But now people on the street called for the Families to go?

The situation was much worse than I thought.

But today, at least, had gone well. I helped Mrs. Bryce, and David seemed improved (if ever so slightly). I could probably get another three excursions to Madame's shop from this Summer dress, then it would be time for my Fall fittings.

Now that I wasn't being watched so closely, I should finally be able to make a proper investigation into Marja's death.

* * *

A line of carriages sat outside Madame's shop. So I got out ten yards up, in the entrance to the alley. Shadow covered the sidewalks and buildings. People bustled about.

A boy of eleven stood on the tree-lined sidewalk in front of a portrait studio, peering towards Madame's shop. He looked familiar. "Aren't you the Memory Boy's brother?"

He nodded.

I gestured towards Madame's place. "What's going on?"

He shrugged. "A lot of men went in. I'm not sure which shop." He stood on tiptoe for a moment. "Can't see from here."

Men? That ruled out Madame's place: what reason would men have to go in a dress shop? A watchmaker's shop lay just past hers; the men probably went there. "It was good to see you."

I went up the alley, then turned left to stroll behind the shops. Even the alleyways were busy: shopkeepers and maids, trash-takers and children. But no one paid me mind as I went to Madame's back door and let myself in.

The hall was silent.

Normally, Tenni rushed to greet me, eager to put on her own clothes. At the time, I thought she didn't hear me come inside.

I raised my veil, went to my private dressing room's back curtain, and opened it.

Madame and Tenni sat on wooden chairs facing each other. Madame looked angry; Tenni's brown eyes were wide with terror.

Two men leaned against the walls.

"Hello, Jacqui," said Tony.

The Interrogation

Sawbuck stood behind me; I ran right into him. "I'm sorry, mum," he said. "But I did warn you what might happen."

I turned towards Tony and his cousin Blitz. The two didn't appear alike except for their smiles, but neither were smiling now.

"Mrs. Spadros, I came to see you," Tony said, "but instead, I find this girl wearing your dress. Who's this girl? Why's she wearing your dress?"

Madame said, "I told you, Monsieur Spadros. This is Tenni; she's under my protection. An orphan. I made this dress for her."

"Don't lie to me, Madame. Don't you think I know my own wife's clothing?" Tony grabbed Tenni's arm, jerking her to her feet. "This ripped at the waist when my wife and I lay together before her maid undressed her — a maid who raised me." He let go of Tenni, who slumped into her seat. "Don't you think I know the stitching of a woman who sewed with me at her side when I was a boy?" He pointed towards the floor. "I spilled red wine on the hem after dinner. This stain and the one on the carpet in my library never came out. This is my wife's dress, and a stranger wears it."

He took a few steps along the curtained entryway. "But that's not the worst of it. My wife, Madame, wears your dress. I remember it from the memorial. Why's she wearing your dress? Where's she gone? I depended on you to be her protector."

He turned to me. "And why do you evade your men? You did the same at the Diamond Women's Club the day of the explosion. Where do you go?"

I stared at him in terror.

"We're going home," Tony said. "Madame, lock your store. Perhaps you'll be more forthcoming at Spadros Manor."

Blitz snorted, uncrossing his arms with a slight shake of his head. I recalled his words the night Marja died: *My loyalty is to the Spadros Family. Who is your loyalty to, Mrs. Spadros?*

Sawbuck took my arm, but his grasp was gentle as he led me past a group of Tony's men loitering in Madame's shop room.

Honor stood stiffly by the carriage, not meeting my glance.

He believes I've betrayed the Family.

Fuck him, I thought. If he and that driver had taken me to the bank instead of locking me in my carriage, I could have sold Anastasia's necklace before gem prices fell. I'd have all the money I needed.

Tony climbed into the carriage next to me.

I said, "Where's Madame? Where's Tenni?"

"They'll be well," Tony said.

He probably put us in separate carriages so we couldn't confer as to our stories.

The prospect of returning terrified me. I didn't think Tony would harm me, but what might he do to them? And how long would they be able to withstand before they told the truth?

I couldn't see Roy or Tony taking kindly to my work. If I confessed to my business and wasn't beaten, or killed outright as any other Spadros would be who stepped out of line, I'd be watched every step I took.

I remembered Madame's little jest then, and my hands began to shake. Even if Roy didn't kill me, Tony could presume that if I left home on false pretenses, changed clothes, and hired accomplices, it was proof of infidelity, easy grounds for divorce.

I wouldn't be safe anywhere in Bridges.

* * *

I sat in my parlor, gloved hands in my lap, as Tony paced the room. Sawbuck stood in front of the fireplace, arms folded.

My gloves were soaked in sweat.

"Why did you go to the zeppelin station? Honor told you we had specific instruction not to go into Clubb quadrant that day."

Tony tricked too much information from me, only to ignore it. "I told you, I had evidence of a bomb. I tried to warn them —"

"By giving your name? Mrs. Jacqueline Spadros, illegally in Clubb quadrant, with knowledge of a bomb? Which you told no one about —"

"I didn't learn about it until I was on Market Center —"

"And why on earth were you there? Why evade your men?"

Why wouldn't he listen? "I was helping Gardena!" I shook my head. "They aren't my men in any case." I had more than sufficient evidence of this already. "They're your men, they're your father's men. Would they have escorted us to meet her blackmailer?"

Tony hesitated, a quick procession of anger, fear, and resolution crossing his face. "Why would anyone blackmail Gardena Diamond? Why won't you tell me what's going on?"

"Tony, I can't tell you that! She risked everything to trust me with this. If I betrayed her now ... it would be wrong."

Gardena had killed her grandfather — as he asked — when his life became pure misery after his terrible accident. And someone threatened to go to her father with the truth.

The fact that she came to me, of all people ...

I faced him. "I will **not** tell you, nor will I tell your father —"

Tony flinched, turning pale. The torture room of Roy Spadros was no secret in Bridges.

"— if that's your wish. So you must decide. Gardena's secret has nothing to do with you, nor with this Family. I'm astonished you would pry into a woman's private affairs this way."

Tony began pacing. "Did you know Pearson keeps record of what goes on in this household?"

This didn't surprise me. But it raised a number of questions.

"For example, in January you told him more than once you were out calling, or going to tea. Yet later he found your driver and footman engaged in tasks around the house."

I gaped at him in horror.

"Where did you go? Who did you see? Was Gardena being blackmailed again?"

I said nothing.

"Regina Clubb brought formal charges to The Commission, claiming she saw you illegally at Clubb Women's Center — and accuses us of spying. Us!" He let out a bitter laugh. "That's rich."

I smiled in spite of myself.

"But on that day, Pearson has a notation that you were visiting Helen Hart. Must I speak to each of these people to verify your locations? Now I doubt your word on several matters."

I never met with Helen Hart that day. I went to Market Center — by way of Clubb quadrant — to investigate David Bryce's disappearance. Tony's little sister Katherine went with me to see the stable-master, who was now dead. Had my actions put her in danger as well?

"And then there's Madame Biltcliffe."

This change of subject made no sense. "What of her?"

His face softened into amusement. "The accountant you insisted upon discovered Madame Biltcliffe charges the Spadros Family significantly more than others using the same services. Is she cheating me? Or is she providing some additional service?"

Oh gods, I thought. Is he going to kill her?

"Was her story about the break-in at her shop true? Or is she allied with our enemies? You're the judge of this. Is it too personal a woman's affair? Or maybe she was being blackmailed as well. Perhaps I should send her and the orphan to my father to learn the truth."

I stared at my hands. "There's no need to involve your father."

Tony stopped, leaning towards me. "What?"

All I had worked so hard to keep secret was being revealed. But I couldn't allow Madame Biltcliffe and Tenni to be hurt on my account. "There's no need to involve your father."

I took a deep breath. "From the age of sixteen, I have employed myself as a private investigator."

The Information

Tony leaned on the back of a chair, eyes wide, mouth open. Then he sat across the low coffee table from me. "But why? Is there something I'm not providing you?"

I considered my bird in its lovely cage. "What if Frank Pagliacci's men shot you during the ambush at your warehouse? By law, all this," I gestured around me, "would revert to your father. He makes no pretense: this is for the protection and benefit of you, and you alone. He has no use or regard for me, other than to provide you with an heir."

Which, if I had any say in it, would never happen. I took a special tea every morning to ensure this. I would never bear a child to be used as a pawn in some Family scheme.

I turned to Sawbuck, who sat beside me. "Would **you** protect me from Jack Diamond? Or Frank Pagliacci? Or 'my men'?"

Sawbuck didn't move.

"I thought as much." I faced Tony. "And even if I were to return to the Spadros Pot I wouldn't be safe. I need means to hire bodyguards until I can purchase a zeppelin ticket."

Tony leaned forward, head bowed, his elbows on his knees. He sat motionless for several seconds. Then he raised his head. "I shall create a will —"

I stared at him in shock.

"Sir," Sawbuck said, "this is most unwise —"

"Shut up, Ten. This is my house, not yours. My money, to do with as I wish. Do you understand?"

Sawbuck's face reddened and his jaw tightened, but after staring at Tony for several seconds, he glanced away.

"I shall direct my lawyers to create a will which gives you everything on my death. Then you can keep our home and select guards of your choosing. My life means nothing if you aren't cared for, whether or not you're able to give me a child." Tony shook his head. "I should've considered this, especially after Master Diamond's outburst at the Ball." He leaned back. "This explains your nightmares. Why did you never tell me?"

I smiled. He had never revealed his nightmares either. "It's of no consequence." Why was he creating this will? Surely he didn't trust me. Was this a test?

Tony sat up. "Ten, ring for some tea. When the maid leaves, stand guard. I want no one overhearing."

Sawbuck rose, not looking at either of us, then stood by the door. I considered the stair at the other end of the parlor and who might be listening already, but it was much too late for that.

Tony said, "Tell me everything. From the beginning."

The door opened. Sawbuck took the tray from the maid, set it between us, then left, closing the door with a sharp click.

I patted the sofa. "Sit by me."

In whispers, I related my desire to be of use, to find freedom from my stifling life under Roy's thumb. I told him I had allies, and disguises, and contacts in various places. I never mentioned names; Tony never asked.

"So you see, Madame Biltcliffe and Tenni helped me. For their assistance, I pay her."

"You mean, I pay her."

I felt abashed. "Well, yes. But I meant no harm. She put herself and ..." I almost said "her maid" but I didn't wish to contradict Madame, "Tenni in danger to help me."

"The girl does look like you from afar. I see how the men were fooled." Tony squeezed my hand. "Go on."

"I never did anything more dangerous than following men suspected of infidelity —" the image of Vig beating the man who tried to violate me when I was sixteen flashed through my mind, but it wouldn't do to tell Tony about that, "until New Years' Eve."

I described my meeting with Eleanora Bryce, whose twelve-year-old son David had to be the child Tony's kidnapped men spoke of. I told him about the Red Dog card Amelia found in my pocket after the Grand Ball, and my horror at seeing one on our front stair, which I felt sure was put there by Jack Diamond.

Tony stared at me. "Several shopkeepers have complained of being harassed by a man fitting his description."

I told Tony about Stephen and Clover of the true Red Dogs, and how appalled they were at the kidnapping. Both Stephen and Herbert Bryce, David's older brother, were later found strangled.

"I've heard rumor of a strangler loose in the city," Tony said, "but I had no idea those boys were connected to our troubles."

I then had a dilemma: what to tell him about Morton? I mentioned a man who claimed to be a Red Dog trey leader, but only as Morton, leaving out his true name.

But Tony said, "And then Master Rainbow appeared, who you knew as Morton."

I recoiled, horrified. "How did you know?"

Tony chuckled. "Pearson mentioned your cry of surprise at seeing Master Rainbow, calling him Morton, and I wondered where you might have met before."

Fear gripped me. What would happen to him?

Tony patted my hand. "I mean Master Rainbow no harm. He saved your life at the zeppelin station, did he not?"

I nodded, heart pounding.

"Go on," Tony said. "I want to know everything. No one will harm you or your friends."

So I told Tony I tracked David to Jack Diamond's factory. Morton took me to the factory on his yacht to rescue David Bryce, yet afterwards David did nothing but rock and suck his thumb.

"I shot Frank Pagliacci that day. But I learned from Dame Anastasia later that he was still alive."

"You **shot** him?" Tony stared at me, mouth open. "And Dame Anastasia knew him?"

I nodded. "He was her lover, and part of her plot to defraud the city. He and Jack Diamond killed her, Tony. The zeppelin explosion was their means of assassination. Jack and Frank mean us personal harm, but I can't prove it. In Jack's factory, Frank said he planned to destroy the Spadros Family, one by one."

Tony paused, hand to his chin. "This explains many things: Master Rainbow's injuries, for example. Again, taken defending you and your friend's young boy." He smiled. "I can't help but feel indebted to him, even if he did deceive me. If you ever do need guards, he would be one to enlist."

He took my hand. "You are the bravest woman I've ever met. To enter Diamond quadrant, rescue this boy ... and actually shooting a man. Who taught you —?"

I shot many more than one that day. But what should I say? Roy threatened to kill my Ma if I revealed to Tony that he had been training me. Did Roy know Ma was still alive? "One of the men dropped his gun when Master Rainbow shot him." I shrugged, looking away. "It seemed easy enough."

Tony snorted. "I wish I had any talent for it." He shifted in his chair. "What I'm trying to say is ... I feel tremendous pride in you, risking yourself to save this child as you did." He turned to me, placing his hand atop mine. "But this business must stop. You've done a great service, and gained valuable information, but you're much too precious to be placed in peril."

"But, Tony —"

"Frank Pagliacci plans to destroy us one by one. He's lured you from your home once already. One day he'll capture you, or worse yet, Jack Diamond will, and I can't even think of that." He ducked his head, trying to capture my gaze. "Will you promise me you'll stop this nonsense? Please?"

Did I have a choice? I couldn't look at him. "Yes, sir."

"Ah, now, none of that. Look at me. I don't mean to order you. I'm not my father. I — I want you to be safe. That's all."

I nodded. My bird was very safe. Yet it would never fly.

* * *

The doorbell rang. After a few moments, Sawbuck opened the door. "The Memory Boy Werner Lead, sir."

Memory Boys remembered exactly what was said, and

delivered messages so secret they mustn't be written.

Tony leapt from the sofa. "Splendid! I'll be there at once." He said to me, "I'll be right back."

Sawbuck closed the door, remaining inside.

I hurried to Sawbuck. "I didn't mention anything from the night you found Marja. I'd appreciate your silence a while longer."

He regarded me warily. "You play a dangerous game, Mrs. Spadros. Trust, once lost, is often gone forever, and hatred soon follows." He glanced aside, then spoke earnestly. "I don't want him hurt. You understand?"

"That's the farthest thing from my mind. But I must learn who killed her." I grabbed his arm. "I must. She was a mother to me. I can't stand aside when I believe this all is connected. But I can't do that with Mr. Spadros hovering."

Sawbuck's face softened. "Pot rags must stick together, eh?"

I had forgotten: he was Molly's sister's son, undoubtedly born in the Pot, just as she and I were. "Yes." Yet I felt disturbed somehow. "One day we must sit, Master Hogan, and have a chat."

He bowed and turned to go; I returned to my seat.

Just in time: Tony stormed into the room. "The unmitigated gall! The effrontery! How dare the man address me in that manner! And to a Memory Boy!" Tony threw his hands in the air and stalked to the fireplace.

This sudden anger surprised me. "Whatever has happened?"

Tony paced, gesturing as he spoke. "Cesare Diamond, that's what's happened. The scoundrel! I ask a simple question, and he proceeds to cast insult. He even insulted **you**! I should call him out ... yes, I shall challenge him!"

"That would be unwise, sir." Sawbuck's voice startled me. "Mr. Cesare is quite skilled with weapons, or so I'm told."

Where Tony was not.

I began to laugh, remembering my encounter with Cesare Diamond on the rooftop at Market Center as we lay in wait for Gardena's blackmailer. "The man is dreadfully rude. Yet he always spoke truth. What did he say?"

Tony turned crimson, his manner instantly cooling. "That's

not important. But —" he took a few steps, then faced me, "it confirms you were with him on Market Center. I suppose I should be grateful for that."

Tony actually considered calling out Cesare Diamond. After telling me at the Queen's Day dinner that we were only at cease-fire with the Diamonds and "nowhere near" ready for war.

To challenge the Diamond heir in the midst of a cease-fire?

Tony was out of control.

Pearson came in. "Dinner, sir." He surveyed us. Normally, we dressed for dinner at seven; we certainly were not dressed for it now. "Should I tell Monsieur dinner will be delayed?"

"No," Tony said. "We'll have dinner now." He grabbed my upper arm. "None of our guests have had time to prepare either."

The way he said it made me suddenly afraid.

* * *

Tony hauled me to our dining room. Tenni and Madame sat glumly across from each other halfway down the long table.

"Please sit," Tony said.

So I sat at the foot of the table, rubbing my arm. Tony took his seat at the head of the table. Sawbuck sat beside Tony, to his right. Morton sat across from Sawbuck, at Tony's left.

A guest sat mid-table. Had Morton risen in Tony's favor?

Sawbuck took Morton's placement as a matter of course. The servants set the soup dishes and retreated.

Madame shook her head slightly when Tenni caught her eye, then nodded once Tony began to eat.

Tenni shoveled soup into her mouth as if famished.

I sipped a spoonful. "Tenni, will your family worry for you?"

Tenni shrugged. "I'm usually home by now. My sister should be there with the little ones."

"I'll have my butler send your sister a message," Tony said.

Tenni started, giving him a frightened glance. "Thank you, sir." She finished her soup, used her bread to wipe the bowl clean as she ate it, then said, "That was very good." She smiled, relaxing, as if she believed dinner to be over. "It's so quiet here."

Several minutes passed as the rest of us ate in silence.

The servants cleared the soup dishes and placed our main

course. Tenni's eyes widened as she stared at her plate. Then she ate as quickly as before, slipping her roll and meat into her pocket.

When I first came here, I did the same, in case they took it away. And I always hid food to bring home to Ma.

Morton said, "Is it noisy where you live, then?"

She nodded. "The factories run all night, men coming and going, whistles and bells." She gulped her milk.

I asked Tenni, "What happened to your parents?"

"I never knew my father well, mum; haven't seen him since my little sister was born. My mother got shot at the grocery a few years ago. It was in the paper."

I nodded. "I'm sorry."

Tenni shrugged. "We never saw her home much, mum. I just started work for Madame. She took me on full time."

Tony froze, staring at Tenni with his emotionless mask on.

Morton said, "How many are at your house?"

"Me and my five sisters, sir. I'm the oldest. The youngest is seven; we make enough to keep her at home." Tenni spoke with pride. "We get off at different times and check on her. She braids twine for the newspaper — five cents every 100 yard roll. Madame showed me how to make gloves for her so the twine doesn't cut her fingers. And I'm teaching her to read. Madame taught me."

"You're a good sister," Morton said.

Tenni blushed. "Thank you, sir."

Tony said, "Mrs. Spadros, may we speak privately?"

"Of course." We went to his study. "How may I help?"

Tony shook his head. "I had no idea this girl was a servant."

"You're upset because you had dinner with a servant?"

"I had a servant at table with a gentleman! What must he think of us? What must the servants think?"

"That you're kind to children? What else would they think?"

"Favoritism amongst servants only causes trouble," Tony said. "I'll explain it to the staff tomorrow. But the maid must go."

Instantly, Tenni had lost all humanity. "Yes, sir."

"Take the dress off her and have it burned."

"Burned? But it's your favorite dress! It's **my** favorite dress!"

"A ..." he seemed disgusted, "... **servant** has worn it, Jacqui, and a shop maid at that. Why would you want to wear it again?"

"May I give it to her? The girl has so little."

"No. Jane will find something suitable for her to wear home."

"You think this poorly of a servant? What of **me**?"

"What do I think of you? You're my wife." Tony grabbed my arm. "If I see your clothing on her again, I'll have her whipped."

Stunned and angry, I returned to the table. Tenni had cleared her plate and was on her second glass of milk. Morton put down his napkin. "Is Mr. Spadros well?"

"Yes. Tenni, let's get you changed. You can go home now."

While changing, Tenni said, "You and Master Rainbow aren't like the others."

I smiled to myself. "I suppose not."

When Tenni and I returned to the dining hall, Madame stood waiting. "Thank you for your hospitality," Madame said to Tony. "Today's been most informative." She took Tenni's hand and left.

I sat. Sawbuck and Morton seemed disturbed. "What is it?"

Tony looked up. "What is what?"

"Something's happened."

"Yes," Tony said. "Something has. I gave Madame Biltcliffe a choice. You'll be retaining a new dressmaker from now on."

I stared at him, outraged. "Did you threaten her?"

"I gave her two options. She chose to withdraw her services."

What was the other choice? "So you've chosen this woman?"

He shrugged. "I'm sure my mother knows someone suitable."

"But Madame's in the midst of work on my Summer dress! You can't cancel an order she's already begun!"

"I'll allow you to visit, Jacqui, but only to finish the dress. You're not to go anywhere else. Do you understand? You're not to venture out without escort."

"I've done nothing wrong, yet I'm imprisoned!"

Tony laughed. "Nonsense. You're free to go anywhere in the city you like, so long as you stay with your guards."

I drained my glass of wine. "Please excuse me."

Morton glanced at me, but I ignored him. If Tony realized he — or Sawbuck — hid my adventures, they too could be in danger.

The Secrets

I carried my blue dress to my room. Amelia cleaned and bound my broken nail, got me changed from Madame's mourning garb into my nightgown, and said goodnight. Then I went into the left side of my closets, to the back.

The paneled wall appeared as any other, but if I pressed on one panel just right, it moved inward far enough for me to slide it up. They'd found all my hiding places except this one.

In the space behind lay an envelope with the money I'd made over the years as an investigator and Dame Anastasia's book on stage makeup. I wrapped these inside my blue dress. If I found a way to escape, a bundle would be quicker to retrieve.

I slid the panel back down, returned to my bedroom, poured a glass of bourbon, drank it, then poured another. I loved the taste, the burning in my chest, the way I felt afterward.

I would never stop working. I couldn't go out anymore, but Tony didn't know my network of informants. And as far as I knew, my mail wasn't being opened.

I could still learn who murdered Marja.

I rang for Amelia. Twenty minutes later, she appeared in her robe and nightgown, hair in disarray. "Yes, mum?"

"I wish to write some post."

"At this hour?"

"I'll post it tomorrow. Please bring paper, pen, and ink now."

As Amelia went rummaging around the room for writing supplies (and, I imagined, my study when finally she left) I paged through the copies of the *Golden Bridges* I'd set aside.

There was little news other than what Tony and Mrs. Bryce had told me, yet much speculation as to the explosion.

I knew who bombed the zeppelin. What I needed to learn was who killed Marja.

Why did I care so much? While I loved my Ma, she was busy owning her brothel; Marja cared for us most of the time. In a way, Marja was more of a mother than Ma ever was.

When Amelia returned, I wrote to my contacts about the facility Marja sent the letter from. Who else worked there? I asked about Marja and who might want her killed. I asked about Josie's uncle, who it seemed she barely knew. Did he have reason to want Marja dead? And I asked about this woman Birdie.

I stacked the letters on my tea-table, then sat in bed with another glass of bourbon. My options seemed more limited every day; each action had to count.

Tony arrived, smiling when he saw me. "I hope you're well?"

"Indeed." I felt luminous. "What intrigues did you concoct?"

He laughed. "Not much, alas." Then he sobered. "I wanted to apologize. You should be able to choose your own dressmaker."

"I'll ask Madame and your mother for recommendations. Perhaps there'll be someone on both lists who'll suffice."

Tony smiled. "Always considering the options."

How might I help Mrs. Bryce? I sipped my bourbon, considering the matter.

I heard Tony's door open, and his manservant Jacob Michaels' voice. Soon Tony returned in his pajamas and slid into bed next to me. "What happened to your hand?"

I shrugged. It still throbbed. "A broken nail, nothing more."

He gently kissed it, then my wedding ring, then the back of my hand.

"I want to help Mrs. Bryce. One of her sons has been murdered and another ruined on our account."

"This Mrs. Bryce ... she's a merchant then?"

"She owns Bryce Fabrics on 2nd Street, Spadros quadrant."

"And you believe Master Jack Diamond is part of the group who took him?"

"Mrs. Bryce says a dark-skinned man with shaven head wearing white came to her door a week before the kidnapping. We saw him and a man who I believe to be Frank Pagliacci put the boy into a carriage." I was too far away to identify either of them. I'd only seen Jack a few times, but ... "She could tell this was the same man by the way he moved."

I compared this man to the man at the Grand Ball. Was this the impostor I saw in Jack's factory? Or was it Jack himself?

"Tell me what happened that night."

Tony's words startled me. "What night?"

"The night which has you wake screaming since we've wed. I know Master Diamond's manservant was murdered, but I must know everything if we're to appear before The Commission."

I felt astonished. "You mean to approach the Patriarchs?"

Tony seemed surprised. "Regina Clubb plans formal protest; I can make one in return. I have now six merchants who describe everything from blackmail to this kidnapping — in Spadros quadrant — by a man fitting Jack Diamond's description. And today you tell me he threatened you here at my home." He shook his head. "This is completely unacceptable. But I must know **why** he targets you, if I'm to help." He glanced away. "This is much larger than you think, Jacqui. Please. Dr. Salmon believes speaking of it might help with the nightmares, too."

It might help with the nightmares? "Very well."

I sat up in bed and told him about the meeting between Roy Spadros and Peedro Sluff that cold winter night just after I turned twelve. Jack's manservant Daniel rushed towards us, shouting what seemed a warning, yet Peedro shot him, claiming Daniel intended to kill Roy.

"This is incredible," Tony said. "I heard the shots but ..."

"You were much too far away to have seen what happened." I was sure Roy planned it that way.

"Such perfidy! Your father hired to kill mine, yet turns on his master to buy favor with a Family? I've heard of such things, but never thought men could be so dishonorable."

I snorted. "You obviously aren't acquainted with my father."

"What happened then?"

"Jack rode up on one of his father's white horses. He wore white even then, and knelt in the mud, weeping for his friend." The anguish in his face haunted me. "Then Jack screamed vengeance on us all —" I faltered, picturing Jack's rage and hate.

Tony took my hand. "I'm sorry you had to see that."

It was my fault. I should never have been there.

Peedro's grip on my arm. Air desperately trying to save me from being sold. Air's body crumpling after Peedro shot him too. The blood.

"Oh, Jacqui." Tony gathered me into his arms. "I'm sorry to cause you grief."

If I told Tony that my father sold me to the Spadros Family then killed my best friend when he tried to stop it ... this would put everything into question, including our marriage.

And Roy would kill me.

I shook my head. Air was dead, and I was sold. None of it should ever have happened. No matter what Eleanora Bryce said, I cast the cards that night.

It was all because of me.

Tony gestured to the portrait of Acevedo Spadros II on the wall. "Ever since you asked about my grandfather, I've considered what he might do. I want to be like him, Jacqui, not like my father." He kissed my hand. "I'll let you help your merchant friend. This is clearly part of Jack Diamond's need for vengeance, and it can't be allowed to stand."

* * *

That night, I pondered how to help Mrs. Bryce. Money was out of the question: too much, and they would become targets. Perhaps recommend her shop to others? Bring food? I tried to imagine what living in such poverty was like. In the Pot, if we had, we shared. The slums didn't seem to abide by such rules.

At breakfast, Tony produced a letter. "We're requested to attend the inquest as witnesses on the fourth of May."

This seemed alarming. "Both of us?"

"Yes," Tony said. "I appear at eleven, you at half past. But we'll likely need to attend other days." He paused, looking aside. "The attorneys say it's best to attend when the other Families do, so as not to give the appearance of controversy."

"This is most disturbing," I said.

Morton, who sat across the round table from us, appeared quite disturbed, yet said nothing.

"My father says this thing must run its course," Tony said. "To be seen interfering in any way would cause more harm than to let the inquest have its investigation."

As usual, Morton wore brown — but the buttons on his jacket seemed familiar. "Where did you get that jacket?"

Morton shrugged. "Your husband's men bought it after I was rescued from the river. Mine was ruined, and I don't dare return for my clothing in case my house is being watched. Your husband has been kind enough to provide me with a new wardrobe, for which I'm grateful."

I hurried round the table to him. "I've seen this button before. I found this exact button on the floorboards of a carriage stolen from Market Center by the two men who kidnapped David."

Morton froze. At the time, he had been disguised, claiming to be a member of the Diamond portion of the Pot as he helped Frank Pagliacci lure me. Did he tell Tony that part? "As you can see, all of the buttons remain on this jacket."

I turned to Tony. "I asked Madame Biltcliffe where the button came from. She said they were hand-carved. Only twenty were made, enough for two jackets. We must learn where your men got this jacket, so we can question the owner to see if he recalls who bought its twin."

Tony nodded. "I'll have them do that at once."

* * *

Tony asked me not to appear at morning meeting. Perhaps he felt the servants might express their true thoughts about Tenni if I were absent.

In any case, I had ample time to walk in the gardens with Amelia's son Pip. He tossed an old baseball to Rocket, our black pitbull terrier.

"How do you like rooming with the men?"

"It's fine." Pip threw the ball, and Rocket raced after it. Then the dog raced back, ears up. Pip threw the ball again. "They helped with the horses while Daddy was gone."

Rocket dropped the ball in front of us. Pip grabbed the ball and threw it, hard. "I'm not going to tend the horses anymore."

"Why?"

Misery crossed his face. "I heard what the men said. I don't want to work for Daddy anymore."

"What did the men say?"

"That it wasn't right for Daddy to stay at the Country House with Mommy and my sisters and send me away. That it wasn't my fault what Mr. Roy did to Mommy."

Rocket dropped the ball at Pip's feet, tail wagging.

Pip stood still, head drooping. "Mr. Roy did something real bad to Mommy, something too bad even for **men** to say." He knelt to hug Rocket. "I think it's why she hates me. But why does she think it's **my** fault? Why did Daddy send me away?" He put his head on Rocket's back. "I don't know what I did to make them hate me."

I crouched beside him. "You didn't do anything wrong, sweetie. Look at me."

Tears glistened in his pale blue eyes.

"You're right; Mr. Roy did a very bad thing to your Ma." I bit my lip, not knowing how much to say. "But the men are right too; it's not your fault."

Pip turned away. "Then Mommy and Daddy are **bad** to blame me. They're **bad** to send me away." He shook his head. "It's not right. I don't want to work for Daddy anymore. I feel hateful when I see him. Both of them."

I lobbed the ball far into the meadow. Rocket raced away. "Come." I held out my hand, and we walked in the garden under the watchful gaze of Roy's men. "What will you do then, if not help with the horses?"

Pip's face lit up, and he let go of my hand, jumping up and down. "Monsieur and Miss Anne are teaching me to cook! I helped roll the pastries, and they're going to show me how to make sausage!"

I smiled. "Monsieur makes the best sausage."

Pip beamed.

"But Monsieur sounds so fierce. Aren't you afraid of him?"

"Oh, no, mum, not at all. Miss Anne says he sounds fierce, like Rocket when he smells gunpowder, but he'd never hurt anyone." He patted Rocket's head and threw the ball. "Monsieur likes me, him and Miss Anne both. They really like me." Rocket dropped the ball, and Pip picked it up slowly, face pensive. "I don't think Mommy and Daddy ever liked me much."

This was heartbreaking.

A cat ran past. Rocket barked, chasing it around the corner.

I put my hand on Pip's shoulder. "I think they love you as best they can, your Daddy especially. He didn't want you to stay with the men. He even came in the house to ask me not to let you go. I could tell it scared him, but he did it anyway." I peered at him, trying to decide what to say. "But sometimes other things make it so they don't know how to love you very well."

Pip nodded, his face serious and pale. "What happened to my Mommy?"

The exact question I didn't want to answer. I let out a breath, shaking my head. "It's her story, and not for me to tell. Maybe she'll tell you someday." I doubted it, but it might keep his questions at bay.

"But **why**? Everyone else knows. They look at me and whisper when they think I can't see."

"I'm sorry. I really am. You deserve to know. But ... maybe someday."

He peered up at me, a young Roy. Was that man ever so innocent? "When I get grown up?"

I smiled. "Yes. When you get grown up, I'm sure they'll tell you. If they don't tell you, when you become a man I'll tell you everything. I promise."

He frowned, then kicked a rock. "It's not fair."

"Yes, dear, I know. Most things in life aren't fair at all."

* * *

Eventually, we went back to the house and Pip went off to his work. I returned to my room, but Amelia wasn't there. So I went to my dresser to put my gloves away.

I normally placed a hair across the locked drawer, but inside, where it would only be disturbed by opening the drawer.

The hair was gone.

I opened the drawer. The five pages of information I wrote back in January with all I knew about Morton was gone. In its place lay a letter:

> My dear Mrs. Spadros,
>
> I apologize for the intrusion, but this was the place least likely to be discovered by others before you found it.
>
> Please don't trouble yourself about the events on the train. I understand your intention was only to create a certain distraction for our flight from the police. While it was a most pleasant diversion,

I laughed. *I'm sure it was, Master Rainbow.*

> I expect nothing more from you and no one will ever learn of it from me.

That he took the time to write reassuring words touched me.

> I have need to tell you more of this woman Birdie who worked with Frank Pagliacci. Yet I can never get a moment to speak with you in private. Perhaps your husband suspects more than a carriage ride to the train station with Miss Diamond occurred last month.
>
> Here's what I observed: she was young and lovely, perhaps your age, with light skin, blue eyes, and jet black hair. But she seemed quite definite in her bearing, as if used to commanding men. I've never seen such a demeanor in a woman before, and it made her rather imposing. She didn't look like any of the Families. Her height, medium, with a fine form. She had long delicate fingers, I remember them well.
>
> She wore red. Her accent was of Bridges; I'm sure

she's not an outsider. But there was something about her which spoke of a difference between her and most quadrant-folk.

This was a cursory observation; perhaps others may give you more detail.

I wish you luck in your ultimate goal to leave the city and be free of the Families altogether. Try not to appear so eager.

If I can get into this drawer, others can too.

Your servant, BR

This is a farewell note.

Morton must have been more disturbed by talk of the inquest than I thought. I closed the drawer, locked it, and tossed the letter into the fire.

A few minutes later, Amelia returned. "Mum, I didn't know you were here. You should have rung for me!" She got me changed and was in the midst of doing my hair when a knock came at the door. "Bother these interruptions!" Amelia snapped. "Who is it?"

Tony's head came round the door. "Pardon my appearance in my wife's chambers, Amelia, but I have words for her."

Amelia turned crimson and curtsied low. "My apologies, sir! I thought you were the footman." She rushed past Tony.

I chuckled. "Come in."

Tony closed the door behind him. "Master Rainbow is gone."

"Could someone have taken him?"

Tony pulled up a chair from my tea-table, sat beside me, and held up a paper. "He left a letter."

"Well, that's a relief. With all that's happened ..."

Tony peered at me, then nodded.

"Did he say why?"

"He can't risk being called before the court or photographed: it would put his life in danger." Tony paused. "In that, I agree. He wishes us only to refer to him as Mr. Graham Morton."

"Surely the staff knows him as Master Blaze Rainbow."

"I've warned the staff that they must not reveal Master Rainbow was here, not even to other members of the Family."

Roy surely knew of Morton's presence and considered him no threat, or he'd be dead by now. "He's been a loyal friend. But I understand his predicament."

"One more item to speak with our attorneys with."

"So we'll meet with them before they appear on our behalf?"

"They've been there from the beginning. They aren't allowed to present evidence, but they ensure Spadros Family interests are protected." He took a deep breath, let it out. "To answer your question, we'll meet with them before **we're** to appear. I hope you've told me everything. I don't relish being surprised in front of those men."

* * *

After Amelia finished my hair, I took care of my mail. As I suspected, there was no one in the city registered with the name Birdie, or anything similar. A nickname?

None of my contacts knew much about Marja. This didn't surprise me. Until a few years ago, she lived in the Pot.

As I pondered my next play, I realized: Pearson would be the best person to ask about the facility. He told me about it in the first place. So I directed him to learn what he could.

Then I went to the veranda to smoke; Amelia followed me. "Mum! Come upstairs, I'll get you into a walking dress."

I spoke more sharply than I intended. "I've worn this dress an hour! I don't need special clothes to walk in my own garden!"

Amelia flushed red and curtsied. "Yes, mum."

I lit a cigarette. To hell with Roy and his constant meddling! At this point I hoped he would try to hit me again.

The sun was high in the overcast sky when Mary Pearson came to tell me that Master Jonathan Diamond was here to call.

"Excellent!" I was going to have him seated outside, but I remembered his health. "How did he look? Is he well?"

"He looks quite fine, mum." An instant later, she blushed.

I smiled at her, amused. "Show him out to the veranda then, and bring tea. Master Diamond prefers his with milk."

I stepped on my cigarette then went to the veranda.

Jon, a tall man of twenty and six with skin so dark as to almost be black, emerged from the house and kissed my hand. He glanced around, the ever-present brown velvet bag of vials at his left hip clinking. "Is Mr. Spadros not home?"

I glanced over his shoulder. "Mary, tell Mr. Spadros that Master Jonathan Diamond has come to call."

Jon pulled out my favorite chair in the corner. Then he sat to my right. "I'm so glad to see you well. I've worried for you."

He was such a dear man. "Likewise."

Mary arrived with the tea-tray. "Mr. Anthony says he'll be down momentarily." She poured for us then curtsied and left.

I blew on my tea to cool it then took a sip. "To what do we owe the honor of your company?"

Jon smiled, turned towards me. "I wished to see you."

I thought I'd ask before Tony emerged. "Is Gardena well?"

"She's visiting friends in the country today."

"And your brothers?"

Jon chuckled. "They're well also."

"What's so funny?"

"You've never asked after them before."

"Well, I've never met them before." I considered the matter. "But I don't believe we were ever formally introduced." I laughed. "The whole matter was strange. Mr. Cesare had nothing but insult, and the rest stood round looking embarrassed."

"That's usually how things occur when with my brother."

I chuckled. "He spoke sharply, yes, but only the truth." I thought about this for a minute. "I think that's why I like you so; you only speak truth to me."

Jon turned away then, and I would swear he looked sad.

Tony appeared. "Jon! How are you?" We all rose, and the men shook hands, then we sat, Tony to my left. "You look well," he said to Jon. "The country suits you."

Jon chuckled. "I hadn't been to see my nephew in some time. He loves trains, so we went to the river for a few days to visit the station. He loved the puppet show there."

Tony leaned forward. "What else did you do?"

"He showed me his animals — pigs, cows." Jon laughed as if

taken by some amusing thought. "He tried to ride a pig and got spilled in the mud!"

I didn't know this nephew Jon spoke of, so the conversation didn't interest me. But Tony hung on Jon's every word.

For an instant, I wished for brothers, sisters, cousins, nephews. Those in Ma's cathedral were my family, but now even they were lost to me. Would I ever see them again?

Jon glanced at me. "How did you like the country?"

A mix of emotions crossed Tony's face ... disappointment and shock, yet a sudden relief?

I smiled at Jon, hoping he might enlighten me. "Please don't stop talking about your nephew's exploits on my account."

"I forgot you didn't know who I meant." Jon leaned back. "The boy you saw on Market Center. Remember?"

"Oh!" I said. "Yes!" I pictured him falling off a pig and chuckled. "That does sound amusing. I hope he wasn't hurt?"

"Oh, no," Jon said. "He's past the age of crying with every spill. He's a sturdy lad with a sunny disposition. One of the happiest boys I've ever seen."

Out of the corner of my eye Tony turned away. "Excuse me." He went into the house.

I turned to Jon. "Is anything wrong?"

Jon gave a one-shoulder shrug, not looking at me. He rested his elbow on the table, his head leaning on his hand. "What have you heard about the inquest?"

Tony was upset about something — but I didn't understand what. "We're supposed to meet with the lawyers soon. Tony seems to be dreading it." I glanced at the open doorway; Tony was nowhere in sight. "He made me speak of my business."

Jon's jaw dropped. "What happened?"

"He and his men caught me coming back from a case —"

Jon gave me a quick startled glance, and I realized I hadn't told him about anything that had happened since the New Year.

"— wearing Madame's clothes. He threatened to send Madame and her shop girl to his father."

Jon put his hand to his forehead. "I'm sorry, Jacqui." He took a deep breath, let it out. "How much did you tell him?"

"About the business, but I mentioned no names. He specifically asked about the night Daniel was killed. I told him what happened, and my father's part in it."

Jon nodded. "But not about Air."

I laughed in spite of myself. "Pandora's deck will never be dealt if I have anything to say about it."

"Jacqui, sooner or later he's going to find out. He deserves to hear it from you. It'll be difficult —" He stopped, then let out a breath, "— very difficult, but so far as I can tell, he's broken off with his father. Things are changing, Jacqui. If you stand with him, the two of you can get through this." Jon turned away. "Would it help if I were there when you told him?"

"Joe says he loves me, Jon. He wants to take me and leave Bridges." I hesitated, not wanting to cause Jon any grief. "I want to go with him."

Jon turned towards me, concern on his face. "Jacqui —"

Tony approached the doors from inside the dining room. I called out to him. "Are you well?"

Tony nodded. "I forgot to tell Pearson something important." He gave a fake smile, sat. "How's your tea?"

Jon said, "Cold, most likely. I completely forgot about it."

Pearson came outside. "Will Master Diamond be joining us for luncheon?"

Tony turned to Jon. "I'd be honored to have you."

So we had luncheon on the veranda, a much more pleasant affair than when we hosted Josie three months before.

Tony seemed to have forgotten whatever it was that upset him so. But evidently he knew the little boy from Market Center. Why did he not say so when I mentioned him before?

The Anniversary

As Jon was leaving, Pearson approached us. "A delivery, sir." Past him outside the open doorway, one of Tony's men held Rocket's leash as they walked down the front path.

"Write if you need anything," Jon said, then followed them to his white and silver carriage at the curb.

In the entryway, four burly young men struggled to carry two black and white urns of polished marble, which held houseplants with large dark glossy leaves. The urns and plants were similar to those in the hallway at the chapel where we were married.

A middle-aged, balding man in rumpled overalls stood nearby with a clipboard. "Where do ya want them?"

"In the parlor beside the sofa," I said, pointing the way.

I said to Pearson, "Who are they from?"

Pearson handed me an envelope holding an embossed card:

To Anthony and Jacqueline

On your anniversary

Roy and Molly Spadros

Today's our anniversary, I thought. Four years. I'd completely forgotten. "How kind of them!" Roy and Molly had never sent an anniversary gift before. Why now? "They must be from your mother: your father would never pick these colors."

Tony chuckled at that. "I'll write thanking her at once."

Tony and I were puzzled when one of Molly's men galloped up: she never sent anything. We felt perplexed when the urns were emptied and found to contain garden dirt and houseplants.

Who sent these, and why?

* * *

Since the Kerrs had some time ago invited us to join them at the racetrack, for our anniversary Tony accepted their offer. We left the gray cobblestones of Spadros, drove through the island of Market Center, and over to Hart quadrant, which had streets of closely-laid deep red brick. It might've been faster to travel through Diamond, or even Clubb, but it was safer to travel this way. In any case, we had several armed outriders with us.

The racetrack was far out into the Hart countryside. At the time, I thought: *This must have been part of the trip Joe took which ended in his terrible fall.*

Tony said, "Any news from Master Kerr?"

I laughed. "Are you reading my mind now? No. I hope that means he's well. Do you think his cast is off yet?"

"So he never wrote you this entire time?" Tony seemed at a loss. "I thought the two of you were fast friends."

Indeed, I loved no one more. But my letters went unanswered. "He's never been a letter-writer."

I wasn't sure he even knew how to write; I hadn't learned until I was twelve, and he was taken from the Pot much later. "I'll inquire when we next meet."

Tony smiled. "I'm sure you and Josie will have much to chatter about as well."

Josie had sent a printed condolence card for Anastasia, which was quite kind under the circumstances.

They're grieving Marja's loss. It would be cruel to expect them to write, when the only mother they knew had been murdered.

* * *

The buildings at the racetrack were red brick trimmed in white, a black wrought iron fence round the whole complex. It reminded me of the fence surrounding the Pot since the Coup.

When we arrived, men dressed in the red and silver livery of the Hart Family unhitched our horses. Our guards flanked us as we followed a man in Hart livery up the red brick steps carpeted in brilliant red to a set of glass-paneled white doors, similar to the doors leading out to the veranda at Spadros Manor.

Silver and crystal chandeliers hung from the white vaulted ceiling several stories above us. Dozens of men, women, and children traversed the cherry-paneled hall while a man's voice spoke rapidly overhead. Many stared at Tony as we passed.

I giggled, taking Tony's arm. "You're quite the attraction."

Tony rarely smiled in public; he was a master at not revealing how he felt. "This building is astonishing. I find it difficult not to goggle like a tourist at the sight."

I patted his arm. "You're doing quite well."

A short, broad flight of white steps rose to a landing with many sets of glass-paneled white doors. These stood open, dozens going through. Our guide led us to an immense stadium.

Horses ran in the distance. Tens of thousands of cherry-stained wooden seats teemed with parasols and top hats, Derby hats, and caps. Children frolicked on the wooden steps, while the man's voice — now broadcast over the crowd — continued its rapid pace. The crowd cheered. "This is spectacular."

"This way, mum," our guide said. Everyone stood waiting.

I turned to Tony. "I suppose now I'm the tourist."

Tony's eyes flashed amusement before his mask reappeared.

We followed to the left, then up a long flight of white steps. Finally we came to glass-paneled white doors.

To our left, picture windows showed the entire raceway. A buffet lay along the far wall. To our right, windows displayed the countryside. The announcer's voice continued its rapid assessment overhead, delicious smells filling the air. The room — thrice the size of our dining hall — was full of people. The tables and chairs were of cherry-wood, with seats cushioned in silver and red brocade.

Charles Hart, portly and red-haired, moved toward us as we entered. He shook hands with Tony, kissed mine. "How good of you to come!" He gestured to the room. "My home is yours."

I glanced back. "Where's Honor?"

Tony chuckled. "Forgive my wife, sir; she has far too much regard for her servants." He leaned toward me. "Our men are well, my love."

A trio of musicians began setting up next to the buffet.

Mr. Hart bent closer, his voice conspiratorial. "The servants' accommodations are the best in Bridges. They can drink a pint and bet on the games, shout when they win and curse when they lose — without having to worry about our tidy disapproval."

I laughed. We were a rather prim lot. "I like you, Mr. Hart."

At this, he seemed touched. "And I like you too, my dear."

"Look," Tony said, "your friends." He pointed to our right.

Joe and Josie sat at a corner table across the room with several others. With her back to the large picture window, Josie made a lovely portrait with her golden curls and clear blue eyes. She nudged Joe, and he looked to her, as if taken off guard.

Joe grasped crutches standing against the wall, gazed at me with those beautiful green eyes, and smiled.

Joseph Kerr's smile held the life and gladness of a summer day, the joy and ease usually only found in the smallest of children. It was innocent and earnest, lighting up the room.

Our eyes met, and I felt that electric shock to my soul.

Gods, how I loved him.

"Mr. Spadros," Charles Hart said. The unease in his voice startled me away from Joe's magnetic gaze. "Perhaps we might sit here? I have a table prepared."

Tony said, "We should go to them, rather than force them to come to us." He took my arm. "Excuse us, sir."

"Not at all." Mr. Hart's face was grim. "Enjoy your friends."

We crossed the room past tables full of people smoking, chatting, eating, and drinking. Most had reddish hair, but some had the straight heavy black hair of Mr. Hart's ancestors.

"Tony, should we have spurned Mr. Hart's invitation?"

"Nonsense," Tony said. "You deserve to be among friends today. Besides, I wish to dine with them."

Surely the reason we visited was to strengthen ties with the Harts? Why else provoke Roy by coming here?

Josie and Joe stood waiting for us.

My heart was pounding, my mouth dry. I longed to caress Joe's soft brown hair, to press his golden body against mine.

Tony shook Joe's hand. "Good to see you up, sir."

Joe reached out, his eyes on mine, and kissed my hand as Tony kissed Josie's. "A pleasure to see you, Mrs. Spadros."

"And I you." I couldn't linger on his hand, as much as I wished to. I took Josie's hands. "I'm so glad to see you."

Josie smiled. "I'm glad to see you as well." She gestured to the empty table. "Would you care to join us?"

I gasped. "Your friends didn't need to leave on our account!"

Waiters took Joe and Josie's plates, swept crumbs, wiped down and set the table. The room buzzed with conversation.

Josie shrugged. "The table has changed twice in as many hours. They wanted to bet a new round."

Indeed, the announcer called for those placing bets to come forward. But why throw money away on a chance to win more?

"Well, then," Tony said, "let's eat!" He held out a chair for me across from Joe, then took a seat next to Josie.

A waiter approached. "What shall I bring you, Mr. Spadros?"

"A selection from the buffet. And wine for the table, please."

"That's very kind of you, sir," Josie said.

Tony laughed. "It's easy to be gracious in someone else's home. Thank Mr. Hart."

Josie seemed amused.

Joe sat regarding me.

I recalled how I touched Tony, and heat rushed to my cheeks at the thought of touching Joe that way. "I hope you're well?"

"Quite well, thank you," Joe said, "all things considered."

They both wore black. Much of the room wore black still, others dark colors such as navy, deep purple, charcoal. Yet most of the room laughed and were merry, betting and drinking.

Tony said, "Did you lose someone in the explosion?"

Josie glanced away, handkerchief held to her face.

Tony said, "Forgive me, I didn't mean to cause grief."

Joe appeared unperturbed. "No one of any importance to us was aboard. A woman who was as a mother to us was murdered the night before the disaster. So we mourn her as we would our mother, if we would have known her."

Tony seemed confused.

Josie said, "Our mother died bearing us."

Tony stared at Joe. "Who would murder a woman? My sincerest apologies, sir. Have the police caught the scoundrel?"

An instant of anger went through them both.

"Marja was from the Pot, sir," Josie said, glancing away. "There was little interest in the case."

If the swarm of police outside Vig's bar after Marja's death wasn't there for Marja, why were they there?

Tony said, "Couldn't Mr. Hart persuade them to investigate?"

Bribe them is what he meant.

Joe said, "She was murdered in Spadros quadrant."

Tony sat back, mouth open. Waiters set large serving platters full of various foods in front of us, along with bottles of wine. But by custom, none of us could eat until Tony did. "How can I help?"

Josie shrugged. The announcer chattered overhead.

Tony glanced around. "I seem to have lost my manners." He spooned food onto his plate and took a bite. "Please, join me."

The look which crossed Josie's eyes was cynical, disdainful, and amused at the same time. And I recalled what she said in February: *I'm not above begging for anything that will help my family prosper. Even from him.* I wondered if she still harbored anger towards Tony for killing Ottilie, Treysa, and Poignee.

We sat eating to the sound of the announcer, the crowd, and rousing jazz music. After some time, Mr. Hart came to the table. "Mr. Spadros! Would you and your wife like to watch the races?"

"Certainly," Tony said. He turned to me. "Excuse me, my dear, I'll leave you to chat with your friends."

Mr. Hart's face went cold.

I smiled up at Tony. "Thank you. I'll be along shortly."

Josie rose. "I'd like some air."

Joe moved to get up, but she waved him off. "I'll just be on the landing." She smiled. "You two have much to discuss."

Josie strolled across the room and opened the door to the landing, the breeze tossing her blonde curls. Tony and Mr. Hart stood at the railing before the picture windows.

I gazed across the table at Joe.

His eyes never left mine. "You look lovely."

I smiled. "Thank you."

"I've missed you. My days are filled with dull exercise."

"Why did you never write me?"

His gaze never faltered. "With the expense of doctors and attendants after my injury, then Marja's funeral, we couldn't afford to send mail. Choosing between pen, paper, ink, messenger fees to your Country House, and food —" he shrugged. "We're grateful Mr. Hart brought us here today."

I recalled Mr. Hart's demeanor just now. "What's happened, Joe? Does your grandfather no longer have an allowance?"

"It's complex." He shifted in his chair. "My grandfather's a proud man. Mr. Hart helps him, but his aid comes at a price."

Ah. I remembered Roy's methods of ensuring loyalty. "I see." Doubtless Mr. Kerr hid his financial difficulties so as not to be further entrapped in Family matters.

Joe patted the table to his right. "Sit by me."

I moved to Tony's seat so as not to appear too intimate. Tony glanced at us, then resumed talking. Mr. Hart stared at us, the stiffness of his posture displaying his unease.

Many in the room sneaked glances at us. The memory of Joe's kiss in the Kerr's parlor two months ago lingered; I gripped my empty glass so as not to reach for his hand.

A waiter came up. "More wine, mum?"

"Ah," Joe said. "You must try their new drink." He turned to the waiter. "Chocolate martinis for us both."

"Yes, sir," the waiter said, disappearing into the crowd.

"Do you remember our last meeting?" Joe said.

His touch, his kiss .... "How could I forget?"

"You seemed intoxicated. I don't want to offend."

"Joe, never doubt my feelings for you. Ever." I took a deep breath, gazed into his eyes. "I've never truly loved anyone else."

The night I gave myself to Tony flashed before me then, and I gripped the stem of my glass, guilt at my betrayal gnawing at me. I faced the room. "I have decided to learn who killed Marja."

He let out a breath. "Damn this leg! I should be out finding her murderer." He spoke earnestly. "You must not do this."

I snorted, amused. "You sound like my husband. He's

forbidden me to continue my business."

"You told him?" He paused a moment. "Did he hurt you?"

I smiled to myself. "He told me I was brave. But I'm forbidden to go anywhere without escort."

Joe hesitated. "It would be safer."

Should I tell him? "Marja sent me a letter before she died, asking to meet. The night I did, I found her shot in the street."

Joe gazed at me, perfectly composed.

Perhaps he'd come to terms with her death. Perhaps it didn't seem real. But the memory of her death had haunted me ever since. "She didn't die alone. I held her hand as she left us." My vision blurred. "Her last thought was for Josie." I wiped my eyes. "I promised her I'd keep Josie safe ... and it occurred to me that if someone's targeting people I love, you're both in danger as well."

He leaned forward. "Did she say anything else?"

I shook my head. "I got there too late for that, it seems."

He rested his hand on my arm; his touch warmed me. "We're safe, Jacqui." He withdrew his hand as the waiter approached with our drinks. "My friends'll guard us until I'm well."

I sipped my drink. It was delicious.

Joe said, "But how can I help? The police won't do anything, and we have nothing to give them."

"I believe my husband wants to help. See if Marja wrote to anyone else, or kept any private notes."

Joe nodded. "I'll ask Josie."

I grinned. And how would he send the information? They had no money. "Expect a package soon."

Joe appeared intrigued. "I can't wait."

Josie pushed open the door, and I could tell she was annoyed. She went to Tony and spoke to him; he left the way she came in.

Josie stood facing the window, arms crossed, then went to a group of younger men and women, who rose to greet her.

Tony returned to our table. "I hope the two of you are well?"

I smiled up at him. "Quite."

Joe said, "I saw my sister speak with you."

"It's nothing," Tony said. "One of our horses stumbled and fell when they brought it to the stable; the doctor's seeing to it.

They told the driver it was just a scratch, but it's best to be safe."

I said, "Poor thing."

Tony said to Joe, "The Dealer has blessed you with a steadfast friend. She only thinks of helping others."

"Sir," Joe said, "let me have the horse you lent us brought to you. I can call for it now. Then you can leave when you like."

Tony seemed touched. "That's very kind, Master Kerr."

Joe said, "I'll see to it at once." He waved to Josie, who spoke to her friends then turned towards us.

Tony said to me, "Would you like to see the racing?"

"Yes," Joe said, "you must. I insist."

"Oh, no," I said. "I'm quite comfortable here." I looked at the large windows beside me. "The view is magnificent."

"Very well," Tony said. "Enjoy the view." He returned to Mr. Hart, who slapped his shoulder and pointed to the racetrack.

Josie had been standing aside. "Yes, Joe?"

"Send for the horse Mr. Spadros lent us."

She seemed unsurprised. "Of course." She went back to her group and spoke in a young man's ear, who jostled two more. The three men walked towards the door and were gone.

I said, "Will you be able to manage with one horse?" Josie seemed so grateful to borrow our horse in the first place.

Joe said, "It's not such a grand offer, Jacqui. We sold our carriage and got one a single horse can pull. I might not be able to ride for some time. So we'll manage." He gazed at me with those beautiful eyes. "To be honest, we can't afford to feed it anymore."

This financial downturn seemed disheartening. *He must feel humiliated.* "I'm sorry."

"Marja. Do you have any idea who might have killed her?"

I shook my head. I didn't really know anything. "It was too convenient, Marja being killed right as I came to meet her." If whoever conspired to kill my Ma discovered that Marja overheard them, they would have killed Marja sometime during the several days between when Marja's letter arrived and I left to meet her. Which reinforced the notion they killed her simply to torment me.

Who knew I was going out? As far as I knew, only Sawbuck, Morton, and Blitz — unless someone else saw me leave and notified the killer. "I fear a spy in my husband's guards."

"The very men who protect you?"

"They're all Roy's men, Joe. Not one is there to protect me; it's all for my husband's benefit."

Joe became quite earnest. "Well, then you must find a way to change that." He glanced around. "Why do they need you?"

I shrugged. "As far as I can tell, for an heir. But any woman would suffice, except for the love my husband bears for me."

Joe's face darkened. "I can't bear the thought of him touching you. I wish I were well. I'd take you where he'd never find you."

I thought of Madame Biltcliffe and her loveless marriage. "I wish you were well, too. But you're not, so we must wait."

Tony kept glancing back at me.

"I'm sorry, Joe — I must leave you for now. I don't think Mr. Hart is pleased that we refused his invitation to dine."

Joe nodded. "I understand."

"Is something wrong? A falling-out between you?"

Joe gazed aside, shoulders drooping. "It was long ago." He waved me on. "You have your duties. Don't worry about me. Please, enjoy your day." Then he held my hand tightly, kissed it. "I'm grateful for this time with you, however brief."

I felt touched. "As am I. Farewell, my love."

"Ah, there you are, my dear," Mr. Hart said as I approached. "A race is just beginning."

I put my arm through Tony's, standing between the two men. A gun sounded far below. The horses ran, the men on their backs whipping them around and around, getting nowhere.

Perhaps they were more like me than I imagined.

At last, one ran faster, and everyone cheered. Or groaned, if they had bet on another, I suppose.

"So what do you think?" Mr. Hart said eagerly.

I shrugged. "Must they whip the horses?"

Tony laughed. "I told you she had her own mind. Even after so long in her company, still she surprises me."

Mr. Hart gazed at me as if trying to memorize my visage, yet his tone was light, soothing. "It's all in fun, my dear. The horses aren't harmed." He gave a short laugh. "They're valuable animals, which I hope to keep in good health for many years."

He continued to look at me, and I began to feel uncomfortable at the intensity of his gaze. The hair on my arms stood on end. I moved to Tony's other arm. "Well, that's a relief."

The day was lovely: a blue sky with white clouds floating high above the faint shimmer of the dome. Tony and Mr. Hart chatted, but Mr. Hart watched me more than the horses.

Why did he keep staring at me?

Mr. Hart turned to Tony. "Might I speak with your wife, sir?"

I said, "My husband can hear anything you have to say —"

"Certainly," Tony said, as if I had not spoken. "Excuse me." He left, disappearing into the Men's Room.

Mr. Hart leaned against the brass railing in front of the large windows. His eyes never left mine. "How do you like my home?"

I glanced away, heart pounding. "You live here?"

He grinned. "The Harts have lived at the racetrack since my grandfather and his brother captured it during the Coup. Next time you're here, I'll take you on a tour of our private quarters."

His tone made it seem much too intimate. "My husband and I would be pleased to visit."

"I'm glad." His eyes met mine. "You're enjoying your day?"

He continued gazing at me. What were his intentions? I glanced away. "Indeed, sir. I thank you for your hospitality."

He took a step towards me, and instinctively I drew back. I considered his wife Judith's past reactions to my presence. Did she believe him to have an unseemly attraction? He was old enough to be my grandfather!

For an instant, he seemed unsure of how to proceed. "You should beware of associating with Master Kerr. His reputation —"

This was outrageous. I stood my ground, faced him. "Sir, if I may. While I thank you for your counsel, you are neither my husband nor my father —"

Mr. Hart flinched, setting his jaw.

"— and I will not shun a man I've known since birth on account of rumor. I'm astonished you would slander a guest so."

Mr. Hart stood stock still, mouth open.

"Why is he here then, if you believe him to be unsuitable?"

Mr. Hart flushed red. "That's none of your concern."

Tony approached us. "Is all well?"

I clung to Tony's arm with both hands, grateful he'd appeared. "Perhaps it's time we left."

Tony shook his head. "The horses aren't ready. Please, I wish the two of you to be friends."

"Then our host must either explain himself or apologize."

Mr. Hart glanced away. "Well, Mrs. Spadros, I don't need to explain myself to you." He held out his hand. "But I apologize for giving offense. It would please me to be friends."

I daresay it would please you to be much more than that.

But I let him take my hand, which he held a bit longer than necessary. Then one of his men called him away.

"Jacqui," Tony said in a whisper, "what did he say?"

"He wants us to shun Joe." I felt so angry I could barely speak. "He brings the man to his table, yet tells his other guests to shun him. What kind of man does that?"

Tony hesitated, then said, "This hasn't been the outing I hoped. I'm sorry."

I squeezed his arm. "It's not your fault. Really. I'm glad we came. It's been a lovely day."

"Perhaps we should sit apart from the Kerrs, so as not to give offense." Tony led me to a table for two by the wall, and there we waited, sipping wine until our horses were ready to leave.

Josie refused to accompany us to the carriage. "Joe's friends will carry him down," she said, "but they're rather flighty. I dare not leave him with them, or he may find himself alone."

Would these men protect him from Frank Pagliacci and Jack Diamond? I gripped her hand. "Watch over him, Josie. I beg you."

"I will." She patted my hand. "Enjoy your trip home."

* * *

We drove through Hart quadrant, over the bridge to Market Center, over the bridge to Spadros, and past the Pot. The shadows had begun to lengthen.

Tony said, "Why didn't you tell me about Helen Hart?"

Had he found out I lied? "What about her?"

"About her illness? I should have guessed you weren't with her when you told me you went with Master Rainbow on his yacht. But —" he shook his head, "I fear I caused Mr. Hart grief."

"I'm sorry, Tony. Josie told me about the baby, and —"

"What baby?"

I stared at him. Did I reveal a confidence? "Josie told me their baby died: it was born too soon."

"Oh." Tony sounded dismayed.

"She made me promise not to tell. No one was to know for fear the papers would learn of it."

Tony's face fell. "Mr. Hart made it sound a terrible illness." His eyes narrowed. "Did he lie to me?"

I let out a breath. "Tony, he may not trust you. I don't understand this split between Mr. Hart and the Kerrs. And ... Mr. Hart kept staring at me. Frankly, I felt uncomfortable."

Tony sounded hesitant. "Jacqui — I don't think he meant anything by it."

Did Tony mean to say I imagined it? Where was his obsession with my reputation now? "Whether he meant anything or not, it was quite rude for him to stare at me so. I have enough people calling me a —"

The carriage turned off the main road. Tony grabbed the speaker tube. "What's wrong?"

The driver said, "Road's blocked, a turnip-cart spilled."

Tony peered out of the window. "What a mess." We started off again, full speed. He turned to me. "Jacqui, you know how much I care about your —"

A shot rang out. The carriage jolted and lurched to the right, as if running over something large with our left wheels, and a horse screamed. Then the carriage jerked backwards. I fell to the left as sand sprayed across my face. Tony fell atop me.

What just happened?

Tony stood. "Are you hurt?"

Shouts and whinnies filled the air; next to my head, a horse screamed in terror and pain. The carriage shuddered.

"No." I glanced at the sky through the window just above Tony's head. "Someone shot at us."

"Yes." Tony helped me to my feet. In the half-darkness, I couldn't tell what he was feeling.

My gun was at home. "What shall we do?"

Tony climbed to the front of the carriage and opened the front window, crouching to peer outside. "I don't see the driver. The horses are tangled." He opened the back window. "Oh, gods."

I retreated from the horse's screams; Tony held me.

One of Tony's men appeared above us. "Are you well, sir?"

"Yes," Tony said. "Someone fired upon us."

"Yes, sir." The man moved towards the front of the carriage, returning a moment later. "Driver's dead, sir. Shot in the head."

I didn't even know the man's name.

Tony said, "Are the wheels damaged?"

"Let me check, sir." He came back. "I don't think so. We've sent for another horse." He grimaced. "Sorry for the noise, sir; we can't tend to the horse until we get the carriage off it."

Honor's face replaced the man's. "Lean on the seat, mum."

I did so, placing my feet on the carriage wall below me.

Shouts, grunts, and groans as the carriage was righted with a mighty heave. I stood, opened the door, and sprang outside. A large crowd of sweating men surrounded the carriage.

"Thank you for your help," I called out. "Find the scoundrel who did this."

Shouts and cheers as men scattered to the buildings.

Tony stood near the front of our carriage. His men assisted the horses, who had many cuts and scrapes on their sides.

The horse lying at the rear of the carriage cried out, eyes wide, its flanks mangled by the carriage-wheels. A bloody mark lay on the cobblestones where it had been dragged by the reins.

Honor shot the poor beast in the head and it lay still.

"That was the horse we lent the Kerrs," Tony said. "It would've been better if it had stayed with them."

A card lay on the ground. It was the size of a business card, but blank. On the other side lay the silhouette of a dog, stamped in red: the mark of the Red Dog Gang.

The Torment

I sat on the sofa in my study, examining the card in my hand. Was this a coincidence? Or were these false Red Dogs claiming responsibility for this outrage?

Tony soon followed. "You're not going to believe this." He sat in an armchair across from me, elbows on his knees, head down. "The turnip truck spilled directly beyond a street under construction. Several men moved the warning signs a few hours ago, filled the hole with sand, and spread cloth painted like cobblestones. In the twilight, the driver never saw the danger."

I handed him the Red Dog card. "It was a trap."

Tony peered at the card, then nodded.

I shook my head. "Someone knew when we left Hart quadrant and our route."

"How can you be sure?"

"This took planning."

I gasped, recalling Mrs. Bryce's sale.

"What is it?"

Where to begin? "Master Rainbow claimed a black-haired woman named Birdie, who he met when he thought Frank Pagliacci was with the District Attorney's office —"

"Wait," Tony said. "Master Rainbow knew Frank Pagliacci?"

Oh, dear. "Master Hogan didn't tell you?"

Tony frowned. "No, he didn't." He shook his head. "Never

mind that. What about this woman?"

I bit my lip. I made Sawbuck promise not to tell, and then I did it myself. This wasn't going to end well.

I took a deep breath and let it out. "He later saw Birdie at the scene of a murder. I believe the person murdered had knowledge of the explosion, and this woman may have tried to silence her. I think Birdie and Frank Pagliacci, or perhaps another of his crew, set the bomb which destroyed Master Rainbow's yacht."

Tony peered at me, a slight frown on his face. "So they were trying to kill those who might identify them."

"Yes. I think your father's after them, which may be why."

If Jack Diamond had set alibis in advance as I suspected, he was more cunning than I thought. Not only did this protect him from Roy, but from Frank as well.

Tony grinned. "Good for him." But then he paused. "So what does this have to do with my driver?"

"We'd best call Master Hogan in."

Tony left to find Sawbuck. Amelia entered with my mail — which I had her put on my desk — and tea. "Master Hogan and my husband will be joining us; please bring tea for them as well."

"It's almost time to dress for dinner."

"We'll take dinner in here."

"Yes, mum."

I had well and truly erred. Once Tony realized Sawbuck hid something of this magnitude he would question what else he'd hidden. Sawbuck hid our adventures the night Marja died from Tony because I asked him to, and would be furious.

Tony and Sawbuck stalked in. "I must apologize."

That stopped them in their tracks.

"I asked Master Hogan to withhold certain events, and he did so out of love for you. No other reason."

Tony turned away, still angry.

Sawbuck blushed.

I stared at him, so astonished that it took a moment to regain my composure. Sawbuck loved Tony, but not as a father or older brother, as I'd thought, nor even as a cousin. "Master Hogan —"

Sawbuck knew that I knew. "Please, call me Ten. If you will."

I felt humbled, melancholy. "I'm truly sorry. For everything."

Tony, still looking away, nodded. He hadn't noticed a thing.

I took a deep breath. "I suppose I'd best begin at the beginning."

The one thing I couldn't do was to reveal Rachel Diamond's intervention to help Ma. Tony's mother Molly had been crystal clear on that account. If anyone knew Ma was alive, it would put her — and possibly Mrs. Diamond — in mortal danger. So I told them the Kerr's housekeeper Marja raised me, Joe, Josie, and my kitchen maids Ottilie, Poignee, and Treysa, who Tony had killed.

Tony turned pensive at that.

Then I described Marja's letter, which warned a mutual friend was to be murdered. I left home the night Tony worked late at the casino to meet with Marja, only to find her mortally shot.

"Good gods," Tony said. "I'm so sorry you had to see that."

I shrugged, but his words were such an echo of Joe's that it touched me. "Master ... Ten found her. The police came, so we ran. But then Master Rainbow told us a woman with light skin and jet black hair — who called herself Birdie — just shot at him."

Tony's jaw dropped. "She shot at him, too?"

*Too? Could a **woman** have murdered Marja? But why?* I nodded, saying to Sawbuck, "But what driver had we that night?"

Sawbuck paled. "The same."

"This evening was no accident, Tony. Our driver saw something that night he shouldn't have, and now he's dead."

If I hadn't gone out that night, perhaps neither of them would have died. My gaze fell to the blood-stained card on the table. How long would any of us survive? "You wanted to know where I went before you found me at Madame's wearing her mourning garb? I visited David Bryce, the boy who was kidnapped."

"Is he well?" Tony said.

I shook my head. "But his mother made a large sale of gray cloth earlier this month to a young woman with black hair. The woman said it was for art."

Tony and Sawbuck exchanged glances.

"Art," Tony said bitterly. He pointed at the card. "Perhaps it's best she not know she met with one of her child's kidnappers."

I shuddered, glancing towards the letters on my desk. "When I spoke with your father at the Women's Club —"

Sawbuck snorted in disdain, Tony flinched, and I let out a sigh. "Yes, I know. But I did learn something."

Tony leaned forward.

"Your father mentioned how he learned of your injury —"

"Oh?" Tony said. "I always wondered."

"An anonymous letter from a young black-haired woman —"

"Ah," Sawbuck said. "Birdie."

"My thoughts exactly." Then I turned to Tony. "Your father agrees to let us examine the letter ... if we go to him for it."

Sawbuck began to laugh. "This is rich! The man won't even help his own son without extracting some petty torment."

Tony shook his head. "Are you surprised? If this is all, let's participate in his petty torment and be done with it."

I wasn't looking forward to this.

"Oh," Tony said, "I almost forgot. Pearson!"

Pearson opened the door and stuck his head in. "Yes, sir?"

"The package."

"Yes, sir." Pearson brought in a medium-sized box wrapped in white paper, handing it to Tony.

Tony offered it to me. "Happy anniversary."

Sawbuck rose, clearly uncomfortable. "I'll leave you, then."

"Sure, Ten," Tony said, his eyes never leaving mine, "thanks for your help." Once Sawbuck left, Tony said, "Go on, open it."

Under the paper lay a stationery box: paper, pens, a small bottle of ink, sealing-wax, even matches. "This is perfect!" Now I could send paper, pen, and ink to Joe so he could write me.

"Amelia told me you enjoyed writing whilst in your rooms."

I felt touched at his thoughtfulness. "Thank you." I put the box on the table and went to him.

He rose, taking my hands in his. "I'm sorry today went so poorly." He cupped my face in his hands, rested his forehead on mine. "My only desire is for you to be the happiest woman alive. Whatever you wish for is yours."

I closed my eyes. *But what if what I wish for is to be free?*

The Rule

The next day, I went to Madame's shop for my fitting. Her store front had been tidied, and she met me out front as usual, but stiffly, without a smile. "Come in."

My outriders dismounted; one went each way, another followed us. Madame turned to Honor and said, "You men aren't allowed in here."

Honor hesitated, but Tony's other man said, "He goes in, or I do. Or we return to the Manor. Your choice."

Madame glanced at Honor. "Better a footman than a thug."

The other man snorted in amusement, then faced the street. After Madame, Honor, and I entered the store, Madame turned the placard to "Closed: entry by appointment only," and crossed to my private curtained dressing room. "He will not come inside."

Honor said, "Certainly not. But men watch each end of your back alley until we leave together." He turned to me. "I'm sorry, mum." He opened the curtain, letting it fall behind us.

Madame whispered, "It would have been better if you didn't come here."

"What do you mean?"

She said nothing.

"I want to continue having you as my dressmaker, very much so. I don't know what threats my husband gave you, but I had nothing to do with it." I turned away. "I hate him for it."

"Ah, cherie ..." compassion laced her voice, "the decision was mine. He wanted me to spy, and I said no." She laid a hand on my shoulder. "Don't be troubled by it."

"But why mustn't I visit? The sentiment against the Family?"

Her sleeve had slid up: a large purple bruise lay on her arm.

"That's part of it," she whispered. "But ..." she glanced at her arm, then flinched away, covering the bruise with her hand.

I felt horrified. "Who hurt you?"

She snorted. "Spadros men. New ones, in Spadros livery. I didn't inform the Family of my 'extra' income over the years."

Shame flooded me, and remorse. "I'm so sorry."

She shrugged. "I still have my teeth, and nothing is broken. I must pay double fees now." She sounded weary. "But I'm alive."

Tenni peeked in. Madame said, "Come in, dear girl, it's safe."

Tenni held the partially-completed dress. After helping me undress, Tenni and Madame pinned my new dress around me.

"May I ask something, Madame?"

"Of course."

"Did you find anything missing? From your files?"

"There were several purchase orders gone — all ones your husband signed."

How would they even know such papers would be there? "Has anyone been in your office? Did any unusual event happen before the break-in? Anything at all?"

"No ..." Madame said, but her eyes gazed far away. A line appeared between her perfect brows. "Yes. There was one thing odd. Several months ago, a young woman asked to be measured. She was to be married in another city and needed notes for her dressmaker. I receive several requests like this each year.

"I measured her as I always do. I brought her to the office, wrote the measurements, then opened my cabinet to take out a folder. Just then, a messenger boy arrived with a letter. I took it, tipped the boy, then turned back, that quickly. I gave the woman my notes, she left." She shook her head. "The letter was blank."

"Can you describe her?"

Madame smiled, color rising to her cheeks. "Very pretty, very young. A lovely figure and straight black hair. Porcelain skin, blue eyes. Ah, a gorgeous girl."

This sounded suspiciously like that woman Birdie. "Do you have her file?"

Madame stared at me, mouth open. "I do."

Honor gave me a surprised glance over his shoulder as the curtain flew open.

Madame returned with a thin file. On the tab: "Eunice Ogier."

A windswept cemetery, an empty grave. Men strained at the winches as they lowered a coffin inside. Molly held my hand. I looked up at her. "This is how we do for our dead."

I nodded. Not left on the street for the rats and crows like in the Pot.

But I couldn't see her inside that box, and I couldn't sit next to her, or comb her hair. I couldn't hold her hand, and no one let me take her rings. They'd never be sold to help her people. I didn't understand.

Eunice Ogier was old, old. She didn't call me a Pot rag like the others. One night, she told me she and her family left the Pot to stay with the first Acevedo Spadros when she was a little girl, back when the Pot was good, just before the war. He told her they would be in his family now. "I'll always remember him for that."

Some nights, she cried about him dying.

Could there be someone else in the city with that name?

Surely not. She had no children. Her relatives died long ago.

Who knew I used the name Eunice Ogier on my cases?

* * *

For the rest of the visit — and on the way home — I pondered the question. My contacts were the only ones who could connect me with that name. An elderly servant at the Country House. A few people in various government offices on Market Center. Thrace Pike. And Mr. Blackberry at the *Bridges Daily.*

Mr. Blackberry was at the Clubb desk for years before he became editor. He'd given me all sorts of information, never asking for anything in return. Could he be giving my information to the Clubbs?

But Ottilie, Treysa, and Poignee had been stealing my letters: they knew this name too. This was the first real evidence they might have been in league with the Red Dog Gang.

I could understand their petty attempts at blackmail. I could even understand stealing my letters out of curiosity. But to send my personal information to someone wishing me harm? What had I done to them, other than offer a better life?

* * *

When I returned home, I went straight to Tony's room. His manservant Jacob Michaels was helping Tony into his jacket when I walked in. "Jacqui? What is it?" Tony said.

I said to Michaels, "Please leave us."

Michaels bowed, shutting the door behind him.

"Why did you kill my kitchen maids? What did they say?"

Tony sat heavily on his bed, not looking at me. "They talked amongst themselves. They — they accused you of giving yourself to the Apprentices gladly, because I was incapable."

"That's the most preposterous thing I've ever heard!"

Tony sounded defensive. "They did say it, Jacqui."

A laugh burst from me in spite of the chaos inside. "First, you are capable, and you know it. Second, I have no desire for Apprentices. Third, in case they had some mad desire for me, the Inventor paid me escort the entire time. Why care so much about what some silly women say?"

*Why did you have to **kill** them?*

Tony spoke slowly. "They swore allegiance to the Spadros Family, Jacqui. I stood outside the kitchen window on a public street and heard them. To speak against us in public is betrayal."

And betraying the Family meant death. I nodded, overwhelmed by grief. "Thank you for telling me."

"Jacqui —"

"I'm going to my rooms now."

Poignee spoke whatever words came into her head, usually biting ones. Treysa and Ottilie went along with anything Poignee said, especially Ottilie, who was younger.

They never understood the danger.

* * *

I ate dinner in my room, with little appetite. And I couldn't sleep. If the men attacked Madame Biltcliffe, who else was next?

Vig Vikenti helped me numerous times, the most recent being

the night I found Marja dead outside his saloon. If something happened to him because of me, I could never forgive myself.

When Tony slept, I put on my robe and went to the door.

Blitz Spadros patrolled the hall, and I waited for the glow of his candle to approach. Besides being our footman, Blitz played piano at Vig's saloon. "Mrs. Spadros, how may I help you?"

"I'm sure you know what's befallen Madame Biltcliffe —"

Blitz shook his head.

"She's been beaten for helping me, and I find myself fearful. Is Vig Vikenti well?"

Blitz glanced away, let out a breath. "Vig was supposed to report his dealings with you to Mr. Roy, but he didn't."

Fear struck me. "What happened? Is he —"

"Dead? No. They broke his nose, destroyed his saloon, but he's alive." Blitz rubbed the back of his neck. "Angry. But he knew the consequences for breaking the rule."

"What rule?"

"You live in Spadros, you report to Mr. Roy. It's the only rule, besides paying fees. Didn't you know?"

Was everyone in Spadros reporting my whereabouts to Roy?

Three of Tony's men were there that night. Sawbuck was Molly's nephew and should be safe enough. It seemed Morton got out of Spadros Manor just in time. "What'll happen to you?"

"Me? I don't know." He grinned, and when he did, he reminded me of Tony. "You can't care about such things when you align yourself against a man like him."

My loyalty is to the Spadros Family.

To the Spadros Family. Not Roy.

"Why **did** you do that?"

He glanced away. "Spadros quadrant deserves better. Bridges has a brutal, bloody past, but we also have a good and noble one."

"A secret Royalist, then?"

Blitz snorted. "You don't need a king to live in peace. People want someone to lead them. But they want to take pride in their leader and be motivated by goodwill, not fear."

What happened to Vig would make him hate the Spadros Family even more than he already did. "Is there a way to help?"

"Vig? Best way to help is to stay away for a bit. I'll let him know you asked."

The way Blitz smiled just then ... Vig's misery when he thought I was using him ...

I sighed. Vig found me attractive, even desirable: many men did. But since the night he rescued me, I feared this might happen. "Tell him I'm sorry. I never meant to hurt him. Tell him ... I remain his true and grateful friend. Say it just like that."

Blitz nodded. "I will." He bowed. "Good night, Mrs. Spadros."

* * *

I closed the door, leaned against it. Tony lay asleep.

They broke Vig's nose? Destroyed his saloon?

I stalked to the bed, threw the covers off Tony. "You promised my friends wouldn't be hurt!"

Tony turned towards me. "What? Jacqui, what's wrong?"

"You promised none of my friends would be hurt if I told you about my business. You lied!"

Tony held up his hand. "Jacqui, wait — what happened?"

"Madame had bruises all over her arms. Your men beat her!"

Tony shook his head. "I never told them to do that. Blitz!"

Blitz entered, stood before us. "Yes, sir?"

"Who's responsible for hurting her friend?"

Blitz glanced away. "Your father's men. I told them not to do it, but they beat the man within a —"

Tony said, "Man? What man?"

I brought my hands to my mouth, horrified. I never told Tony about Vig. What was Blitz doing?

Blitz looked between me and Tony. "Were you not speaking of —" He frowned. "Who did you mean?"

Tony grabbed Blitz by the collar. "What man?"

Blitz glanced at me, afraid, then back at Tony. "The saloon owner Vig Vikenti. Wasn't that who you meant?"

I put my hand on Tony's arm. "One of my contacts, Tony. A friend, nothing more. Vig saved my life more than once."

Tony let his arms drop to his sides. "My wife was in a — a **saloon** — and you never told me?"

"No, sir."

"Tony," I said, "it was the —"

Tony punched Blitz in the face, knocking him to the floor. "What the hell do I have you guarding my wife for?"

I grabbed his arm. "Tony, stop! It was when Marja was shot."

Tony turned to me. "Why were you there? How long have you known this man?"

I shrugged. "Since I was sixteen. Tony, I asked Blitz and Ten not to say anything. You were so upset all the time, and —"

Tony growled, flinging my hand off his arm. "Everything you do makes my problems worse." He confronted Blitz, who still lay on the floor. "How long have you known about this?"

Blitz sat up, giving Tony a wary look. Blood lay on his lip. "It was the night you were out late. In February."

I glanced at Tony. Some message had passed between them. "As I said, it was the night my friend Marja was shot. Ten and Master Rainbow were there too. They followed me."

"Who saw you there? What else haven't you told me?"

I sat, telling the story: disguising myself, arriving at Vig's saloon, talking with his mother. I said, "Blitz, is his mother well?"

Blitz shook his head. "She's dead, mum. The doctor said it was her heart. The strain of all those men destroying her home —"

I leapt to my feet. "Gods damn you to Hell! This is what Vig gets for helping me? Get out, both of you."

Tony pulled Blitz to his feet then turned to me. "Jacqui, we didn't hurt your friends."

"You promised my friends wouldn't be harmed. Nonetheless, two are beaten, and another is dead. So you have no power to promise anything."

Tony didn't meet my eye.

"Get out," I told Tony. "I don't want to see you."

After Tony and Blitz left, I locked the doors, then got my cigarettes, a glass, and a bottle of bourbon, then sat in bed.

Vig's mother helped me since I was sixteen.

How could she be dead?

The Game

The next morning, I felt weary and my head hurt. To my surprise, a letter came from "Eunice Ogier," but was actually from Thrace Pike about "the information you requested." The letter was addressed from a residence on Market Center. His home?

At breakfast, Tony's knuckles were torn and bruised, yet unwashed, unbandaged.

If he wanted his hand to fester, that was not my concern.

The whole house must have heard the argument, but no one said anything. At breakfast, Tony said, "Jacqui, I had nothing to do with your friend being hurt. But you said two of your friends were beaten. Who was the other?"

He truly didn't know? "Madame Biltcliffe."

"I gave orders for her to be left alone! I'm going to get to the bottom of this." He left his breakfast half-eaten and stormed out.

So I ran morning meeting alone, then wrote to Mr. Pike with a time and place to meet.

When I called Pearson in to give him the letter, he said, "I've learned more about the facility you were interested in."

I gestured to the armchair across my desk. "Please sit."

He glanced at it. "I'd prefer to stand, mum."

He rarely ever sat in my presence. "Very well. What have you learned?"

"The facility's managed by a man named Shigo Rei. It

employs 78 workers in three shifts, mostly menial laborers." He shrugged. "There's nothing unusual about it."

"Are all produce distribution centers owned by the Clubbs?"

"The ones they deliver to. This one handles grain."

What an excellent way to learn about a quadrant! The Clubbs were sly indeed. "Thank you, Pearson, that'll be all."

I wrote to my contacts asking them to learn more about this Shigo Rei. A strange name, but Josie did say he changed it to hide the fact he was a Kerr.

That he changed his name didn't surprise me. After the Coup, the traitor Xavier Alcatraz hunted down the Kerrs, placing their heads upon spikes at Market Center. What fierce hatred he must have had for them! How did any of Joe's family survive?

* * *

During luncheon, Tony said, "The men assigned to Madame Biltcliffe's street deny hurting her."

"She said they were new men, wearing Spadros livery."

Tony frowned. "Spadros livery?"

I nodded. "They told her she had to pay double or they'd beat her again."

Tony gestured to Pearson. "You hear that?"

Pearson nodded.

"Make sure it's taken care of."

I felt confused. "Make sure what's taken care of?"

"Jacqui, our men only wear livery on specific occasions. Someone's impersonating us."

It dawned on me. "The black cloth!"

Tony stared at me down the length of the table, mouth open. Then he put his hand to his forehead. "First they steal our money, then they threaten and beat our merchants, then they ruin our name." He dropped his hand to the table. "What do they want from us?"

* * *

After luncheon, we went to Spadros Castle.

Spadros Castle wasn't one, any more than Spadros Manor was a manor. But that never stopped Roy from building it. A fortress, rather than a home with any artistic appeal.

I shivered as I entered. Although the damp chill of the dim entryway might have caused my reaction, I doubt it.

The servants, ancient and bowed, never spoke as they ushered us down pale gray halls. The parlor windows let in the gray light of a cloudy afternoon. Although Roy built Spadros Castle five years ago, it felt old, from the furniture to the decor.

This cold room matched Roy Spadros so well. Did Molly roam these pale halls with her silent servants?

Tony and I stood before the unlit fireplace. A portrait of Tony's little sister Katherine hung above it, three feet wide and four feet high.

"Astonishing," I said. "I didn't know photographs were ever made this big."

"It's not photography," a woman's voice said.

Molly Hogan Spadros, a beautiful raven-haired woman of fifty, gave me a warm smile when she caught my eye. "Hello, Jacqui." She clasped my hand, her long red sleeves brushing against my fingers. "So wonderful to see you."

She kissed Tony on the cheek then pointed at the picture. "Roy drew that from memory."

Katherine's picture hanging there was beyond dispute; the pencil-marks showed plainly. This man had vast talent: why had he squandered it in violence?

Roy entered the room, thirteen year old Katherine Spadros bounding in behind him. "Jacqui!" She hugged me around my waist, her auburn curls atop my corset. "I'm so happy to see you!"

I wrapped my arms round her, kissed her hair. "And I you."

"Hi, Tony!" She hugged him. "Can we play croquet? Please?"

Tony smiled. "Ask Mama, not me."

"Perhaps after we finish here," Molly said.

"Aww."

Molly frowned. "If you behave, Katie, and do as you're told."

Roy Spadros stood motionless, blue-ice eyes staring out from a pale, expressionless face. He wore a wool jacket and pants the color of midnight in winter, and a white vest with a texture which reminded me of fallen snow.

I expected rage at my defying his orders, guilt or evasiveness about having his men attack my friend.

But all he said was, "We'll go to the garden."

Katie skipped up to her father, chattering away.

Molly took Tony's left arm, I his right, and we strolled after them. "I'm glad you're feeling better, Jacqui," Molly said. "We've worried for you."

I hadn't been ill; I simply had nothing to say. So far, speaking hadn't made things better.

Their veranda was the same as our own, down to the shade of pale gray. In place of gardens, sheep grazed an expanse of lawn; an ancient man leaning on a cane herded them away from a target range as we approached. Roy's men stood watching for intruders.

We strolled along the grassy field. To our right, a white wrought-iron table and six matching chairs sat under a lawn umbrella, a croquet set neatly stacked on the ground beside it. We sat around the table.

Roy glanced at Tony's bruised hand. "Brawling, I take it?"

Tony frowned. "Where's the letter?"

Roy didn't smile often, but he did then. "To the point. I approve." He gestured to a maid; she handed him an envelope, which he put in his pocket. "Let's have tea. Converse. We are family, after all."

Katherine said, "Daddy, I don't want tea. Can I go play?"

"Certainly," Roy said.

She ran across the field, arms spread wide, and headed for the sheep, scattering them. A maid brought a tea-tray, set it before us, then began to pour.

"What do you want from us?" Tony said. "You have us here. What game are you playing now?"

"It's been a while since I played a game," Roy said. "An excellent idea." He sipped his tea. "If you want the letter, you two can play. Whoever wins may not show it to the other one."

Molly looked confused.

I frowned. "What sort of nonsense is that?"

Tony shook his head, chuckling. "Let him have his fun."

Roy looked at Tony sideways. "Well, then. You can go first."

He pointed towards the target range. A new paper had been laid upon the target. "Shoot six rounds."

Tony glanced at me, his face pale. He didn't like to shoot. He wasn't good at it. He never practiced. He hated loud noises. And I think he just realized what I told him earlier: I could shoot too.

All of Roy's men stood watching.

Roy planned to humiliate Tony in front of his men.

I smiled at Tony. "I'm sure you'll do fine."

Tony stood with trembling hands and took out his revolver. "Very well." He walked the twenty yards to the range, lifted the gun, pulled back the hammer, and I could see how nervous he was by his stance. He fired and missed.

Roy stood up, faced him. "Again!"

Tony took a deep breath, fired, and missed.

"You're heir to the Spadros Family!" Roy took a step towards Tony. "Again!"

Tony fired, hands shaking, and missed.

Roy stalked over to Tony and bellowed, "Again!"

Tony fired, and it wasn't even close.

"What're you going to do when I'm not here to protect you?"

I rose. "Stop it!"

Roy said something in a language I didn't understand.

Tony's face went white: he fired and missed even worse.

I ran to Roy. "What's wrong with you? Do you want your men to hate him?"

Roy yelled, "Again!"

Tony fired, and it clipped the side of the target. "There," Tony said, voice trembling. He threw his gun on the grass. "Satisfied?"

I grabbed Roy's arm. "Leave him alone."

Clicks from all directions. Every gun that every one of Roy's men held now pointed at me.

I put my hands up, backed away. Tony rushed to my side.

Roy waved to the men; they returned to whatever they were supposed to be watching. "Temper, my dear ... you always did let your emotions run away with you."

"You had your fun," Tony said, his voice shaking. "Give us the letter and let us go."

"But Jacqui gets to play, too," Roy said. "It wouldn't be fair otherwise."

Tony turned to me, whispering, "You don't have to do this. We can get the information some other way."

"I don't see how." I let out a breath. "I don't think he means to hurt us."

Tony held both my hands, closed his eyes for a moment. "Just do your best."

"How touching," Roy said.

The chairs had been moved to the side and an open box of ammunition lay on the table. Roy took his revolver from his belt and handed it to me. "You asked about shooting a moving target."

Tony glanced at him in disbelief.

Why would Roy hand me his weapon after what just happened? "What?"

I ducked away as Roy's hand lashed out. "Go!"

I ran, only a second later grasping what he meant over Tony's outraged shouts. I angled towards the target, raised Roy's heavy revolver in both hands, and fired. I didn't do as well as I hoped, but in all my years of practice, I have never missed a target.

Roy's men held Tony, who struggled, shouting at us both. Roy walked to the croquet set, picked up a ball, and threw it at me. "Run!"

The ball narrowly missed my leg, pulling at my dress as it passed. I fired again, doing better.

"Now back towards me!" Roy reached down for another ball.

I had to watch him, watch the target, watch for Tony, who flailed mightily, and avoid tripping on my dress.

"Shoot!"

The ball glanced off my corset, knocking the air from me; I hit the paper's edge. Tony screamed at Roy, but I barely heard him.

"Shoot, damn you!"

I shot, with better aim this time.

"Back up!"

Back and forth, at angles, reloading as I ran, grabbing ammunition from the table as I dodged his blows. After the heavy croquet balls were gone Roy threw mallets, hoops, and might have thrown the chairs if I displeased him. But he nodded: the session was over.

I ached all over. "This is more difficult than I thought."

Roy grasped my face in his thick hands, but this time his touch was gentle. "You've done well." Then his eyes narrowed. "Don't defy me again."

I stood there, stunned, as he walked away. Roy seldom gave praise, and had never praised me for anything without comparing me to someone who did better. "Wait." I stalked over to him. "You sick bastard. I want my damn letter."

He snorted, handing it over. "I mean it. Don't show it to him. I'll know if you do."

What could possibly be in there? "I thought you'd be angry."

"Why should I harm you?" He gave a small smile. "You're destroying yourself better than I ever could."

What the hell did Roy mean by that?

Tony ran to me. "Are you hurt?"

I shook my head, putting the letter in my pocket. "Tired," I panted, "probably in need of a bath. But unharmed."

Tony turned to Roy. "I meant what I said. We're done. I'm through with you."

Across the field, Katie stood watching.

Suddenly, Molly stood behind Roy. "Katie, do you still want to play?"

"Here I come," Katie said, running up. She stepped between myself and Roy and faced him. "Daddy, if I argue, will you have men point guns at me too?"

Roy's face softened as he leaned over. "You're my very own darling girl. I'll never let anyone harm you."

Molly looked as if she might be sick.

Tony grabbed my arm. "You play your games then."

"Bye, Tony," Katie said in a plaintive voice.

Tony never looked back.

In the carriage, Tony sat, his face turned away.

I said, "What do we do now?"

"Were you taunting me?"

I peered at him. "What?"

"Were you taunting me, back in February, when you asked me to teach you to shoot?"

"No! I wanted to learn to shoot better. I didn't dare go to your father after you denounced him. Yet I should have killed Frank Pagliacci. I thought maybe you —"

"That I could teach you something, anything you didn't already know?" He let out a bitter laugh. "All this time, I thought I was keeping you from the harsh edges of this terrible world. Instead, I find you're well in the thick of it!" He ran his hand through his hair. "It's as if I don't know you."

I've humiliated him yet again. "It's not that, Tony."

He didn't speak for several seconds, and when he did, he sounded weary. "What am I supposed to think? You shoot better than I ever could. The staff loves you. The people love you. You've got my own cousins hiding things from me. Do you want the Family, Jacqui? Is that what this is about?"

"Are you mad? All any of us want is for you to be happy." I moved to sit beside him in the carriage. "My fondest wish is for us both to be happy."

Well, my second fondest, but it was good enough.

I kissed his poor bruised hand. "But **you're** not happy. Your eyes are full of fear and guilt. You have nightmares, and you still don't eat enough." Whatever bothered him had something to do with Gardena Diamond, but I didn't know what. "Something's terribly wrong, I can feel it, yet I don't know how to help you."

He put his arm round me. "I'm sorry, Jacqui." He kissed my forehead. "I don't know how to help me either."

The Intent

We sat like this for some time, then I asked, "What did your father say when you were shooting?"

Tony and Roy — and sometimes Molly — spoke this other language from time to time, but never before when they thought I might hear.

Tony hesitated. "He told me, 'What will you do when it's time to protect her? Let her die?'"

I recalled Tony's nightmare a few months back of me lying cold and still.

"He's trying to cause me harm and upset in any way he can." Tony leaned his elbows on his knees, his face in his hands. "If I didn't know better, I'd say he tried to drive me mad."

That seemed unlikely — but it wouldn't help to say so. "What language do you and your parents speak?"

This seemed to cheer Tony somewhat. "Italian. We've spoken it as long as I can remember."

"Did your family not teach you Italian?"

My cheeks burned. "I was born in the Spadros Pot, Gardena. I said so at our dinner."

She blushed. "Forgive me. I meant the Spadros Family."

Gardena's comment back in February now made sense. Why would they **not** teach me?

Ah. For the same reason I didn't teach Kouri-Vini to Tony. Or why Zia used hand signs with Morton. *In case you might be false.*

I smiled, thinking of all the secrets held behind spoken walls.

Tony smiled back, and I wondered at his and Gardena's secret. "Gardena told me her family speaks Italian as well."

Tony gave a short fond laugh. "Her mother knows many languages." His face sobered. "Or at least, she used to. But Mrs. Diamond had a passion for pre-Catastrophe cultures, and a notable one was based in Italy.

"I've never been there, but she and Gardena went for a whole year when Gardena was fourteen." He paused, as if in thought. "Or maybe fifteen. I think it was to get her away from the war between our Families."

This made sense. My mother kept me inside that long year, as men fought and died. I was glad to stay inside, mourn Air's death. And avoid Roy's men.

The air smelled of morning as I sat playing jacks near the open doorway. Golden light slanted in, tiny motes of dust dancing in it. Snores filled the air.

Hands grabbed me from behind, and I screamed in terror.

My eyes stung at the sudden memory.

Tony put his face in his hands. He sounded defeated, ashamed. "Which of course, you know of much better than I."

I moved across from him, took a deep breath, let it out. "It's of no consequence."

Tony said nothing. But then, he didn't need to say anything. There was nothing he could say.

He couldn't protect me from what I'd already seen and done.

I opened the letter. It was written in a woman's hand, different from all those I had seen so far:

> I will take everything you hold dear, spawn of
> Spadros: your home, your wife, your family, your
> bastard heir. Even now your brother lies beaten by my
> men. I can strike you anywhere, at any time, and it
> will never stop until I've destroyed you.

Brother?

I remembered Dr. Salmon's tale of Acevedo Spadros II, Roy's

father, his liaison with Tony's mother Molly, and their plan for her to marry Roy.

I suppose they felt it a good way to move her into the house, to have their affair in front of Mr. Acevedo's wife without anyone knowing.

I stared at Tony in shock.

Roy was not Tony's father at all.

"What is it?" Tony said. "What does it say?"

Don't tell him. I'll know if you do.

I shook my head. Tony adored the man he thought to be his grandfather. In the Pot, nobody cared who sired a child, but here, it seemed vital. "Believe me: you don't want to read this."

Tony let out a bitter laugh. "And my father knew **you** would read it."

What will Roy do to Molly? "Oh, gods."

"What?"

"They mean to destroy your mother, too."

Fear overwhelmed me: I almost had the carriage turn round. Yet I realized that Roy had this letter for months now. If he meant to harm Molly, he had many chances to do so.

He must have already known of her betrayal.

I crumpled the message, shoved it in my pocket, and put my face in my hands. "You asked what they want. Now I know. They mean harm to everyone, down to your lowest servants. They mean to utterly destroy the Spadros Family."

Yet a young black-haired woman sent this. Birdie?

That must be one trusted secretary. A female secretary was unusual enough, but the woman must be part of their inmost circle to be allowed this kind of information.

Tony said, "I want nothing more than to read this letter. Yet I fear to do so."

"He told me he would know if you read it. I believe he would." What would Tony do if he learned what his mother had done? This could destroy their relationship. "I wish I never had. This is not something you want to see."

Tony shuddered. "I remember the false note my father got, supposedly from me, and the things it contained. You're right; I wish to see no more." He kissed my hands, gripping them tightly. "Why would my father let you read such filth?"

I shrugged. Why indeed. He could have refused to let me read the letter even after I won his little game. "Who knows why Roy Spadros does what he does?"

Tony leaned his elbow on the base of the carriage-window and looked away, hand to his chin. "I meant what I said. I want nothing more to do with him."

The carriage arrived at Spadros Manor, and we returned to our rooms to change into house clothes. I locked the letter in my drawer before I did anything else, but Morton's warning loomed ever-present in my mind. I had a safer place for this letter, once Amelia was off on an errand.

This letter gave me great pause. The person who wrote this knew the Spadros Family's most intimate secrets: Amelia's violation, Molly's affair. Yet instead of making these things public, they taunted Roy with the knowledge.

Who would feel safe enough — or was mad enough — to taunt Roy Spadros?

The Launch

After luncheon the next day, we set off for the yacht launch in a stony silence. Tony hadn't spoken to me since returning to the Manor, and I wondered how long he meant to continue.

I wasn't looking forward to this event. Tony never told me why he feared going, which worried me no end. And since this was the first time I'd been to any event by the Clubbs since last I saw Nina ... I had no idea what to expect.

Armed outriders came with us, but more this time, as we traveled north, crossing the "betters' bridge" to Clubb quadrant.

Sandstone cobbles paved Clubb quadrant streets in front of golden-brown buildings trimmed in oak and brass. When we reached the main street out to the countryside, we turned left, towards quadrant center.

Outsiders, strangely dressed, even women wearing trousers! Some had oddly cut hair in unnatural colors. Exotic dogs, brass follow-carts piled with parcels, or silver-toned mechanical men accompanied them, clanking and hissing as they went.

Our carriage turned right, towards the marina. The streets teemed with delivery trucks and golden-haired pedestrians. Clubb Family carriages in brass-trimmed oak pulled by gold champagne horses wearing brown and golden tack choked the streets. We turned right, then left — after our outriders stopped traffic — into an enormous entryway. Golden roses filled the central area as our carriage rounded it.

To our right stood the boathouse, a large edifice of sandstone and oak. A golden carpet led up to an oak-stained stair with brass banisters, then a large set of glass-paneled oak doors. Men in golden-brown Clubb livery opened the doors as we approached.

Inside, panels explaining the history of Bridges' waterways lined the walls. Mock-ups of champion boats stood behind glass. A large historical craft hung from the high oak rafters.

Alexander and Regina Clubb came across the wide hall to greet us. Both golden-haired and (at minimum) in their seventies, they appeared — and moved — as a couple twenty years younger.

Mrs. Clubb grabbed me by the arms, towering over me. "I'll not have my Nina become a woman-lover, especially with a Pot rag."

The memory stopped me; Tony moved past me to greet them.

"Welcome," Mr. Clubb said, and shook Tony's hand.

Tony wore his public face. "A pleasure to see you."

Mr. Clubb took my hand in his and kissed it, the metal of his mechanical left hand buffeted by the gloves we wore.

I stared at it in amazement: I would never be able to tell it was anything but real by its movements.

Mr. Clubb smiled. "So happy to see you again."

The man was handsome, even if he was terribly old. How did he manage to look so well? "And I you."

Tony kissed Mrs. Clubb's hand, then she took mine.

For a moment, I felt disoriented: we were the same height now. She seemed so terrifying before.

But today, she smiled. "I'm so glad you could attend." She retraced her steps, still holding my hand. "I can't wait for you to see our new yacht."

I fought the urge to snatch my hand back. Why was I remembering these things, having these feelings, now? "The *Ace of Clubbs*. What does this signify?"

Mrs. Clubb glanced away with an ironic, amused laugh. "Our beloved son, of course."

His name, Lancelot, derived from the Holy Cards, a Jack variation. Shouldn't he be the Jack of Clubbs? And if they intended to give Lance this honor — the highest and lowest of them all — why not name him Ace? As old as Alexander and

Regina Clubb were, did they expect more children? But ... he **was** the youngest. And their heir. "You must love him very much."

She smiled, color rising in her cheeks. "We do."

Attendants in Clubb livery opened the doors onto a wide dock of polished oak where a party lay spread: food, drink, musicians, and well-dressed people from all four quadrants.

To my relief, Regina Clubb let go of my hand. "Enjoy," she said, disappearing into the crowd.

My eye immediately went to Jonathan Diamond. He said a word to his companions, raised his water glass, and came to us.

Tony said, "I didn't know you got an invite to this shindig."

Jon laughed. "We're all here, it seems." He pointed to a very pale Helen Hart, who sat under an awning with her Inventor husband Etienne, a dumpy auburn-haired man in his fifties wearing his odd spectacles. As usual, he had his nose in a book. Helen, dressed in black, sipped her tea in silence.

Surely Jon's twin Jack didn't attend. Heart pounding, I took Tony's arm and said to Jon, "Who else is here?"

Jon glanced over my shoulder. "Turn round and you'll see."

So we did. "Gardena!" Relieved, I hugged Jon's younger sister. "I'm so glad to see you."

Gardena Diamond's raven curls were up-swept under a black hat with navy blue feathers in it, matching her navy blue gown. Jon wore a cravat matching his sister's dress, pinned with the symbol of his Family in white.

"Miss Diamond," Tony said in a flat voice.

Gardena didn't smile or meet Tony's eye. "Mr. Spadros."

Oh, dear. Whatever went on between them at Queen's Day dinner ... had not been resolved in the slightest.

A stern voice said, "There you are." Cesare Diamond, a man in his early thirties, gripped his sister's arm. "Your presence is requested." He ignored us as he yanked Gardena aside.

"That man infuriates me," Tony said.

Jon laughed. "He generally has that effect."

Tony twitched. Evidently, he had forgotten Jon stood so close by. "My apologies." Tony let out a breath. "Your brother delights in displaying his disdain for my wife and I." He glanced over.

Cesare lectured his sister, who didn't appear to be taking it well. "Not to mention everyone else."

I took Jon's arm. "When will the launching take place?"

"Oh, any time, I'd think, now that we're all here," Jon said.

Regina Clubb proceeded out, followed by eight of her daughters. They wore the same navy blue dresses as their mother, had the same golden hair, thin faces, and haughty demeanor. Mrs. Clubb spoke on a megaphone. "Welcome to the launch of our newest craft, the *Ace of Clubbs*!"

Applause followed. Jon flushed, appearing embarrassed; Tony's jaw clenched.

"Our daughter, Apprentice of the Dealers Kitty Clubb, is here to offer the blessing."

Surprised murmurs rose as Kitty Clubb strode forward, dressed in a pale green robe with a white scarf of the same material which completely covered her hair. Everyone rose — Helen Hart, with help — and bowed or curtsied.

"So she did join the Dealers," Jon said. "How remarkable."

Kitty raised her hand. "We thank the Floorman for the bounty provided to create this vessel. May the Dealer richly bless those it carries, bringing them safely through the rounds to come." She lowered her hand, and everyone murmured, "So be it."

"Thank you, Blessed Apprentice," Regina Clubb said. "Launching the yacht is our son and heir, Master Lancelot Clubb."

A man of three and twenty with thick straight golden hair, Lance Clubb hesitated, then stepped forward. He grasped the champagne bottle, tied to a boom which jutted a foot from the grand yacht's deck, and launched it at the side of the craft.

The bottle struck full on, yet did not break.

Everyone laughed; Lance turned bright red.

"No matter," Mrs. Clubb said. "Let's try this again."

Men scrambled to retrieve the bottle.

Arms held high, Lance flung the bottle towards the yacht as if it offended him and it broke, spraying champagne over the dock. We cheered, and he turned towards us with a sheepish grin.

"I could almost like the man," Tony murmured.

"What?"

Tony seemed startled. "Nothing. My pardons."

Why would Tony dislike Lance? Even though the man was a year our senior, he had something of a young child about him, as if he hadn't yet matured. I found it endearing.

Mrs. Clubb said, "Please accompany us on the *Ace of Clubbs* for its maiden voyage." We followed up the wide gangplank past photographers and reporters barred by a pair of golden ribbons.

The *Ace of Clubbs*, although vastly larger in size, reminded me of Morton's craft the *Finesse*, now in pieces at the bottom of the river: white with an oak interior. The *Ace of Clubbs* had immense golden sails with the Clubb symbol embroidered in golden-brown. Brass railings and gold bunting adorned the sides.

Men untied golden lines. The yacht cast off, moving out of the marina. The day was cloudy yet calm. A perfect day for sailing.

"I rather like boats," I said.

Tony gazed at me with a curious expression, then nodded. "I'm not so fond of them, but the company is diverting."

Did Tony just flirt? He rarely did so, usually when intoxicated. But he had nothing to drink today, so far as I'd seen.

Jon laughed from behind us. "Indeed."

Tony's face reddened. "You must come forth, sir, or begone."

Jon moved in front of us and bowed. "My apologies."

"You two are incorrigible," I said. "We must have other conversation than upon my few virtues."

"Never mock yourself," Jon said. "You are the most glorious lady present."

Music began from inside, to the aft.

"Would you like some drinks?" Jon said. He gave a quick glance over my shoulder: Gardena stood some six paces back.

"Nothing for me," I said, "unless you wish to bring something when you return."

Tony followed our glances. "I'll accompany you." The two disappeared below.

Gardena came to meet me, suddenly pensive. "I wanted to thank you for your kind welcome. I fear your husband wishes me gone." She paused, her head downcast. "I don't blame him: it was wrong to strike him, to say what I did that night. I regret it all."

I took her white-gloved hands. "It would help, I think, if you told **him** these things. He has high regard for you, and your disagreements wound him."

She turned to lean upon the rails. "I know. I wish things had occurred differently." A glossy black curl fell beside her dark brown cheek. "I think we all feel that way at times."

Well, I certainly did. I wasn't sure how to make things right between these two, but a plan was forming in my mind as far as my situation. "There are always things which can be done, Dena. It just takes the strength and courage to act."

"If I act, people are hurt. They may die. If I don't act, people are hurt, but different ones. All people I care for. No matter what I do, I feel as if I am betraying someone." She shook her head. "You of all people deserve better."

I had no idea what she meant, but she seemed in such distress that I dared not ask. "Is there a way I can help?"

Gardena smiled a fake smile, then her eyes reddened. "Just be my friend, Jacqui, for as long as you can."

The navy blue dress Gardena wore was the same one I borrowed the day we met to catch her blackmailer. "You and Lance dressed alike. Was that coincidence?"

Gardena smiled fondly. "His mother. She wishes the city to become accustomed to the idea of us together, before —"

I recalled Marja's note: *They plan to kill your Ma too.*

"Jacqui," Gardena said, "what is it?"

"A sudden fear came upon me." I told her about Marja: who she was, what she meant to me. I told her about Marja's note warning me of a plot to kill my mother. "That was how I knew I must get my mother out of the city."

Gardena's eyes filled with tears. "We sent her to her doom! Oh, Jacqui, I'm so sorry." She pulled me into a tight embrace.

I'd added more sorrow to Gardena's hand, yet I couldn't reveal that my mother lived without also revealing her mother's part in it. "You helped me when I had nowhere else to turn. For that I'm grateful."

She nodded, wiping her eyes.

"Marja sent the message from a produce distribution center in

Spadros quadrant owned by the Clubbs."

Gardena peered at me with a slight frown.

"I believe she overheard someone there. It stands to reason that they — or someone who worked for them — killed her."

Gardena's face went from confusion to disbelief. "You think the Clubbs killed her? That they killed your mother? Why?"

I shook my head. "I have no idea. My husband won't let me out of his sight, or the sight of his men," several of whom stood on deck watching me, "so it's been difficult to learn more." No one was in earshot. "Have you gained their confidence?"

"You want me to spy on the man who courts me?"

"I don't want you to do anything you feel is wrong. But if the Clubbs plotted against them ..."

Gardena took my hands. "I understand. If someone hurt Mama ... I don't know what I might do." She stood motionless, then gasped. "Surely they — no. I can't believe they would ruin their own building and kill hundreds of people just to target one woman." She shook her head. "Why not shoot her? Even if your mother were in a rival Family, this is beyond monstrous."

I hadn't examined that aspect of it. "Someone must be using the Clubbs, then. I don't have any other ideas."

Gardena stood in thought, then her face changed, as if she had come to some decision. "I'll see what I can learn. They don't talk much around me, but Jon is Keeper of the Court. Perhaps they've spoken to him."

And his twin, Jack, was allied with Frank Pagliacci. Fear gripped me. "You mustn't breathe a word of this to Jack."

Gardena seemed confused. "Why not?"

How much could I tell her? At the doorway to the cabin, Jon and Tony were emerging. "It's all too complex and there's no time. Please, trust me. Your life may be in danger if Jack learns you know of this."

She frowned. "You and Jack have your differences, but —"

"Dena, Jack's threatened to kill me and destroy my family."

Gardena's hands flew to her mouth, eyes wide. "Surely you don't believe this? I won't believe it." She shook her head. "I'm sorry, Jacqui, but you're wrong."

Tony and Jon threaded through the crowd towards us. I grabbed her arms. "Promise me, Dena."

She glanced away. "Very well."

"I don't want anything to happen to you. Jack might not harm you, but his companions are dangerous beyond measure."

She peered at me. Then she nodded. "I promise."

Jon handed a wine glass to Gardena. "We come bearing gifts."

Tony offered me a glass of bourbon, neat, and I smiled at him. "My favorite."

"So I recall."

"Excuse me," Gardena said, disappearing into the crowd.

Tony smiled at me. "Did you have a nice chat?"

My eyes met Jon's. Why didn't **he** do something about Jack? "Yes, it was lovely."

"Excuse me." Jon moved in Gardena's direction.

Tony and I sipped our drinks as we sailed upstream towards the Rim, the yacht tacking back and forth as we went.

I recalled my speculation that Gardena's blackmailer was allied with Frank Pagliacci. Indeed, the timing made me certain of it. "I believe Gardena's in danger from the men who target us."

Tony said nothing for several seconds. "A police official once came to me with an astonishing story."

"Did you not hear me?"

"A woman named Zia Cashout claimed you knifed her in the streets of Market Center dressed as a scullery maid. But you were at Dame Anastasia's house helping her pack. Were you at Dame Anastasia's house?"

I gazed over the water. "Of course." For about an hour, then I went many places that day. Including Market Center, dressed as a scullery maid. "Why would this woman make such a report?"

"I don't know. She disappeared soon after."

"So why did the police go to you?"

"They were concerned about your safety and reputation, and thought I should know." The water reflected in Tony's eyes made them as pale as Roy's.

"That was kind of them."

"Indeed." Tony clearly questioned my story.

I wished I didn't have to keep lying to him, but if I told him where I was, he would ask why. And on that day, I visited Thrace Pike and his grandfather, and then Mr. Jake Bower. I didn't think Tony would be happy about either visit.

That I had anything to do with Thrace Pike — a man who made public statements against my character — would upset him. That I went to an investigator's home (even though it was also his office) unescorted would alarm him no end.

I didn't want Tony to learn of my visits to Mr. Pike until I found out what Mr. Bower's financial documents contained.

"Tony, you must listen. That letter ... I — you don't want to know what it contains. But they know too much —"

Alarm flashed through his eyes. What was he so afraid I might learn?

"— and I fear for our friends. They wish to destroy us, Tony. Not just kill, or make afraid. Destroy."

Jon approached us. "May I speak to Mrs. Spadros?"

Tony blinked. "Why, of course." He moved a few feet away, clearly curious as to what Jon might have to say.

Jon didn't meet my eye. "Do you carry your weapon?"

"Of course." Jon gave me the pistol years before.

He relaxed. "Good." He paused, head down, hands on his hips. Then he straightened. "May I ask a question?"

I grinned. "You just did."

He let out a short laugh. "Well. I suppose so!" Then he sobered. "This is a serious matter, Jacqui. Did you have your weapon on your person at the Grand Ball?"

It was ten minutes from my entrance time. I went into the toilet-room, Amelia helping me with my dress. When Amelia saw my calf holster, she drew back in alarm. "You're not to have that here!"

I smiled, amused. "Don't worry, Amelia; I won't shoot anyone."

I nodded. "Of course."

"When Jack advanced upon me, why didn't you draw your weapon? Or move away? Why'd you come to my side instead?"

I gaped at him. "My only thought was for your safety."

Jon spoke fiercely. "This will be your undoing, Jacqui! You

must **not** forget your own safety! Certainly not over mine."

His demeanor startled me. "What did Gardena say, Jon? Something's upset you."

Jon appeared surprised. "Gardena said nothing." But then he put his hand to his forehead, shook his head. "I have no proof. It could've been said in jest. But I overheard something just now ..." he dropped his hand to his side, "and it made me fear for you. Promise me that if you find yourself in danger, you'll care for **yourself**, rather than rush to the defense of me or anyone else."

I touched his cheek. He was such a dear man. "I promise." I dropped my hand to take his. "And you must promise to protect yourself and Gardena. You may both be in danger."

Jon grinned. "We're Diamonds. We're always in some sort of danger." He kissed my hand. "Be at peace. My sister's well cared-for, never fear."

* * *

Jon and Tony went off on some adventure, and I gazed over the water, considering Jon's words. What would it be like to grow up in a Family, constantly in danger?

Mrs. Clubb approached with a brown-haired woman wearing forest green. "Inventor Cuarenta, may I present Mrs. Spadros."

I curtsied low. "It's an honor to meet you, Inventor."

The Inventor held out her hand. "Please call me Lori."

She was perhaps twenty-five. I gave her my hand. "Jacqui."

"There!" Mrs. Clubb said. "I wish you to be friends." Mrs. Clubb moved into the crowd without so much as a fare-you-well.

I chuckled. "That was rather abrupt."

"I believe she has other guests to attend," the Inventor said.

"I meant no offense."

She smiled, her tone light. "None taken."

I'd never spoken with another quadrant's Inventor before. In fact, I thought doing so was forbidden. "Was there some topic you wished me to bring to my husband?"

"No," the Inventor said. "But you might help nonetheless."

This surprised me. "Oh? In what way?"

"Mrs. Clubb tells me you grew up in the Pot."

The sail creaked overhead. "I did."

"More to the point, in the Cathedral."

"However did she know that?"

Lori Cuarenta smiled. "She knows just about everything. Was there a place in your Cathedral more revered than others? Where you weren't allowed to play? A special door, or a secret room?"

That also seemed abrupt, and I felt wary. What did she want to know this for? "Surely the women there could answer your questions far better than I."

"I'm told the Clubb Inventor may not visit the Spadros Pot."

That had to be Roy's doing. "Well, other than the altar, which is revered for obvious reason, I don't know of any such place."

The Inventor shook her head slightly. "What obvious reason?"

I stared at her. "Do you not know? The Dealers used to cast the Holy Cards upon that very spot."

Kitty Clubb spoke behind me. "It's true. Since the downfall of the Cathedral, the Dealers no longer cast the Cards as we did."

Her voice startled me. "Kitty! I mean, Blessed Apprentice." I curtsied, as did the Inventor. "How good to see you!"

Kitty gave me a wry smile. "I grow tired of people calling me that." She took our hands. "It's good to see you both."

They must know each other well, I thought, given the similarity of ages. What would friendship with an Inventor be like? "You've been reading." Last time we met, Kitty didn't even know the Cathedral still stood.

Kitty blushed. "I have." She turned to Lori Cuarenta. "Mrs. Spadros has been most patient with my unschooled questioning."

"I wish I could help further," I said, not wanting the questioning to resume. I caught Tony's eye and smiled: our signal for conversations we wished to be extricated from.

He nodded, picking his way towards us.

"I was astonished to see you," I said. "I thought you were cloistered for your first year."

Kitty grinned. "What Mommy wants, Mommy gets." She gestured at a woman wearing an emerald green robe and scarf, then laughed. "I'm allowed out, with a minder."

Tony approached us and bowed. "Ladies, please excuse my

interruption, but I have need to speak with my wife."

I took Tony's arm and went the other direction. "Thanks."

"Who was the woman with Kitty Clubb?"

"Their Inventor, with an inordinate interest in the Cathedral."

Tony's eyes narrowed. "As I recall, Miss Clubb had quite an interest in it at the dinner."

She did, upsetting the entire table when Tony forced me to give answer to her questions. "As did you, if I recall."

Tony stopped. "I should never have pressed you that night; I regret doing so."

I smiled at him. "All is forgiven." I drained my drink. "I've found that not all questions should be answered." Yet there were still too many unanswered questions for my liking.

Why were the Clubbs so interested in the Cathedral?

What did Marja overhear in their warehouse?

Was she killed to keep her silent? Was it a random shooting? Or was it simply another of Frank Pagliacci's distractions?

Gardena was right, of course. The Clubbs would never waste time killing a brothel owner in the Spadros Pot. And to do so using a zeppelin explosion?

I examined the glass in my hand, put it on a passing waiter's tray. "I should stop drinking so much."

Tony gave a slight smile. "That's a good idea."

The Documents

The next morning, I received a letter from Mr. Paul Blackberry, the current editor of the *Bridges Daily*:

About your inquiry, madam — these are known merchants for the quadrant in question:

The Ladies' Emporium

Blind Button Dealers, Inc.

Mississippi Paper Co.

Big Bet Mining Supply

Open Stakes Trainers

The Dealer's blessings upon you. If you require anything more, you have only to ask. — PB

What a list! I rewrote it, removing Mr. Blackberry's information, and passed it to Tony at breakfast. "These are the shops which claimed Mr. Hart didn't pay them," I said. "I believe our enemies used false invoices to steal from them as well."

Tony shook his head. "I should have asked Mr. Hart about this at the racetrack! Perhaps he'll allow us to speak with his merchants, or at the very least, share what the scoundrels stole."

Oh. I'd forgotten these were in Hart quadrant. "That would

be helpful, I'm sure." But I chuckled as I pictured Mr. Hart's reaction to our having such a detailed list. We'd be lucky if we got information from the Harts anytime soon.

* * *

I told Tony I wished to go to the river for luncheon, so his men cleared a wide section of the beach, with guards stationed to keep onlookers away. The men brought a changing cabana, and Tony put on his swimming suit. While Jane and Mary set up a picnic for us on the rocky shore, I slipped on some bathing-shoes to wade the gentle surf.

The promenade remained open, and many strolled past. Fortunately, the reporters hadn't found us yet.

After luncheon, Tony and several of his men returned to the water. I had Amelia put my boots back on. "I might promenade," I told Sawbuck. "If you think it safe."

Sawbuck grinned. "I let it slip we'd be bathing at Straight-Draw," an exclusive beach on the other side of the quadrant, "so it'll take a while for them to find us here." He gestured for four of Tony's men to follow.

I strolled the promenade, parasol in hand, guards flanking me. Under a tree, a thin young man with straw-colored hair wearing a dark brown suit sat at the far end of a bench reading a newspaper. He wore brass-rimmed spectacles tinted brown.

I sat at the other end of the bench, fanning myself. My guards stood more than far enough away not to overhear.

"Good day, madam," Thrace Pike said. "I feel quite the spy."

I held my fan up to hide my amusement. "I could think of no other way to meet."

"My grandfather is furious."

"Why?"

"He believes you planned to defraud him."

I went to Doyle Pike — or rather, to Thrace Pike, who turned the matter to his grandfather — about collecting debts for Dame Anastasia Louis. Doyle Pike agreed to receiving one percent of the take. "It's not my fault you didn't get the money."

"My grandfather hasn't hired enforcers as yet. Although nothing he did would surprise me."

"But Dame Anastasia's dead!"

"His point exactly." He turned the page.

"Wait," I said. "He thinks **I** killed her?"

"Surely not. But —" He shook out the newspaper, "he did valid work, which you refuse to pay for."

I considered this. "We had an agreement."

Thrace Pike shrugged. "Back to the point, please, madam. I have little time. My grandfather believes I'm attending my daughter, who I told him was unwell." He turned the page. "The documents. Your husband pays a tremendous amount to Diamond Manor every month in the name of Gardena Diamond."

This news astonished me. "Are you certain?"

"I am." He sounded distressed. "I could scarce believe it."

"What ... why would my husband do such a thing?"

"I can think of several reasons."

"Such as?"

"The most likely is blackmail."

Gardena did urge Tony to tell me something vital. But why would Julius Diamond — or whoever was blackmailing Tony — want money paid to Gardena? "None of this makes sense."

"Perhaps Miss Diamond provides some service we know nothing about," Mr. Pike said.

"I can't think of what." And why keep it secret?

He crossed one leg over the other. "There's a third option, which may be what Mr. Bower referred to."

Something in Mr. Pike's voice made me afraid. "What?"

"I hesitate to mention this, madam, as it's too horrible to imagine that a man would treat you so."

"I shall inform you at once if I become too distressed."

"Your husband could have a secret family."

It took everything within me not to laugh aloud. Tony had been the most devoted husband possible. And he seemed so eager for a child. Why would he want children so badly if he already had some? "What if it were true?"

"Once a man signs betrothal papers, the marriage can only be broken if both families agree before the wedding takes place. Once married, no other alliance may be entered into unless divorce is finalized." He turned the page. "Now, yes, men do break their vows, and there might even be children. But for a man to take from his estate to provide for them?" I saw Mr. Pike shake his head from the corner of my eye. "He would be subject to criminal action on behalf of his heirs present and future."

"So what happens to the woman in this circumstance?"

"She certainly would have cause to file for divorce, but —"

"No, the other one."

"Well," Mr. Pike said, surprised, "she certainly wouldn't be accepted in society any longer. If married, her husband would immediately divorce her."

"Oh?"

"Some men might reconcile with a repentant woman, but her reputation would be permanently tarnished. They would probably need to leave the city to have any hope of living without constant scandal. An unmarried woman's father, though ...."

I knew he suspected Gardena, which infuriated me.

"To preserve his reputation and that of his heirs, her father must denounce her and turn her out at once."

"But where would she go?"

He shrugged. "She could go the Pot and continue her whoredom there, I suppose. It's a pity for the child, but —"

"That's quite enough." Why should a woman suffer so for falling in love? "I wish to hear no further."

Mr. Pike didn't speak for a few moments. "Very well, madam. Will there be anything else?"

Why was this happening now? "Are you acquainted with a man named Frank Pagliacci?"

"No, madam. Should I be?"

"No. That'll be all for now. Thank you. Please speak of this to no one. I'll contact you should I need further assistance." I rose without looking at him and continued on, my guards following.

The idea of Tony keeping a secret family was utter nonsense.

Yet none of the other reasons made sense either. Why would Gardena blackmail Tony? Why would she insist on him telling me the truth if she was?

But then I stopped, facing the shore. What if it were Julius or that insufferable Cesare who blackmailed Tony, using Gardena to hide the money's final destination?

I began walking back to Tony's cabana. This was more plausible. But was Tony capable of anything so terrible that he would submit to blackmail to hide it?

When I approached the cabana, Tony emerged fully dressed.

"How was your swim?"

"The water's just right." Tony seemed more relaxed than I'd seen him in a while. "And your stroll?"

"Lovely."

Tony offered his arm. We began climbing the rocky slope back to our carriage.

I said, "I'd like to luncheon with Gardena sometime."

He hesitated several seconds. "Very well."

"I'll bring her to Spadros quadrant, if it helps."

Tony chuckled. "It would."

"I'm sorry I've caused such turmoil. I feel I've lost your trust, and that distresses me."

"Ah, now." He stopped, took hold of my hands. "You just did what you felt necessary." He reached up, tucked a loose strand behind my ear. "You've lost none of my regard."

Sawbuck walked past. "I don't know about you two lovebirds, but I'd like to get somewhere cooler." He gestured to the carriage. "What do you say?"

* * *

On the return trip, I pondered Mr. Pike's findings. The most logical conclusion was blackmail. First Gardena, now Tony. Could this be part of the Red Dog Gang's plot?

Tony said Joe told him that the Diamonds started the Red Dog Gang. Morton said someone suborned the original Red Dogs to frame them for murder and kidnapping. All the evidence about the blackmail attempt against Gardena pointed to it being a way to keep me from reaching Anastasia in time to prevent her death.

But this felt much more dangerous than that. Tony was terrified of even discussing the subject.

I'd forgotten to ask Mr. Pike how long this had been going on.

Perhaps someone pressured Gardena into being involved, using her grandfather's death or some other misdeed as leverage. Perhaps she wanted me told so as to break the blackmail. Then Tony might win free. But why would Tony **not** want me told?

When we reached the Manor, I invited Gardena to luncheon a few days hence. We couldn't visit the Spadros Women's Club: since Roy's intrusion, most ladies of high stature refused to attend without armed guards, which the Club didn't allow.

I picked a highly-rated restaurant in Spadros, The Culbertson, where both men and women were welcome, then had Pearson set up a reservation. Gardena could bring her brothers or other guards as escort, and I could speak to her in public.

* * *

Over the next few days, I spent most of my time considering the matter. Gardena never would be around Tony for more than a few moments, and then only when Jonathan was present. Tony and Gardena always acted cross with each other. Sometimes Tony seemed afraid of her. And Cesare hated Tony as much as his father Julius did.

A lot of things went on in the past between these two Families: murders and betrayals on both sides. But Tony was in the Family — anything, no matter how horrible, might be covered up. If one went on rumor, Jack Diamond was a murderer many times over. Roy Spadros routinely tortured people to death. Yet they both walked free, even prospered. What could Tony possibly have done which he would be so afraid of revealing?

* * *

I went to the restaurant, and there Gardena was. Maids escorted us to a table and poured tea.

The room was full. Two of Gardena's brothers sat behind her at another table, sipping tea as they waited to order. A buzz of conversation filled the room, which would drown out anything I might have to say.

Gardena said, "To what do I owe this honor?"

"I needed to speak with you."

Her demeanor seemed perfectly innocent. "Whatever about?"

"I just received some disturbing news. I'd hoped you might assist me."

She smiled warmly. "However I can help, Jacqui. You have only to ask."

I leaned forward. "Why do you receive monthly stipends from Spadros Manor?"

Gardena stared at me in horror. "How did you learn of this?"

"What has my husband done?"

"You promised you wouldn't ask!"

"That was when I thought it a simple disagreement. But ... blackmail? Dena, if I'm mistaken please tell me."

Gardena took a deep breath, let it out. "Do you remember the boy you met on Market Center with my cousin Octavia?"

I nodded. Yet I felt perplexed, not making any connection between two children and our topic. The boy, perhaps four, looked like Jon; the girl — seventeen or so — had light skin and long blonde curls.

"The boy's name is Roland. He's my son."

I felt surprised. "You have a son? He's a lovely child. But why did you never speak of him? And why pretend he belonged to your brother?" And what did this have to do with payments?

She shook her head. "I begged Anthony, but he wouldn't tell you." She paused for a long time. "His name is Roland Spadros."

The Decision

Roland ... Spadros? "I don't understand."

Then I stared at Gardena, aghast.

Roy Spadros had violated Amelia, forced her to bear little Pip, terrorized and hounded her. Her entire family had gone through anguish and turmoil for a decade because of it. "Did Roy Spadros hurt you? Is that what's going on?"

Gardena stared at me, mouth open, her demeanor moving from shock to fear, then to a horrified realization. She pressed her hands to her mouth for several seconds, and her eyes reddened.

My heart pounded. I hoped she would trust me. And I decided if Roy had hurt Gardena, I would go to Roy's house and kill him. I would concoct a pretext, get past his guards and cut his throat. I didn't care who saw, or what happened afterward.

I'd wanted to kill him for ten years, and this was as good a time as any. Such a monster didn't deserve to live.

"No, Jacqui," Gardena said, "I've never been allowed near Roy Spadros without many guards, and ... and now I understand why." She looked away. "I understand many things now."

Gardena sat motionless as conversation from the other tables swirled round us. "I think I would take my life rather than bear a child of his." She took a deep breath, hesitating, not meeting my eye. Then she faced me. "Roland is Anthony's son."

I feared that this might be the case, but never let myself believe it. "Why?" *Why hide it? Why lie?*

Gardena rounded on me, but she spoke in a whisper. "Why? Why? Because I wanted a child! No man was **ever** good enough for my father. I feared ending up alone, unwanted, unloved, never allowed to have children of my own."

But Tony loves you. "Tell me how this happened."

"I was almost 20! I'd been forced to turn down ten suitors in one year, men I would've been happy to wed. I saw a copy of the *Golden Bridges* — they called me 'the Diamond spinster' —"

I felt a surge of anger. Those men tossed sticks of dynamite as if they were toys.

"— and I felt humiliated, Jacqui. I felt desperate. I didn't know what else to do.

"I knew Anthony wanted me. At the Grand Ball, I took him to a closet, and he lay with me ..."

Five years ago, I thought. Tony would have been 17. Was I at that Grand Ball? I couldn't remember.

"But my father caught us, and only my father's fear of Roy Spadros kept him from killing Anthony then and there."

She put him in such danger! "How could you have toyed with my husband? And why did you not marry him?"

"We were both afraid," Gardena said. "I'm fond of Anthony. More than fond. I was prepared to marry him. That's what I thought would happen. How could my father do otherwise? He would be forced to." She gave a small smile. "That's how Cesare was born, to hear the servants tell it. My grandfather insisted they marry when my mother was found with child."

Then she sobered. "But Anthony feared his father's wrath. I shouldn't have blamed him. He was so young. Your betrothal was already announced and he felt unable to break it. He feared his father would kill me and take our son if he learned of him."

This explained much. "Now I see the Clubb Family's plan."

"What do you mean?"

I sighed. This would hurt. "Your son is an heir to Spadros and Diamond. All Lance needs to do is make Roland love him, and the Clubbs have three quadrants. The Harts could do nothing."

I recalled the news article in the *Golden Bridges* a few months ago about the meeting between Mrs. Regina Clubb and Mrs.

Judith Hart at the Clubb Women's Center. This was why Mrs. Judith Hart was so upset. Mrs. Clubb must have brought her there to brag of their victory.

Hurt crossed Gardena's eyes. "Jacqui, Lance isn't like that. Could it be possible that he courts me because he **loves** me?"

"Does he know about Roland?"

"Well, yes, but —"

"Lance may be the Blessed Floorman Himself, Dena, but his parents most certainly are not. They're behind this."

Gardena stared at her table settings in dismay.

The waiter approached. "Would you ladies like to order something to drink?"

The enormity of it all fell upon me like a rock. Tony had a son I knew nothing about. When had he planned to tell me? Would I have gone to my grave not knowing?

"I don't think so," I said. "I'm sorry, but I must go."

"Jacqui," Gardena said, "please, wait ..."

I glanced at her brothers; they glanced back at me. I could just imagine the exchange: pay up or something might happen to your son. And she went along with it. "No, Gardena, I've heard all I wish to." I gestured at the table. "You may put whatever you like on our tab." I felt bitter. "That seems to be what you're used to."

The waiter turned away, embarrassed.

Gardena stared at me, stricken. I felt ashamed for speaking to her in this way, angry at her, angry at everyone. I left her standing there in the restaurant as everyone watched me go.

* * *

At the carriage, Honor faced away, talking to the driver, and jumped when he realized I stood behind him. "Oh! I'm sorry, mum. Did Miss Diamond cancel?"

"That's none of your concern," I snapped, immediately regretting it at the shock and hurt on Honor's face. "Forgive me, it's been a trying day."

Honor took on a mask rather like Tony's, staring straight ahead. "Yes, mum." After helping me inside, he closed the door.

The carriage started off. Filled with guilt, shame, anguish, I drew the curtains around me and wept.

Tony lied about everything. He didn't marry me because he loved me so much; he was forced to marry me by his father. He clearly would rather have married Gardena.

He lied as to why he wanted a child so badly — was it pride? Was it another way to hide that he already had an heir, that he didn't even need me for that?

I'd been trapped at Spadros Manor all these years for nothing!

I wiped my face with my handkerchief. Tony loved me. He could never be that false.

Perhaps Gardena lied to cover up some other misdeed. After all, she did kill her own grandfather. Perhaps Roland wasn't Tony's son, yet he was being tricked into believing the boy was.

Honor knocked before opening the door, and he led me to the porch in silence. Pearson opened the door. "Good day, mum."

"When is my husband expected home?"

"In an hour, mum."

After Amelia got me changed into my afternoon dress, I said, "I wish our rooms to be undisturbed until my husband arrives. When he returns, please ask him to come directly to my room."

Amelia gave a sly smile, then she sobered. "Yes, mum."

Once she left, I went to my sideboard, filled a waterglass with bourbon, and took a long drink. I gazed at the photo of Acevedo Spadros II, who Roland — and Tony — looked so much like.

Somewhere in Tony's belongings would lie clues to the truth.

I waited until Amelia's footsteps were down the stairs, then went into Tony's bedroom. I locked the door to the hall so no one might enter his room taking me unawares. Then I began to search. Closets, pockets, boxes of memorabilia ... a large locked drawer next to his bed. Retrieving my picks, I went to work.

Before me lay a small lifetime's worth of information about a boy's small life: portraits, framed and stacked. Doctor's notes. Pictures drawn "to my Daddy." A curl of black hair in tissue.

I wanted to weep all over again.

At the bottom of the pile, I found a birth certificate for Roland Anthony Spadros. A square portion of the right upper corner was cut away. I'd never seen a birth certificate before, so the cut-away portion puzzled me.

I moved Tony's tea-table near the drawer. Then I placed the photos upon it, the larger in back, the smaller in front. Underneath everything sat a locket of a young Gardena holding baby Roland in her arms. This I placed in the center, my heart heavy.

I heard the door to my rooms open. "Jacqui?"

I sat on his bed. "I'm in here."

Tony came in slowly, face wary, flinching at the open drawer and the table full of portraits.

I turned the table so it faced him and spoke with a calm I didn't feel. "Who is this boy?"

Tony's face went white. "How dare you go through my things like this!"

"Who is this child?"

"That's none of your concern!"

"Why are you sending money to Gardena Diamond?"

"What I do with my money is no concern of yours."

"My lawyer tells me it is entirely my concern."

"Y—your lawyer?" Tony looked as if he might faint.

He never thought I would find out.

"To answer the questions you should be asking: One, I was made aware of certain transactions between Spadros and Diamond Manors; Two, I went to Gardena Diamond —"

Tony took a step forward. "Jacqui, I can explain —"

This made me even angrier. "How could you possibly explain this?" Disgusted, I said, "And three: Gardena has told me all."

Tony's demeanor became that of a man terrified by some sudden thought. He whispered, "Not here. Please. We don't know who listens." He rushed to put the portraits away and lock the drawer. He tried to take my hand, but I shook it off. He never trusted me. Not once. "Let's go out to the gardens, Jacqui. Please."

So I followed him out to the gardens, then turned on him. "She told me all, Tony. All that you have not told me in the five years since you asked me to marry you. That you love and desire her. That you never wished to marry me —"

"That's not true —"

"— but felt forced to for fear of your father. And that you have a son you never told me about, even when Gardena begged you to."

Tony stared at me in horror.

"Did you think I would harm him? Did you think I would reveal him to your father? Or was I not good enough to know about him? All the times you've chided and harassed me, had your men follow and spy on me. You were so worried about what I was doing, what I kept from you, and yet here you've kept the most important thing in your life from me. When were you going to tell me? Would I have gone to my grave, not knowing? Would I learn from some tabloid, some chance meeting —"

Tony flinched. So he knew I saw Roland on Market Center.

"— and learn the truth? Why am I so untrustworthy in your eyes? What defect have I that I can't know the bonds of love my husband has, that I have to learn of his son from his mistress?"

He went pale. "Jacqui, it's not like that —"

"Not like what? You don't spend time with your true family, speak Italian with the woman you love and her son? You never even tried to teach me!" That hurt almost as much as anything else. "Perhaps you have some secret hideaway you use those times when you say you're out late tending to the Business."

Tony said, "I've never seen Roland, Jacqui. I wasn't even allowed to name him. And Gardena's never allowed me to touch her again." His shoulders slumped. "After the dinner, a letter came with the last photo: 'This is all you'll see until you tell her'."

I felt as if cold water had been thrown upon me. So Gardena **had** blackmailed him, there at the last. That was why Jonathan was so angry at her on Queen's Day.

I drew him to the arbor, where two chairs and a small white table stood. I sat across from him, leaning my arms on the table. "Tell me what happened."

"What happened? I was young, and stupid, and too much in love." Tony sounded disgusted with himself. "Several weeks later, I slipped my guards, just as you do. The Diamonds captured and blindfolded me, then told me Gardena was with child. They said I must marry her or sign their paper — but what choice was there? I couldn't risk harm coming to her. I was barely of age, terrified of my father learning, so I consulted no one. But I must pay, and there's nothing in the paper as to what I get in return!" He sounded close to panic. "I took them to a secret court after the dinner; my lawyer provided every argument he knew. But it's no use. I can't see my son, and if I try I may be prosecuted." His voice broke. "My own child! I see pictures of him, and he of me. Or so they tell me. Who knows what he thinks!" He put his head in his hands. "He must think I abandoned him. That I care nothing for him. It's unfair. It's unjust."

"Well," I said. "This is a situation." The Diamonds took advantage of his youth, his fear, and played it. "But now that I know, perhaps Gardena can persuade her father to relent."

"He hates me, they all do."

"Not Jon. And not even Gardena. She said she's fond of you." *More than fond.*

Oh, gods, I thought. She loves him too. "She understands now why you refused to make things right." I reached across the table, held his hand. "So this is why the nightmares."

Tony shook his head. "I know you hate me, Jacqui."

I let go of his hand. Did I hate him? I felt crushed, angry, abandoned, betrayed. "You lied to me."

Tony went on. "You're right. I lied. You should have known everything before you agreed to this madness."

A pang shot through me: I had never agreed to any of this.

"I gave money to them instead of keeping it safe for my lawful heirs." He gave me a small sad smile. "Which I believe you'll give me someday — if you'll let me." He paused, suddenly downcast. "You have every reason to hate me."

I leaned forward, cupped his face in my hands. "But I don't hate you for **this**."

I had other reasons to hate him; sometimes I did. But I didn't want to think of my forced marriage, my meaningless life in this gilded cage, my murdered friends, his threats. I didn't want to think about Joe, who I had to see under false pretenses so he wouldn't be killed too.

I must never speak of that: Joe had to be kept safe at all costs.

"In the Pot, none of this would mean anything. You're providing for your child. You sacrificed your dearest wishes to protect Gardena and your son."

Tony stared at me, mouth open. "Y—you're proud of me?"

I nodded.

He took me onto his lap. "Oh, Jacqui, I love you so much."

I laid my head on Tony's shoulder; he wrapped his arms around me. And I thought of Joe's words two months earlier:

"So he defies his father. He takes you and leaves Bridges. And then what? Are you going to stay with a man, sleep with a man, who you feel for only as a brother? Why?"

I felt as if I woke to a strange land with no guideposts.

I waited for Joe's leg to heal. I wanted to stop the men who kidnapped David. I wanted to learn who killed Marja. But the real reason I stayed? Fear of Roy Spadros.

At first I didn't understand what Roy sharing a humiliating secret meant. Roy's only motivations involved causing pain. But then I realized he caused me pain by sharing his secret. He'd cause Tony and Molly pain if I revealed it. Either way, he'd won.

My marriage to Tony was a torture set by Roy many years ago. But the torture had unwittingly extended, not only to Gardena, but to her entire family.

I could no longer play this game. There was only one way everyone could be free.

I had to leave.

The Change

I'd thought of leaving before, and even made plans for it. But when I firmly decided to leave as a definite act of will, a tremendous weight lifted from me.

Tony asked, "What is it?"

I kissed his cheek. "Things will turn out well. You'll see."

Of course, all the other reasons I couldn't leave still remained. But it felt manageable: remove one card — mine — and the game was won. And yet I felt a great fondness for Tony, as if he were already free of me and happy.

Perhaps I was mad, but it was a beautiful madness, where everything seemed so clear.

Tony gazed into my eyes: his heart lay bare. "You're a better woman than I ever imagined. I promise never to hide anything from you again."

Then madness passed; grief and anger returned. I rose, turned away. "Let's go inside." So I went through the gardens and to the veranda, Tony trailing behind.

Tony said, "Where would you like to take tea?"

"Is it that late? Here will do." I hadn't faced Tony, nor did I wish to. "I'll return shortly."

I went towards my rooms. I needed to think.

How was I to find money for four zeppelin tickets? Surely Joe wouldn't leave his sister to face the Spadros Family alone. Tony would stop at nothing to learn where we went.

When I entered my room, Amelia said, "What's wrong?"

I fell into her arms and wept; even now I couldn't say why.

Amelia just let me cry. Once the storm passed, she took hold of my upper arms. "Now tell me what happened."

Amelia helped raise Tony. I remembered her tears at his broken rib, how she wept the night I almost killed him with opium. I laughed bitterly, shaking my head. "You don't want to know." Amelia loved Tony more than her own son: to learn what he had done, what the Diamonds had done to him .... "There are things I can't tell you, Amelia."

She smiled. "I know, mum. But if ever I might ease your troubles, I'll do it gladly. You've been kinder to me than any mistress should be, and for that I'm grateful."

I stared at her, dismayed. "One day we must talk." Then I sighed. "But today, my husband wishes tea on the veranda."

Amelia nodded. "Come wash your face; your makeup needs fixing. Once you're ready, I'll take care of everything."

Cold water and deep breaths eased my face and mind. As Amelia redid my makeup, I forced myself to list the things which needed doing. I had almost enough money for one zeppelin ticket. Perhaps I might find a case, or borrow the money for more.

Might the bank be willing to extend me a loan, with my apartments as collateral? They were in my name, after all.

But the bank would want to know why I needed a loan, and surely would notify Tony — or worse, Roy — to ask permission.

Or perhaps I could see a broker to ask about the value of the apartments. But how to do so without involving Tony? He'd wish to know why I would sell the apartments so soon, especially since they were the only thing I had left of Dame Anastasia.

But I still had her makeup book. If I were to disguise myself well enough to fool Tony's men, I might fool a property broker.

"There!" Amelia spoke proudly. "Stand tall and smile, and no one will ever know you shed a tear."

* * *

During tea, I considered the matter. A female broker would be scrutinized more closely than if I approached the bank myself. Someone would contact Tony or Roy to confirm my identity.

I decided honesty might be the best policy here. Or at least forthrightness. "I wish to renovate my apartments."

Tony sat reading some mail. "Oh?"

"I'll need to take a loan on the bank."

Tony smiled. "No need — I'll give you the money."

If I were to steal from the Spadros Family, they would never stop hunting me. "Are you certain? I could take the loan, and establish credit. I've read that —"

Tony burst out laughing. "A married woman? Taking loans, establishing credit? You sound like some widow merchant." He smiled fondly at me. "There's no need for such things. Write a list of what's needed, and the amount, and I'll give it to you. Or contract it out and have the bills sent to me." He went back to reading. "Whatever you wish."

"Very well."

This was a mistake. If I made a list, Tony — or his accountant — would want to verify how the money was spent. Not only a mistake, a dead end.

Perhaps inspiration might come to me later. In the meantime, there was something else I needed to bring up. "I know you said you didn't want me working on cases anymore, but ... I must learn who killed my friend Marja. She was as a mother to me."

Tony glanced at the servants. "Might we discuss this some other time?"

I had forgotten they stood there. "You're right, of course."

* * *

After tea, Tony and I met with three Spadros Family lawyers. Tony's father Roy wanted to meet with us as well — or so Tony said — but Tony refused to have him here.

The men sat in armchairs in Tony's study; we sat on the sofa. Tony posted Sawbuck to keep anyone from listening.

A Mr. Primero Trevisane spoke, the other two taking notes. "I've managed to place you and your wife at the end of the proceedings, which went well with the inquest's wishes."

Tony's eyes narrowed. "If I recall, this means they wish to build their case on testimony we might give, to prove us false."

"Yes," Mr. Trevisane said. "Yet we can hear and counter their evidence." He opened a thick folder. "Servants were questioned first: those in attendance at the explosion and of all four Families."

"Four?" I said.

"Since the allegation of collusion has taken place," Mr. Trevisane said, "the inquest has been made aware that this could be a Hart plot to defame the three Families so accused."

I laughed. "An idea likely from the Clubbs." Everyone stared at me. "It's no secret they bear animosity towards each other."

"Indeed," Mr. Trevisane said. "In any case, the questions seem irrelevant. What fuel runs the heating in Spadros Manor? When is Mrs. Spadros 'at home'? Have there been any incidents?"

"Such as?" Tony said.

"The dismissal of three kitchen maids from the Pot. It angered many that instead of hiring their own, Spadros Manor would bring this sort," he glanced at me, "to serve in such capacity."

Tony said, "A mistake which has since been corrected."

"But your butler revealed the theft of letters from your wife." He turned to me. "Perhaps you can enlighten us on this matter."

"I never thought to examine them. If I may, I'll fetch them."

"Of course, Mrs. Spadros. It would be helpful."

I poured a drink and began searching. I found the letters stacked at one end of the window-seat in my study. "They're all personal correspondence. Must you read them?"

Mr. Trevisane pursed his lips, frowning. "I'm sorry, Mrs. Spadros, but they might contain something important." He conferred with the others in whispers. "If you would care to read them? Perhaps some detail might help."

I opened one. "A notice of an appointment with my dressmaker." I set it aside. "A personal note inquiring after my health." That was from Jonathan. And then I scanned the next envelope. "I don't recall getting this."

Tony leaned forward. "What is it?"

"A letter from Jo — Miss Josephine Kerr." I'd never seen Josie's handwriting before then; all her cards and envelopes so far had been embossed. But it seemed familiar. I tore the envelope open and glanced at the top: dated from before the Grand Ball.

They intercepted my mail!

But how? All mail was supposed to go through Pearson. "Does Pearson keep a record of the mail?"

Tony rang for Pearson.

Why would they take a letter sent from Josie?

Pearson entered. "Yes, sir?"

Tony said, "Mrs. Spadros has a few questions for you."

Pearson closed the door, taking several steps into the room. For the first time, he seemed uneasy. "How can I help, mum?"

"Do you keep a record of mail?"

He glanced between Tony and I. "What sort of record?"

"When a letter leaves. Where it's sent. When one arrives."

"Yes, mum." He surveyed the room. "Do you need it?"

"Yes," Tony said. His face never changed, but he was angry.

I turned to Mr. Trevisane. "I fear these women were stealing my mail for longer than we thought. They may have been gathering information about who I have contact with."

Tony nodded. "Might they have also taken mail you posted?"

"How would they do that?"

Mr. Trevisane said, "One might only bribe a messenger boy to have access to all sorts of information. We never use them except for the most routine correspondence."

"Hey, you need be giving us more money." Poignee stood in front of me in my study, hands on her hips. Ottilie and Treysa stood beside her. "You wouldn't want us telling Mr. Spadros about your romp with Joseph Kerr, now, would you?"

They blackmailed me to bribe messengers for my letters?

Tony said, "The will?"

"Oh, yes, sir," Mr. Trevisane said, opening another file from his case. He handed over a stack of papers. "Your signature on the last page, sir, then we can witness it."

He was going through with this?

Tony scanned the papers then signed. "Arrange a bank account for my wife. Place the income from her apartments there."

The lawyers gaped at Tony. "Why sir," Mr. Trevisane said, "a woman? Holding a bank account? Why, it's preposterous! We'll have to consult your father —"

Tony's expression didn't change. He reached into his left

jacket pocket, removed his revolver from its holster, then placed it on his leg, the barrel pointing towards the man. "I didn't hear you correctly. Are you my attorney or are you my father's?"

Mr. Trevisane glanced at the revolver. "Y—yours, sir."

"Then pray carry out my wishes. Without involving my father." He pointed the gun back and forth at the three men, not raising it from his leg. "Or I will know who to call to account. Make sure the bank understands this as well, because I'll hold you responsible should he hear of it."

The three turned pale, then nodded. Tony replaced his revolver in its holster.

I glanced at the fireplace, where Tony shot Duck after the man betrayed him. I could never forget the pool of blood there.

I'd been to the bank on Tony's behalf many times, and of course I had Anastasia's lockbox. But I'd never had a bank account before, and I didn't know whether to be excited or afraid.

Pearson returned with two of his sons, each carrying a large stack of ledgers. "This is for the year so far, mum."

And it wasn't yet May! "Bring the six months prior." I turned to the men. "That was when the women were most saucy to me," I gave Tony a quick glance, "which is why they were dismissed."

These men had no business hearing the real reason.

Pearson glanced between us then said, "Yes, mum." The three left, returning — in two trips — with six equally large stacks.

Pearson wouldn't recognize some of my mail, but Tony would wonder why I wrote to (for example) Thrace Pike. I needed to see what was in the ledgers before Tony did. "This'll be like finding a needle in a haystack. I keep record of correspondence; I'd be happy to search for missing mail." I didn't keep any record, but it was the best way to control these records I could think of.

"That would be helpful," Mr. Trevisane said. "In the meantime, let's turn to the matter of your appearances at the inquest. The Four Families will appear in the audience three days from now, when the public is invited to speak."

I almost laughed at what was unspoken: to give the impression of caring about their opinions.

"Deep mourning would be best for the duration of the

inquest. You're only allowed to enter and exit during a lull in the proceedings, or in case of emergency. You do not rise except when a judge enters, on exiting, or if need be to allow another to pass."

"Judges?" Tony said. "I thought this was merely an inquest."

"Well, yes," Mr. Trevisane said. "But since I don't know the future, I thought it wise to educate your wife on these matters."

Tony seemed put out. "Very well."

I said, "What's a judge? How will I know one?"

"The man in charge of the proceedings," Mr. Trevisane said.

Tony put his hand on mine. "Just do as we do."

Mr. Trevisane continued. "When appearing as a witness, answer the question asked, nothing more. Make them draw the information from you. Unfortunately, we're not permitted to cross-examine, but they'll ask if there's any information they've neglected. This is where we must determine your exact words."

* * *

After a half-hour of this, they left.

Pearson brought a note for Tony, who read it, then kissed my forehead. "I'm off to Market Center. I'll visit the Chief of Police about your friend. Master Kerr said there was little interest in her case." He grinned. "Perhaps I can persuade him to take interest."

"Oh," I said, impressed.

I went to my study, setting the stolen letters aside. On the desk sat three more: from Joseph Kerr, Jon, and Gardena.

Seeing Jon and Gardena's names sent me into a rage. What did I have to say to them? How could they explain themselves? They'd not only lied to me, they'd betrayed Tony! I crumpled the unopened letters, throwing them into the freshly-lit fire.

At that moment, I wished to see neither one of them again.

Joe's letter I opened as if sent from the Floorman himself, amazed at having a part of him with me. He wrote with large, printed letters, as a young child might.

> I hope you're well. Please visit tomorrow after
> luncheon. Look forward to our meeting. — Joe

I hugged Joe's letter, imagining his beloved face pressing upon my chest. I felt such joy that I kissed the letter, leaving a lipstick mark. Then I locked it in my desk. *Soon, my love, soon.*

I went to the door. "Pearson, please notify the bridge guards that we're not at home if the Diamonds should call."

"Yes, mum. For how long?"

"Until we say otherwise. And I'll call on the Kerrs tomorrow after luncheon."

"I'll have the carriage ready. Will there be anything else?"

"My cigarettes, and a bottle of bourbon." I was celebrating.

* * *

Ledgers sat in neat rows between my desk and the fireplace.

I poured some bourbon, opened a ledger, and began reading, stacking the ledgers on the other side of my desk as I went. They detailed comings and goings, arguments in the hallway and packages delivered. Many entries were about mail, or meetings with people who came calling — about both Tony and myself!

Then there was a note:

Mr. Anthony surprised me whilst writing. We conversed.

We conversed? I daresay you did. Tony must have been furious.

I called Pearson in, a ledger open, waiting until he closed the door and stood before me. "Why do you listen outside my door?"

Pearson stared straight ahead and said nothing.

I rose, coming round my desk to walk past him. "I've trusted you since I was a small girl. But now I find you've made notes on me. Listened at my door. You're reporting to my husband, but only after he discovered you. Who do you really report to?"

Pearson's jaw clenched, but he said nothing.

"It's insupportable. You've betrayed me, my husband, everyone. Yet you're not the only one doing so. Do I have to dismiss my entire staff?" I stood in front of him. "This will stop."

"I can't, mum."

"Well, it must."

His nose reddened. "I'm sorry, mum, I can't."

I had never seen Pearson so distressed in my life. "Why?"

He hesitated a full minute, glancing at me from time to time, becoming more agitated as the seconds passed. Then he spoke in an anguished whisper. "Mr. Roy has my mother."

His mother?

"When my family was made gift to Mr. Anthony, he took my mother as hostage." He turned aside. "To spy on my own Family **is** insupportable, mum, but I can't take the chance."

I spoke without meaning to. "Why would he do this?"

"I don't know." He sounded adrift. "I'd never betrayed him, even in my thoughts. I've been in the Family since birth. Mr. Roy and I were boys together in this house." He retrieved his handkerchief and wiped his nose. "You and Mr. Anthony are dear to me as my own children. You mustn't think I betrayed you."

"Oh, Pearson." I put my arms around his, resting my head on his left shoulder. "Forgive me for not trusting you." I let go, came round to face him. "Do you have proof she lives?"

"She sends letters. And I visit her when you and Mr. Anthony are out. I saw her last month. She appears well." His jaw clenched. "But she belongs in the home Mr. Acevedo gave her."

I took a deep breath, let it out: no idea came. But I had to do something. This was wrong. "If it's in my power, I'll win her free."

He froze. "Mum, you must do nothing. He might kill her."

I nodded, whispering, "Someday I'll kill him, never fear."

He smiled sadly, shaking his head. "Were all my sons combined half so fierce." His shoulders drooped. "But I suppose lambs are best for the servant's lot."

I placed my hand on his shoulder. Jane, Mary, his sons ... they must be terrified. "None of you deserve this."

He stared at the floor. "I'm glad you told Mr. Anthony where you've been going. He fears for you."

I sighed. Tony seemed to be fearful of everything.

"I remember when he was a tiny boy. Such a happy child. He adored his brother. But I'll never forget the way he stared at Master Roy Acevedo's body — after it happened. He found him. Even though Mr. Anthony was but two," Pearson shook his head, "I fear the sight changed him."

The Map

The doorbell rang.

"Please excuse me, mum," Pearson said.

I stood in the middle of the room, trying to make sense of what he'd just said. Tony found his brother's body?

I knew almost nothing about the boy, not even his name, until Pearson said it just now. But the way he'd been spoken of over the years made me feel as if something terrible had taken place.

Poisoning is what everyone said.

But who would poison a child?

* * *

Pearson came in holding a silver tray containing a full bottle, a glass, a silver case containing my cigarettes, and a letter. "This just arrived, mum. From the Inventor."

Whatever could the Inventor want to mail **me** about? Pearson lit a cigarette for me. "Thank you, Pearson, that will be all."

I poured a glass, took a long drink, then opened the letter.

Maxim Call wrote with a flowing hand, full of flourishes. From what I gathered, they weren't having any more luck finding the controls to this new piling than they had with ours. They'd spent a great deal of time repairing the lift mechanisms and were just now able to descend safely to the observatory.

"Now that we know the sort of thing we're looking for," the

Inventor wrote, "the process should go more smoothly. I may stay here to compare the readings on this piling with yours, but that shouldn't take more than a few months. In the meantime, I've had my men search for others in the city. It's a pity there isn't any sort of map —"

Map?

I lay upon the floor in the midst of Ma's cathedral as the sun rose.

Four buttresses rose from the floor of the huge round structure to meet in a grand domed window of stained glass. But in the ceiling lay smaller windows, spaced evenly through each quadrant. Each of these smaller windows - still larger than I was - held an array of yellow, gold, and red, which reminded me of flowers.

I never understood what these meant until now. "Pearson!"

He peered in, face concerned. "Are you well, mum?"

"I must speak with the Inventor immediately. It's urgent."

"I'll send men to find him, mum."

"No, fetch Amelia. We must go to him."

Amelia produced a deep purple gown I hadn't worn before, and placed the elderberry shawl atop it. "This will do for now. I don't expect the Inventor cares much for formality."

"This dress is lovely," I said. "When can I wear it again?"

"After the inquest. You'd think you lost a parent, or Mr. Anthony himself, the way they force you to deep mourning."

"I suppose it's for the best." I still mourned many people, yet I wondered if continuing to appear in public wearing mourning garb brought Dame Anastasia to mind more than it should.

* * *

Tony would have approved of our entourage: Honor had accompanied him to Market Center, so Blitz escorted us, armed, with a full set of outriders. Blitz bowed when I approached, a wry grin on his face. "Mrs. Spadros."

"Good evening, Blitz." He helped me into the carriage. "This excursion isn't likely to be as diverting as others we've taken."

He chuckled and closed the door.

While on our journey, I thought about Tony, Jon, Gardena, and everything they were involved with. I didn't belong with these quadrant-folk, unraveling the fruits of their twisted schemes. I was one of the Dealers' Daughters, a direct descendant of the women who survived the assault on the Cathedral during the Coup. My place was with them.

But as long as Roy Spadros ruled, I didn't dare try to return home. He'd threatened to burn the Cathedral with everyone in it should I step back into the Spadros Pot, and at the time, I believed he might do it.

My only other option was to leave with Joe, sending what aid we could from a place of safety. But if what I knew helped Inventor Call repair the city, at the time, I felt glad to offer it.

This second piling lay under a home near 143rd and Book. A maid in her forties opened the door. Her eyes widened. Then she fled, leaving the door open. So we stood waiting.

"Well?" A man said in the distance. "Did you let them in?"

Footsteps approached. The occupants, an elderly couple, gaped in astonishment. "Mrs. Spadros?"

"I'm here to see Inventor Call. May we enter?"

"Of course!" They made way, bowing and curtsying as we passed. "I apologize for our foolish girl," the man said. "I think you quite flummoxed her. This way!"

They led us through their luxurious home to a wide, well-stocked pantry. At the back of this was a door, which opened on a narrow flight of wooden steps down to a storeroom large enough to encompass the entire house, with thick supports at intervals. In the center of the floor, a large trap door lay open.

The man pointed to it. "My father built this home. My parents kept the door locked, and when they turned in their cards, I never thought to look."

I grinned at him. "You hold quite a treasure."

Blitz said, "I'll fetch the Inventor, mum; there's no need for you to dirty yourself."

I so loved the curling orange steam which rose from the magma. But I would only become sweaty, and there was no time to bathe before dressing for dinner. "Very well."

Tony's men brought down straight-backed chairs and a dark wooden tea-table, and I sat to await the Inventor. After some time, he emerged, muttering under his breath.

He let out a short laugh when he saw the table and chairs in the midst of the storage room. "Am I called away from my work to have tea, then?"

I rose, curtsying low. "Inventor, I have urgent news for you." I glanced around. "Blitz can stand guard; the rest of you, out. This is not for Mr. Roy's ears."

One man let out a laugh. But they filed upstairs without protest and the door was shut. Blitz stationed himself at the bottom of the stairs, a good ten yards from us.

I gestured to a chair. "Please, sir, sit."

Maxim Call appeared intrigued. "What's your urgent news?"

I leaned forward. "I believe I have your map."

The Inventor's face became that of an excited schoolboy. "Praise the Dealer! However did you find it?"

So explained that I grew up in the Cathedral, and shared my recollections of its skylights. "I don't know what else it could be."

The Inventor shouted, "Monte! Get up here!"

Feet ran up metal stairs, and a dark-haired Apprentice emerged. "Yes, Inventor?"

"Pen and ink, at once." Inventor Call turned to me. "Tell me of the smaller circles. Were they all the same?"

"I think so. It's been so many years since I lived there."

He became solemn. "I'm astonished you're here."

"You didn't know I was from the Pot?"

"No one's ever mentioned it."

I found that hard to believe. Everywhere I went, ladies of rank used my birthplace as a reason for scorn. But Maxim Call seldom mixed in social circles. "And what do you think now?"

"This is the most exciting discovery imaginable!" The Inventor took pen and ink from his Apprentice and set it down before me, along with several large sheets of paper. "You must draw every detail. This knowledge could save the city!"

By the time we returned, it was past time to dress for dinner, so Amelia put me in a simple, easier to assemble gown. I had refused to let Amelia fuss with my hair earlier, so all was ready.

I hurried downstairs; Tony stood waiting. "I hear you had an exciting time."

Amused, I took his arm. "Inventor Call near leapt with enthusiasm. I brought a map of his beloved pilings."

We strolled past our sun-room, turned towards the dining hall. "Where did you find it?"

I tapped my temple.

"Oh," Tony said, impressed.

"We should speak of this later," I said, glancing at the servants around the long table.

* * *

As we sat in my bed, I told Tony of my recollections of the Cathedral. Yet I refrained from specifics, not knowing who listened. "Inventor Call didn't know where I came from."

"It's not widely known," Tony said.

"But all the ladies of standing know, and I imagine their gentlemen as well."

"Nevertheless," Tony said, "Don't volunteer it."

"What have I to be ashamed of?"

Tony kissed my hand. "Nothing. But there are those who would take offense, and I wish everyone to love you as I do."

Yet you didn't trust me with Roland. He never explained why he feared telling me about his son. "Do you believe me to be allied with your father?"

"What makes you say that?"

I hesitated. "Certain things you've hidden. Yet you asked if I wanted the Family." I couldn't understand how this even crossed his mind. A woman Patriarch? "I just want to understand what you're thinking. At times, I don't feel I know you."

He wrapped his arms around me, his face in my hair. "For a long time, I've been almost mad with fear," he murmured. "For you, for Gardena, for my son. Even, I suppose, for myself."

I recalled what Pearson said about Tony finding his older brother's body. What would that sight do to a child?

Tony cradled my face in his hands. "I've been a fool. You've had much more to fear, yet instead of learning to protect myself as

142

you have, I've let my fear come close to destroying us." He dropped his hands. "My father was right. You were right. If I don't find a way to be a different man, I'm condemning us to death. If not now, then when my father's time comes." He snorted. "Why should men follow me if I can't control myself?"

"Tony, listen to me. You have men who'd follow you into the Fire." I thought then of what Jon told me on the Clubb's yacht. "But you must think of yourself first. Make yourself strong, and trust that others are strong as well." I placed my hand on his cheek. "You don't have to protect the whole world."

Tony laughed, and for the first time, he seemed happy. He put his hand on mine. "I don't know why my father chose you for me, but I'm grateful." He straightened as if coming into some insight. "I must be worthy of respect if my father's men are to follow me one day. Perhaps they despise me now, but there must be a way to earn their allegiance without becoming my father."

I nodded. "A good intention indeed."

Tony pulled me close, kissed me.

This surprised me so much I stiffened.

Relax, breathe, you can do this.

Tony caressed my hair. "What's wrong?"

Oh, gods. "You surprised me, that's all."

He smiled, moving his arm around my waist. "A good surprise, I hope."

Does he suspect I don't desire him? I forced myself to smile, closed my eyes. *Joe, where are you?*

I let out a sigh, forced myself to relax.

Tony — Joe moved his hand up my leg, kissed me.

Joe ... the way he smelled, his soft hair, the way he touched me ...

I wrapped my arms around my beloved Joe, pulled his golden body to me. Kissed his beautiful face. "Yes." Joe's lithe body moved atop me, between my legs. I wrapped my legs around his muscled back, pressing him closer to me as he moved inside. Joe's breathing, his moans, only made me want him more. "Yes. Oh, gods, yes."

The Reaction

I awoke panting, bathed in sweat. Tony lay sleeping peacefully, and I felt grateful I hadn't screamed.

I lay back on the pillows, aching from my earlier encounter.

I didn't know who I was anymore.

Was I going mad? Why did I tell Tony yes? Was it Tony I told, or Joe? Who was I intimate with? What would it do to Tony if he learned my yes was a lie?

Then, with horror, I remembered the time Tony lay with me in his study. I said, "I love you," aloud, but it was to Joe.

I had never lied to Tony: I never told Tony I loved him in all the years we had known each other. But should Tony ever learn the truth, he would believe me to have lied to him. He loved me. The truth would cut like nothing else ever could.

I rolled away from Tony, curled into a ball. Tears streamed to my pillow, yet I held my hand over my mouth to keep from making a sound. What was I becoming? What had I done? What could I do?

* * *

The next morning, Tony brought flowers from our gardens as I sat drinking my "morning tea."

I smiled, my heart heavy. "Set the vase on the dresser."

He sat across my tea-table from me. "What tea is this?"

I forced myself to hide how uneasy I felt. He had never come in this early before, not to mention sitting at my tea-table.

He removed the lid, sniffed it. "I don't believe I've smelled this kind before."

That tea was how I kept from bearing him children. Did he suspect? "A formulation my mother made for me, long ago." I poured the rest in my cup and set the empty pot down. "It reminds me of her."

For a moment I felt sad. Did she ever think of me?

Tony reached across the table to take my hand. "You've never spoken of your mother before."

She sent me away, and I'll never see her again. I shook my head, unable to speak.

"I'm sorry," Tony said. "I only wished to make you smile." He kissed my forehead. "I'll speak no more of it. Enjoy your tea."

When the door closed behind him, I lay my head on my arms and sobbed. At that instant, I felt like Pip. I was Ma's only child. Why did she send me away?

I recalled the disgusted look on her face when she turned away, as the carriage took me from her for the last time. What did I do to make her hate me?

It wasn't often I cried like I did that day. Sitting on the street bench with David Bryce. The morning after my wedding, when I realized what I'd been sold into. The day I heard of Nina's death.

I stood, my back pressed on the wall beside the open door, listening.

"Did you hear? Miss Clubb's dead. Yes, Miss Nina. I heard it was at her own hand."

When they sent me home that evening, I sat in our back rooms at Ma's cathedral and wept the whole night. I was fourteen, and I felt my life was over.

* * *

After luncheon, I went calling on Joe and Josie, grateful for the chance to be away from the Manor.

As the carriage rattled along, I remembered that lonely bereft girl and smiled. She never knew that in a few months time a certain boy would take interest.

Joseph Kerr never paid me much mind before then, but one afternoon I sat outside the Cathedral smoking and he came over to see me. I found myself telling him everything — about Nina, the

Spadros Family, Jack Diamond, even Air.

From then on, we were inseparable.

Joe got me cigarettes; I got him some of Ma's bread. He brought me into the plans he and Josie made for our street gang, the High-Low Split. I'd sneak out once Ma fell asleep, then Joe and I would kiss in the moonlight. He never tried anything — I told him about Ma's patron, the Masked Man, and how he'd forbidden me from entertaining any man, even in the Cathedral.

We shared a bottle of moonshine one night. I might have been fifteen. "They got plans for you," Joe said.

"I wish I knew what."

"You ever seen the man's face?"

"Never." I described him: blue eyes, light skin, a brown leather mask, a dark cloak — sometimes black, sometimes brown. Dark brown leather boots. But nice: the clothes would fetch a lot. But no one dared touch him. He was that sort of guy. Scary, if you didn't know him, but always kind to me.

"Wearing brown. With blue eyes. Could he be a Clubb spy?"

I never considered such a thing. "I dunno."

"Damn spies." Joe shook his head. "I hate Clubbs. All of them. If it weren't for the Clubbs, my ancestor the King coulda left the city, him and his whole family." He spat. "My grandfather's parents never woulda ended up here. We coulda gotten help, come back," he raised his fist, "taken what was ours by right."

The Clubbs seized the zeppelin station during the Alcatraz Coup, trapping the Kerrs in Bridges.

"But then you'd be a king or something." I laughed. "You wouldn't even know me."

He put his arm round me with a grin. "No way I could ever resist knowing you." But then he sobered. "I wouldn't let the Cathedral be like this. The Dealers should be here casting the Cards, giving little kids their Blessings like in the old days." He took a drag on his cigarette. "One day I'll make this right, Jacqui, you'll see."

* * *

Joe and Josie came into their parlor together, Joe walking with a cane!

I jumped up. "Oh! I'm so glad you're doing well."

Joe shrugged, dejected. "I can walk." He winced when putting weight on his leg. "I still have to be careful. The doctor claims the bone is sound enough, but everything hurts."

Josie laughed. "He frets like an old woman these days. The doctor says he heals remarkably well."

"I'm relieved."

Josie placed a chair next to the sofa. "Sit close to the end."

Joe sat in the chair beside me. "It's better with a firm seat."

Josie went to the sideboard. "I got this to celebrate." She brought over a bottle of fine wine and three glasses.

"How wonderful!" Remembering their finances, I opened my handbag. "Let me contribute for the cost."

She smiled. "Thanks, Jacqui." Josie poured the wine, and we toasted Joe's newfound ability.

"Just like old times, back in the Pot," Joe said. "The three of us together, sharing a drink." He stretched like a cat. "Life is good."

Josie sat across the table from us and spoke quietly. "Joe told me of your idea. It seems reasonable."

For a moment I felt confused.

Joe leaned over to speak in my ear. "To leave here."

"Ah," I said. Josie was obviously worried about being overheard. "I had a question about Marja."

Josie nodded. "Yes, Joe told me. It sounds as if she sent the letter from her work." She leaned forward. "Do you still have it?"

I shook my head, remembering my joy at Joe's letter. "I'm so sorry. I burned it." How was I to know it would be the last thing they had of her?

Josie sighed, leaning back. "Don't fret. It's only —"

"You wanted something to remember her by. I understand."

She nodded, looking away. "Think nothing of it." She gave me a happy, relieved smile, then stood. "I'll play a bit," she said with a sly grin, "so you can talk without me around."

Joe laughed. "You are a dear."

As she began to play, Joe intertwined his fingers in mine. "I don't know what I'd do without Josie." He kissed my hand. "She's taken care of me through everything."

"I'm terribly grateful for her," I said. "It's good to see her doing so well through it all." Enduring this place, Joe's fall, and now, Marja. Yet we'd survived it. Feeling a surge of fondness, I hugged our clasped hands to my face. "I love you so much, Joe."

We held hands as Josie played. I felt so safe, so at peace, so loved. Everything was right when Joe was near.

"Jacqui, I've learned who started this Red Dog Gang your husband spoke of."

"Oh?"

"The Clubbs, Jacqui. I have it from a reliable source."

"I thought you told my husband the Diamonds started it."

Joe caressed my hair. "He must have been mistaken. Mixed me up with someone else. I said no such thing."

It wasn't like Tony to misspeak. Or was I mistaken? "Are you sure? I don't understand. Why would the Clubbs hire children to throw rocks at their own —"

He gazed into my eyes, which flustered me. "If they wanted to blame someone else for it, this makes perfect sense," Joe said calmly. "And they've used Hart colors. They could claim he began it, and everyone would believe them."

I recalled the Golden Bridges article in February. "People are already saying it." I read back over the article in my mind. "The Clubbs said it. The article said they planned formal protest."

Joe shook his head. "The scoundrels! Mr. Hart may be many things, but he doesn't deserve this."

"Why does he dislike you so much?"

Joe gazed towards Josie, and she gave a slight nod. "You saw him at the racetrack, Jacqui. He knows how you feel for me."

I could hardly believe my ears. "He's jealous? But — he's married! And," the idea disgusted me, "**old**."

Joe laughed. "That he is. Never fear: once we've left Bridges, he'll never bother you again."

I kissed his hand, moved by his words. Then he leaned over and kissed my lips, softly, his hand cupping my face.

If only you were well. If only we might leave here. If only I didn't have to go home, face Tony, endure my wife duties tonight.

If I could keep my mind on Joe, they weren't so bad. But

before that ....

And how could I keep lying to Tony? Keep dodging his questions? Every day, every night meant more pain to come. I had to get away from here. I gripped Joe's hand, gazed into his eyes. "You **must** recover quickly!"

He smiled his glorious smile. "I have no other wish, if only to leave with you sooner." He paused, growing somber. "But we must plan this carefully if we're to escape without suspicion..."

Escape. The word once said made this feel more real.

"You're better at such things. What shall we do? And when?"

I clasped his hand. "We must gain tickets for the zeppelin."

Joe nodded. "Yes."

I took a deep breath. "But I don't have enough money."

"Never fear," Joe said. "I may have to call in some favors." He glanced away. "I may have to do more than that."

The way he said it made me fear he might return to the Pot of an evening to sell himself, as he did when he was a boy. *People'll pay top rate to fuck a Kerr*, he once told me.

He caressed the side of my cheek. "But I **will** get them." He glanced at the clock. "Our grandfather will be home soon."

Josie said, "I'm so glad you could visit." She came over to hug me, speaking in my ear. "I'm even happier at the thought you might be my sister soon."

Sister.

I'd forgotten: one might marry without papers, once past the Aperture. I hugged her tightly, kissed her cheek. "I'm glad too."

In the carriage, my mind was a-whirl. How might I gain the rest of the money for my zeppelin ticket?

Selling the apartments was out. I had other things I might sell. But to who?

They would have to be small things, sold very discreetly. If rumor arose that Mrs. Spadros was selling off her belongings, it could create the impression that the Family was in financial difficulty. A scandal was the last thing I needed.

More importantly, I had to keep this from Tony. There was a limit to what he could withstand. Granted, he'd been more generous than I imagined about my deceptions, but if he got the idea I meant to leave ...

I didn't know what he might do. And that terrified me.

The way he almost lazily shot his man Duck, bound and blindfolded as the man was, just for making a sound when Tony told him not to ....

It was as if Tony lost the ability to care about anything once he realized the man betrayed him, even the danger to everyone in the room — including himself — should the bullet ricochet.

If he reacted like this with a man's betrayal, how would he react to mine?

The Money

I sat at my desk going over my possessions in my mind. They were too costly to sell at any of the normal outlets, and reputable dealers would wonder why I sold them. If I tried to disguise myself, was able to sell an item, and Tony found it on someone else, they might be in danger.

I felt deflated: another avenue blocked.

I rang for Amelia. "Is the afternoon paper here yet?"

"Why yes, mum. I'll fetch it at once." She brought it in, her face puzzled. "You've never asked for it before."

I opened the newspaper to the zeppelin schedule. The zeppelin ran all day and night, although with fewer flights after dark. Meal service, bar, sleeping rooms — these flights sounded magnificent. I imagined lifting from the ground, flying.

The paper listed the current prices. I almost had enough for one ticket if we went to the least expensive city. I tapped the paper with my pen, circled the price. I didn't like Joe selling himself to get our tickets, but no other ideas came to mind.

Perhaps once the account was set up at the bank, I might withdraw that money. Well, most of it. If I closed the account, Tony might hear of it. How long would that be?

Pearson came to my study and knocked. "A Mrs. Gertie Pike here to see you, mum."

After a moment, I remembered the stout woman married to Thrace Pike. Whatever might she be doing here? "Seat her in the parlor, Pearson, I'll be there at once."

Gertie Pike was twenty, somewhat thinner than I remembered, but she wore the same ugly gray dress she had the last two times I saw her. Her hair, straight, blonde and lank, her skin sallow, her teeth uneven, her eyes too close together. But she loved Thrace Pike and their child dearly, although I saw little in the man to warrant such interest.

Mrs. Pike stood in the middle of the room, her coat still on, slowly turning to face me when I came in. "It's all as he said."

Evidently she'd read her husband's pamphlet, which detailed — without naming me, fortunately for him — an afternoon in January when I tried to seduce him.

This was going to be awkward.

I forced myself to smile. "What a pleasure to see you. Would you like some tea?"

"Yes, mum, thank you."

I rang for a maid; Mary Pearson came in. Mary, like Gertie, was twenty, although just turned, with straight blonde hair. Unlike Mrs. Pike, Mary was pretty, with rosy cheeks and a bright smile. She curtsied. "Yes, mum?"

If my guess was right, Mrs. Pike didn't eat well. "It's almost tea-time; set it up here." It was actually twenty minutes before tea-time; I hoped Monsieur wasn't too put out by it.

After Mary left, Mrs. Pike said, "I don't wish to impose."

"Nonsense. Mr. Spadros is out today; otherwise, I'd have to take tea alone. You do me great service."

"Thank you, mum."

"How's your daughter?"

"She's well, mum, thank you."

The hem of her skirt had dragged in mud recently; the stain still lingered. "How may I help you, Mrs. Pike?"

"You contracted my husband to perform tasks for you."

I chuckled. "On the contrary — he volunteered."

She stared at me, mouth open. "Aren't you going to pay him?"

That was a fair question, especially in light of their poverty. "As I said, he volunteered to do this for me. So I hadn't considered the matter."

"And now that you've considered the matter?"

I sighed, feeling melancholy. "I'm not pleased with what he found, but it was helpful."

"Then I ask that you pay him, not his grandfather."

"Why do you ask this?"

Mary came in with tea, slices of cake, and a small crock of butter. "There wasn't time for icing, mum. I hope butter will do."

"It's lovely, Mary; please thank the kitchen staff for it."

She curtsied. "I will, mum."

Mrs. Pike took cake, spreading it with butter, then sat regarding me. "You're an odd woman."

I smiled, selecting my cake and tea. "How so?"

"You're ready to take any advantage, even over someone far your inferior, yet you're kind to servants. It's unusual."

My inferior? Did she not know I was a Pot rag? "I suppose I'm in an unusual situation." The saltiness of the butter was lovely with the warm sweet cake. "I enjoy it when people speak truth. You find it so seldom."

She ate her cake, sipped her tea. My answer seemed to embolden her. "Then I'll speak truth." When she spoke next, her voice shook. "What are your intentions toward my husband?"

I blinked. "What?" A laugh burst from me. "I have no intentions towards him whatsoever."

Mrs. Pike glanced away, cheeks reddening. "It's just that —"

"You read his pamphlet."

"Yes, mum." The way she spoke made me think she had more to say but decided not to share it.

"Then it was unwise for you to visit. It's likely my staff has read it as well."

She turned crimson.

"Why don't you want me to pay his grandfather? Is he not your husband's master?"

She shook her head, agitated. "My husband did the work without any instruction or aid, yet his grandfather will take the great share, leaving us with a pittance. It's unjust."

So it was. "Is that why your husband became a reporter?"

Her head drooped. "His grandfather would have nothing to do with him so long as we were Bridgers." She paused, rubbing her ring finger. "My husband believed he could do good work at the *Bridges Daily* ..."

"But ..."

Mrs. Pike didn't meet my eye. "It's corrupt; real news never sees daylight. It's what the Families want printed, nothing more."

She was such a foolish girl — much too trusting. I hoped she survived long enough to see her baby grown. "Mr. Pike was right to leave if he felt unable to do good work there."

She finished her cake, drained her cup. "May I have more?"

I smiled at her. "Have as much as you wish." She reminded me of Tenni, with thin arms and a child's honesty.

Mrs. Pike put a second piece of cake on her plate and slathered it with butter.

"How did you and Mr. Pike meet?"

She blushed. "We grew up together, mum. In the Bridgers. It's our way." She took a deep breath. "It's a blessing, being as I am."

"Whatever do you mean?"

She snorted in amusement. "I know what I am: an ugly woman. Don't deny it! Here, I'm a pitiable creature, secretly ridiculed and scorned. Ugly women are doomed to live at home as a burden to their fathers, or sent off to try to join the Dealers. But in the Bridgers, it's the pretty girls have the most trouble. All the men want them, yet none are allowed to pay them court." She gazed off to the side. "Most pretty ones run off. But I had many suitors." She smiled to herself. "I could pick any I wanted."

I frowned. "You get to pick?"

"Of course! We receive the man's attentions, bear the children, raise them, keep the home — it would be cruel to force a man on us we didn't want! That's why I'm so blessed." She smiled, pride clear on her face. "I chose the best, the kindest, the most righteous man of them all." Her expression became fierce. "And I won't have him toyed with, by you or anyone else."

Oh, dear. I might need Mr. Pike in the future. "I most sincerely apologize for any distress I've caused." There! That should mollify her. "As a token of goodwill, I'll pay him for his work, at your grandfather's stated rate. I recall the paper Doyle Pike presented to me the day I sat in his office. It said, 'For retrieval of documents: ten dollars,' did it not?"

"Ten dollars?" Her eyes widened in dumbfounded wonder, as if learning she had hit the jackpot at our casino. "Oh, thank you, mum. Thank you so much."

The Investigation

The next morning, the *Bridges Daily* had an article on page 3:

Warehouse Manager Found Shot

I stared at the few lines about Joe and Josie's uncle. He was forty. The police thought he surprised a robber.

First Marja, then Joe and Josie's uncle. How many more people would die for their connection to me?

At breakfast, I showed the paper to Tony. "He worked for the Clubbs. Marja worked for him."

Tony frowned. "Do you think this is related?"

"Tony, he's Joe's uncle. Marja overheard something in his warehouse and tried to warn me and now they're both dead. I don't know what to think."

Tony peered at the paper. "It says here the man's name was Shigo Rei. You say he was Joe's uncle?"

"Josie said it." She also said the man changed his name to hide the fact that he was a Kerr. An investigation into his past might harm others in his family. "Maybe the man was their mother's brother." In either case, this would make him a Pot rag too. How did he get a job working as a manager?

Tony sat, hand to his chin. "I should never have involved the police. This is a Family matter." He shook his head. "I have too much to do right now to deal with this. I'll have Ten assist you."

"Oh," I said, both surprised and hesitant.

Tony grinned. "You might need another gun. Or a fist, should it come to that. There may be a time where a huge group won't do, and I'll feel better knowing he's looking after you."

Interesting. So Sawbuck wasn't just Tony's right hand man, but his enforcer as well.

* * *

Right after morning meeting, we left for Market Center.

The courthouse on Market Center was an imposing white edifice which sat upon a base of red brick, almost obscured by the press of the crowd. Shouting reporters, camera-men flashing their photos, men calling out words, shaking their fists, holding up banners in support or derision.

Our men made us a path. Black wrought-iron banisters guided us up the white stone steps to a grand hall whose doors stood open beyond majestic pillars. Inside, an expansive lobby tiled in golden stone teemed with people. Our guards pushed through the throng, who parted more readily than those outside. We climbed the wide curving steps to our left, to a private room where we might observe the proceedings. It did most resemble the boxes at the Opera House.

So many people sat down below that I felt afraid at the thought of being called before them. A man spoke loud and eloquent from a podium on the lower level, with a group of men seated on a raised stage before him intently listening. The room itself was lit brightly, but no lights shown on the box itself, throwing us into relative darkness.

The Hart Family sat in front of us, the Clubbs beyond them in front of the Diamonds. None seemed to notice our presence.

The Diamond Family sat on the far side of our assigned row, with Jon closest. He focused on the proceedings, apparently unaware of our entry. I glanced at Tony, who smiled. "Go ahead."

So I moved to sit by Jonathan Diamond. While grateful that I didn't have to sit near Gardena, or worse yet, her dreadful oldest brother Cesare, for the first time I felt uneasy in Jon's presence. His mad twin Jack Diamond was absent, for which I felt relieved.

My procession down the row caught the attention of the Diamonds; they glanced over yet did not rise. I folded my hands in my lap and watched the spectacle before me. I didn't understand most of what was being said, but the man at the podium seemed enraged.

"I must speak with you," Jon whispered.

I didn't move. "Why did you lie to me?"

Out of the corner of my eye, I saw him lean forward. "I have loved you more dearly than you know, Mrs. Spadros —"

He'd never called me that in a private conversation before, and it stung.

"— but if you chide me now, when I was forced to choose between the life of my sister and a possible insult to your feelings, then ... you're a different woman than I thought."

I felt ashamed of myself. "Forgive me."

He didn't speak for some time, and I sat in misery, hearing nothing that was said. Of course, Jon was right. He'd always spoken truth to me, which was why his deception cut me so deeply. It felt as if a support had dropped from under me, a betrayal on top of all the others which composed my life.

Yet what if he had told me the truth in February? Who might have been listening? What might Roy Spadros do to Gardena and little Roland? Gardena might now be dead at Roy's hand, with Roland a hostage, the Diamond Family helpless to stop whatever Roy might do to or with the child.

I wiped my eyes with my handkerchief and sighed. "You're right, as you always are."

"I care nothing about being right. Only about those I hold dear." He paused. "Which is why I must speak to you."

"Speak, then."

Judith Hart turned round and glared at us.

"Not here," he whispered.

Another man stood up, burns on his face. He spoke of loading the cargo, described the zeppelin lifting off, his shock and pain after the tremendous explosion which followed. The chamber, full of people, stood silent during his speech. After he spoke, the crowd murmured, some applauding.

Then a man in the center of those on the stage struck a small hammer on a block of wood. "We shall recess until 3 pm."

I gave Tony a questioning glance, and he said, "Luncheon."

Was it that late already? The clock to the wall at our right chimed noon, and I stood, laughing. "Long luncheon."

"Indeed," Jon said from behind.

I followed Tony along the row and out to the hallway. Roy and Molly were already partway down the stair.

Jon grabbed my arm and pulled me aside, out of sight of the stair. Tony followed.

"There's too much you don't know," Jon said to us. "Have you conferred with your attorneys?"

"Some," Tony said. "But they've told us nothing, other than their assurances that the inquest goes well."

"It's not going well at all," Jon said. "I'm not allowed to speak with your attorneys," he glanced around, "and as Keeper of the Court, I shouldn't be seen speaking with you either."

"Jon, whatever are you talking about?"

Tony shook his head, finger to his lips.

"Admit no fault in this whatsoever," Jon said. "I wish you could deny being there, but it's too late for that now." He turned to me. "You shouldn't have laughed up there in the box. Too many people saw you. Keep a sober demeanor when in public from now on. Say only what the lawyers tell you to. Your life depends on it."

"But why?"

Cesare Diamond called sharply from down the stairs, "Jon!"

Tony's jaw tightened, but he said nothing.

Jon glanced towards his brother's voice. "I must go. Did you get my letter?"

"Yes, but —"

"Just heed what I wrote and all will be well." He hurried off as fast as he ever did, which was a moderately rapid walk.

Oh, gods, I thought. *I burned the letter.* "Jon, wait!"

Tony put his hand on my arm. "Leave it be, Jacqui."

"But Tony —"

"He's Keeper of the Court, Jacqui. He mustn't be seen to favor us. The lawyers can answer any questions you have."

I shook my head. I didn't even know what to ask.

What had I gotten myself into?

* * *

When we returned home, I had Pearson find Sawbuck and ask him to attend me at his convenience. After getting changed, I found the scrap of paper Marja held in her hand when I found her dead, and brought it to my study.

Spread out upon the desk, it was the size of my palm. Dirty, with smudged pencil scratches upon it, the scrap had been ripped from cheap paper. Newsprint?

I remembered Mr. Blackberry telling me that Dame Anastasia and someone fitting Frank Pagliacci's description were in the *Bridges Daily* giving Mr. Durak their false interview. They could have gotten a piece of newsprint from there.

But I couldn't read whatever might be written on it.

I held the paper up to the light. A knock came at the door.

"Come in," I said.

Sawbuck stuck his head in. "You wanted to see me?"

I put the paper down. "Yes! Please come in."

Sawbuck pulled a chair over, sitting across my desk from me. Which felt strange.

I said, "We need to talk."

He bit his lip and nodded, not meeting my eye. "I realize what you must think. But I've not betrayed you."

I let out an amused laugh. "That wasn't why I called you. But I'm curious: how did you come to be here?"

Sawbuck smiled fondly. "Aunt Molly has ever doted on me. Even as a small boy I visited often." He pointed over his shoulder. "I used to bounce on that sofa. I don't recall Mr. Anthony's birth, but they tell me I was taken with him even then."

"You were what, six?"

"I suppose. After Master Roy Acevedo was murdered, Mr. Anthony's father chose me as his protector."

"A boy of eight?"

"I was large for my age, yet as a child, I could be at his side where men might not be allowed." He shrugged. "Perhaps it was too much responsibility. But here he is, alive still."

"And here you are."

"And here I am. Alive still." He gave a wry grin. "Which is

some feat in Bridges."

Especially as someone opposed to Roy. But perhaps Roy let Sawbuck live, knowing every day spent beside the man he loved but unable to speak of it would be torture. I nodded.

"What can I do for you, Mrs. Spadros?"

"Has Roy Spadros said anything about our driver's death?"

Sawbuck sat motionless, staring at me. "No, he hasn't."

"Or our visit to the Harts?"

His jaw dropped. "You don't think —"

"That he had our driver shot? No. But with the way he feels about the Harts —"

Sawbuck let out a breath. "He might leave Mr. Anthony to his own devices. As punishment."

"I thought so." I tapped my pen on the blotter, laid it down. "So we're on our own."

"Until the old codger decides a new torture is more fun."

"Indeed." I held up the paper. "This was in Marja's hand when we found her." I handed it to him. "Can you see anything?"

Sawbuck scrutinized it, held it up to the light. He shook his head. "Nothing." Then his eyes narrowed, and he sniffed it.

"Onion?"

"No," he said, handing it back.

I sniffed the paper but didn't smell anything. This had to be in her hand for a reason. "Let's try anyway."

I went to an electric lamp and turned it on, placing the paper over the bulb. A message began to appear in brown. "Not onion." A caramel odor wafted through the room. "Sugar water."

The writing was tiny, block-printed:

I KNEW YOU'D FIGURE THIS OUT.

I BELIEVE YOU TOO DANGEROUS

TO KEEP ALIVE. BUT I NEED HIM.

SINCE HE WANTS YOU, WE'RE BOUND

TO EACH OTHER A WHILE LONGER.

He? He who?

WHEN I'VE DESTROYED THE SPADROS FAMILY,

WE'LL KILL THEM. THEN WE'LL TAKE THE CITY

AND YOU WON'T STOP IT. YOU'RE MAKING THIS

A CHALLENGE. SO I'LL GIVE THIS ADVICE:

DON'T CHASE OUTSIDERS.

YOUR FED WILL BE DEAD

SOON ENOUGH.

The Trouble

I frowned, shaking my head, and handed the scrap to Sawbuck. Why go to the trouble of leaving this message? And why speak of Zia — who I did chase down, but she got the worst of that encounter — as if she were my ally?

"He's playing with you," Sawbuck said. "I've seen this sort before. Fancies himself a master criminal. Likely he's a cold-blooded killer who's read too many spy novels." He snorted. "But who's the Fed? Someone after Master Rainbow?"

I nodded. "A woman —"

Sawbuck raised an eyebrow.

"— named Zia Cashout. Pretty, with red hair. They worked together. But he didn't know she was a Fed until her friends tried to kill him. He thinks they destroyed his boat."

"Well, if that's not the strangest thing I've ever heard, I don't know what is," Sawbuck said. "How do you know her?"

I went back to my desk. How much could I trust Sawbuck? "Master Rainbow introduced her first as his maid, then his sister. She was with him when he brought me to rescue the boy."

Sawbuck nodded.

"But later she made it clear she was in league with Frank Pagliacci." In love with him might be more accurate. I pointed to the paper. "Which makes this puzzling."

"Perhaps they've had a falling-out," Sawbuck said. "And

you've not heard from her since?"

I shook my head.

"Wait," Sawbuck said. "This is the woman the police think you knifed on Market Center."

Why did I mention her name? "So my husband did tell you."

Sawbuck chuckled. "Did you really knife her?"

"Not intentionally." It was the first time I'd actually cut anyone. "If I'd have known she was a Fed, though ...."

Sawbuck leaned forward. "Why do you keep lying to him? What haven't you told us?"

I sighed. "None of it matters now. I was trying to help Dame Anastasia, and ... well, now she's dead."

Pearson knocked. "Two packages for you, mum."

In the hall, a big bouquet of lavender sat next to a package addressed to me. Inside were two thick round white candles, six inches long, carved on the surface as if covered with lace. There was no return address or note. "Where did these come from?"

"There was no card on the flowers, mum," Pearson said. "Perhaps the messenger lost it. Where would you like them?"

"In the parlor, please." I detested lavender, and white was my least favorite color. But it was so rare for anyone to send me a gift that I didn't have the heart to throw them away.

Thunder rolled in the distance. I went to the front door and opened it. The air smelled of rain.

"Mrs. Spadros," Tony said behind me, "would you assist me?" Tony had shed his coat and hat, and rolled up his sleeves.

I laughed. I'd never seen him like this. He appeared ready to engage in some physical labor, which of course we had servants for. "Whatever with?"

"Come," he said, and took my hand.

I glanced over my shoulder. "Thanks for your help, Ten. We'll speak on this matter another time."

Sawbuck grinned at me. "My pleasure."

Tony led me through the house and out to the back gardens, where a target stood ready. "You must teach me to shoot."

"Me? Can't Ten teach you?"

"He's tried." Clouds scudded past overhead, while black storm-clouds loomed in the distance. "I thought maybe ..."

I smiled. "Very well. First, you must put in earplugs."

"Already done."

He handed me some, which I put on. Then I brought him to the closest mark. "Stand one foot in front. Your left should be good, since you're left-handed. Which eye do you see from?"

Tony stared at me blankly. "I don't know."

"That might be your trouble. Hold a finger up to cover the middle of the target."

When Tony did so, I said, "Watch the target. Close one eye, then the other. The finger which stays still is your sighting eye."

"Oh!" Tony let his arm drop. "Why did no one ever tell me?"

I shrugged. "Not everyone is good at explanation, I suppose." Roy probably loved to see him fail. "Now the gun."

I showed him how to stand, how to hold the gun. "Now, it's going to be loud. Make everything else but the target go away."

Tony sounded out of breath. "Very well."

"Now slowly squeeze the trigger."

Hands trembling, he did so. "I hit it!"

I grinned at him. "That you did."

Pearson came to us. "Master Joseph Kerr and Miss Josephine Kerr to call, sir."

Tony holstered his gun. "Seat them in the parlor." He took my face in his hands and kissed me. "I love you so much."

I batted his hands away, laughing. "You silly man — you smell of gun! Let's go inside."

As we walked back, large drops fell. "They got here just in time," Tony said. "A few minutes later and we'd all be drenched."

Hand in hand, we ran back to the veranda.

Joe and Josie sat in the parlor on two armchairs facing the sofa, rising when we entered, Joe needing his cane to do so. The sky was dark, and rain battered the window.

Jane came bustling in. "I'll light the lamps for you, mum."

Josie gasped. "Your candles are lovely. Are they new?"

Jane looked put out.

I smiled. "Go ahead and light the candles instead, Jane, if you would." I sat by one of the large glossy houseplants in its marble urn at the end of the sofa. Tony sat beside me. "To what do we owe this honor?"

"Why, you've come to our home," Josie said. "It's only right that we visit in return."

"Thank you for your card of condolence," Joe said to Tony. "We didn't know our uncle well, but ..."

Tony smiled. "I'm grateful that you've come." He rested his hand on mine. "She has so few callers." His smile faded. "I'll remember who's been kind to my wife and who's shunned her when I'm in charge of this Family."

The scent of lavender wafted in the air, mixed with gun oil. Jane lit the first candle.

"Is your father well?" Joe said.

Tony shrugged, taking his hand off mine. "As wicked as ever. But enough about us. I'm glad you're here. I spoke with the Chief of Police about your friend's murder."

Lavender ... candle wax ... gun oil ...

Lavender sprigs lined the aisle, a bunch at each pew as I walked towards him, and I clutched a bundle in my hands to stop their shaking.

I still felt the cold imprint of Roy's gun as I walked, not meeting anyone's eyes.

Jane lit the second candle. My lips tingled, and I licked them. Swallowed. I didn't feel well at all.

"He understands that finding her killer is of high priority."

Tony smiled and took my hand ... then we climbed the steps. "We are gathered today to join this man and this woman in holy matrimony."

The smell of candle-wax mixed with lavender ...

"But I'm going to have my men on this as well. And the matter with your uncle. This affects my wife," Tony placed his hand on mine, "which makes it a Family matter. You can rest assured, we'll learn who did this."

The room was filled with bunches of lavender as Tony undressed me in the candlelight. I couldn't look at him. Couldn't bear to feel his touch.

Jane started towards the door.

"We're truly grateful for you help, sir," Joe said.

The lavender ... the candles ... Tony touching me ... the smell of the gun ...

My stomach lurched. I managed not to spoil my dress or the sofa — except the arm — but the potted plant was worse for wear.

Everyone cried out, except Josie, who told Jane to bring a wet cloth. I lay draped across the sofa's arm panting, bathed in sweat.

Tony knelt beside me, smoothing my hair. "My poor dear."

Pearson came in. "I'll call the doctor."

"That would be wonderful, thank you." Tony sounded happy, which infuriated me. "Have the men bring the plant outside. The rain should wash it clean."

"Yes, sir."

Josie said, "We should go." She placed her hand on my hair. "I hope you didn't catch ill with this weather."

I squeezed her hand. "Don't fret. Our doctor is excellent."

Joe stood by my feet, gazing at me calmly. "We'll return another time, when you're well." He mouthed, "I love you."

Tony, kneeling beside me, focused on my face, never saw it.

I still felt faint. "Have a safe trip."

Tony carried me upstairs and laid me in bed.

* * *

Dr. Salmon sat beside my bed as he examined me. He chuckled at the moonstone on its chain around my neck.

"What's funny?"

"Your husband gave you that."

"How did you know?"

"I did an investigation into these 'miracle gems' when they first went on the market." He fingered the stone, then laid it on my chest. "One of the moonstone's claimed powers was to increase fertility."

This astonished me so much I laughed.

Dr. Salmon gazed at me soberly. "My dear girl, I've never betrayed you. And I never will. I hope someday you can bring yourself to trust me."

So he suspected my morning tea. Could I trust him? Should I confess? But he had no proof, and who might be listening?

Then he took my hand. "Tell me what happened."

So I told him how the smells made me so ill.

The rain beat upon the windows, and I recalled that he attended my wedding. Did he guess as to why I fell ill? But he spoke kindly. "What can I do to help?"

My eyes filled with tears. All I wanted right then was to go home and see my Ma. "Perhaps a day or two of rest?"

He placed his hand on my forehead. Then he called Tony in.

"How is she?" Tony seemed almost giddy.

Dr. Salmon gave Tony a sad smile. "She's never fully recovered, and has developed a case of nervous exhaustion with severe irritation of the stomach. She may eat whatever she finds soothing, but rest as much as possible for the next few days."

Tony stared at me in shock.

After he left, Tony knelt by my bed, holding my hand. "All this time ... ill ... and you never said anything? How could this be? I should never have pressed and agitated you so." He put his forehead on the bed beside me. "Oh, gods. I—"

"Shh," I said. "It's not your fault." I moved over in bed. "Join me." Taking off his shoes and jacket, he did, and I held him to my breast, stroking his hair. "None of this has ever been your fault."

Tony fell asleep in my arms. I lay staring at the ceiling.

If I left with Joe, it would destroy Tony. Even though he loved Gardena, he trusted and relied on me. I was everything to him. He never intended me harm — in fact, the opposite. He had never so much as raised a hand to me, ever. None of this was his fault.

But could I spend my life pretending I loved Tony, when Joe had a way out?

* * *

Presently, Tony awoke, going off to tend to something or other. Yet I lingered, grateful for the chance to relax in privacy. All too soon, Amelia came to check on me. "A package, mum."

It was a new copy of the *Golden Bridges.* The top story:

Third Body Found In Train Tunnel

A third body was found in the train tunnels
under Market Center this morning.

Our Inside Reporter, speaking with a source
on the island, confirms the body belonged

to a man of seven and twenty who recently died of strangulation. This source also confirmed this man was an associate of the infamous Dame Anastasia Louis.

The number of her associates missing numbers two dozen. Six and ten so far have been found dead throughout Bridges, all of strangulation.

Sixteen dead? All of strangulation? "Good gods," I said. Amelia said, "Has something happened, mum?"

Were they targeted by an angry bankrupt? Or has the scoundrel many call the Bridges Strangler resumed his grisly work? All the deaths so far are recent, which suggests the villain keeps the men captive for an extended period before their murders.

So far the Police have not seen fit to acknowledge this menace. We advise all young men — especially those associated with the deceased lady — to travel in groups until the madman is found.

I handed her the paper.

"I'd never heard this," Amelia said. "It's preposterous. How could such go on without any warning about it?"

"Perhaps the Families don't want a tourist to bring this news to the Feds," I said. "I believe the Feds would have jurisdiction over a multiple murderer, would they not?"

"Ah," said Amelia. "I wonder what the Families plan to do."

"That's an excellent question."

* * *

After a while, I got up, telling Amelia I'd be taking dinner in my room. Presently, Tony came in, Pearson and Honor following. They set up a small table and chairs, with various foods for me.

"How kind of you," I said.

Pearson said nothing. Honor bowed. "My pleasure, mum."

Once they left, we began eating.

"I'm glad you're feeling better," Tony said.

A knock came at the door. "Come in," Tony said.

One of Tony's men entered. "Sir, about the coat."

Tony gestured with his chin. "Go ahead, sit down."

The man gave me a glance, then pulled up a chair from my tea-table and sat across from us. "Thank you, sir. I talked with the manager there at the shop. He didn't remember the coat at first, so we hunted down Master Rainbow —"

"You've seen him?" I said. "How is he?"

He glanced back and forth between us, then shrugged. "Seemed fine to me, mum. Anyways, the manager remembered the coat once he saw it. Said a red-haired gal picked it out."

Was this Zia? "Did he remember anything else about her?"

The man frowned slightly. "Not that I recall." He glanced at Tony, then at me. "Something you want me to ask?"

I leaned forward. "Was she an outsider? Have an accent?"

Tony said, "You know this woman."

I nodded. "An outsider. She had a heavy accent, and liked to move her hands when she talked."

"The manager said none of the sort, mum." He let out a short laugh. "Seems like he would've: that one liked to gab."

How many women did this man Pagliacci have? "What did Master Rainbow say when he heard the description?"

The man shrugged. "Don't know, mum. Just gave me the coat. He weren't there when we talked. Anyway, the manager said he'll search out the invoice and send it by."

Tony nodded at him. "That'll be all. You've done well." Once he left, Tony said, "What is it?"

"Frank Pagliacci collects women as the Harts do racehorses."

Tony laughed. "It would take all one's energy to keep them from learning of each other. I wonder how he finds the time."

I snorted. Tony had put a remarkable amount of energy into keeping me from his connection with Roland and Gardena. "Let him collect his horses, then. Perhaps it'll keep him busy enough to make a mistake."

The Trick

Two days later, Joe and Josie came calling. When I saw Joe in my parlor, my heart thudded in my chest, but I made my voice light. "How wonderful to see you!" I sat next to him at the end of the sofa, while Josie sat beside me. "Would you like some tea?"

"No, thank you," Josie said. "How are you feeling?"

"Better," I said. I had the lavender removed, the room aired out, and I had no further problems. I reached up to touch the plant between me and Joe. "I fear my plant won't recover, though." The potted plant had wilted, in spite of all attempts to cleanse its soil.

Joe grinned. "It's just a plant."

Josie moved to the window. "What a lovely view you have."

Josie was such a dear, giving us time to speak privately. "Thank you." I turned to Joe. "There's something I wished to ask." I hesitated, not wanting to remind him of how rude I was to him. "Do you remember when you called on us in January?"

Joe blinked. "I suppose."

"Did your coachmen notice anything peculiar?"

"Why, no," Joe said. "Why do you ask?"

His gaze flustered me. "I — we had reason to fear an intruder on the grounds that day. Might my husband speak with them?"

Josie stood gazing out of the window. "We had to let them go. But I can send their names, if you wish to contact them."

"I hope nothing was taken," Joe said.

I smiled at him. "Nothing of the sort." I gestured to Josie. "You're welcome to look at the art book there."

"Thank you!" Josie sat in the window seat, eagerly paging through the book.

"Josie loves art," Joe said. He took my hand, whispering, "As much as I love you."

I clasped his hand in mine. "I desire nothing more than to leave with you. This place is a madhouse. I fear I might go mad as well, should I stay here."

Joe leaned forward. "Have you been harmed?"

I shook my head. "I can't speak of it, even if I had time." Should I ask? I peered in his eyes. If anyone was trustworthy, it was Joe. "I can't leave my Ma in Bridges —"

A flash of surprise crossed Joe's face.

"She's a knife to my throat as long as she's here," I said. "We must find a way to bring her with us."

He nodded, his gaze downcast. "I don't know if I can get that many tickets. It's a terrible large amount for one ticket, let alone four. Do you have any money at all?"

I stared at my hands. It was a dreadful risk. If anything happened — Joe getting waylaid, Ma refusing to go, an unscrupulous ticket agent — I could lose everything I had saved these six years. But I couldn't leave Ma here — any minute, someone might learn she was alive. "Wait here."

When I opened the door, Pearson said, "Mum, are you well?"

"I need to fetch something," I said. "I'll return straight-away."

"But is it not something your maid could fetch for you?"

I hurried up the stairs, locked the door behind me, then went to my hiding place in the back of my closets. Ten dollars (in ones) for Thrace Pike. Pennies for the taxi, change for Mrs. Bryce. The rest I placed in my pocket, returning the bag to its resting place.

I placed the cash into a large sealed envelope. I wrapped a newspaper around the envelope and brought the newspaper to Joe. "Keep this safe. It's all I have in the world."

He gazed at me soberly. "I'll guard it with my life."

* * *

Tony was out, so after the Kerr twins left, I took tea in my rooms, Amelia serving me.

"Amelia, please fetch me onion."

She blinked in surprise, then said, "Yes, mum."

She returned with a saucer filled with minced raw onion. "For your sandwiches, mum?"

"No, Amelia." I smiled at her. "Did you never write secret letters as a child?"

Amelia laughed. "I never did, mum. Not much time for that."

She'd worked ever since her father died when she was eight. Perhaps I could show her some fun. "Bring my stationery box."

I crushed the onion with the back of my teaspoon until the juices flowed. Then I wrote a note to my Ma in ink:

A friend will visit.

Amelia said, "What nonsense is this?"

I grinned.

I then took out a new pen, dipping it in the onion juice. Underneath, I wrote:

When the owl flies

The letters were faintly wet on the page.

Amelia said, "What does this mean?"

I chuckled. It was something we said in the Pot: *when the owl flies, he doesn't come back.* "Well, that's the second half of the secret. My reader will know what I mean, but someone else who finds this won't." I put down my pen. "That's odd."

"What, mum?"

The message Frank — or perhaps his leader — sent could've been read by anyone who thought to search for a secret message. The police, even. And it wasn't coded. How could he have been so sure I'd be the one to read it? "Ever tricked someone, Amelia?"

She smiled. "That reminds me of when I was a young girl. A man would follow me in my sweeping every day. Not walk past — when I moved down the road, he'd be watching me. Finally I went behind a tavern and found Peter with the horses. He was tall as he is now, so I thought he was a man grown. I told him about the man and he hid me. The next day when I went to work Peter came too, told the man he'd thrash him if he came round again." She laughed. "The man never knew Peter was just a boy."

"And that's how you met."

Her cheeks colored. "Yes, mum. That's how we met."

"I feel certain someone is tricking me. But I don't know who or why." I sealed the note. "Have Pearson fetch the Memory Boy. I have a message for him."

"The third part of the secret?"

I grinned at her. "Yes. Please inform me when he arrives."

After a few hours, Pearson notified me of the Memory Boy's arrival. I went out to the front porch with my message.

Werner Lead was maybe seven, with white-blond hair and a bright red jacket. The left chest and right shoulder sported a circular white patch with "MB" written upon it in red. His two brothers stood behind at the bottom of the steps.

"Good day," I said.

"Hello, Mrs. Spadros," Werner said.

I handed him the note, and his eyes went wide. "I've never taken a note before."

I chuckled, leaning over. "Hand them that. Tell them it's from me. But here's the real message: My favorite flowers."

"My favorite flowers. Yes, mum. Where to?"

"The message is for whoever is in charge at the Cathedral now." I handed him a dollar.

"Okay, mum. Thanks!"

But he came back two hours later empty-handed. "I gave the note to them, and the men brought it inside. A woman came out and I told her the message. But when I asked if there was a message to return, she said no."

Was this woman Ma? "What did the woman look like?"

"Oh, very old, mum, blue eyes, with straight white hair. She walked with a cane and men helped her."

I nodded. Not Ma. Ma and Molly were close to the same age. I pictured Ma's brown skin, curly dark hair, dark eyes. Did this mean they kept her safe? "You did well. Thank you."

* * *

Three days later, I went to Madame Biltcliffe's shop for the final fitting of my Summer dress. I might never have a chance to wear the dress until next year, should the zeppelin inquest go on much longer, but Tony was true to his word.

Madame came to greet the carriage, but ushered me and Honor inside without a word. For once, her office door stood open. Several racks were missing, and those that remained held a smaller selection. Did she have to sell some of her goods to pay her newly increased fees? I should have written to tell her that the men who attacked her weren't Spadros men, but impostors.

She led me to my private dressing room. She ignored Honor, then dropped the curtain to shut him out. Tenni curtsied when I entered. My new dress hung on a rack in the corner.

"I hope you're well, Madame?"

Madame gestured for Tenni to help me out of my dress. "I'm well, thank you." Madame's manner was stiff, formal.

"Has anyone been back to hurt you?"

"No. They did not return."

"I like your shop's new appearance. More open."

Madame gave a fake smile, not meeting my eye. "Thank you."

Tenni helped me into my dress and the two of them began working on it in silence.

I wondered what happened, but I didn't want to pry in case it was personal. "I forgot to ask the last time I was here: I'd like your recommendations on a new dressmaker."

Madame nodded. "The list is on my desk."

"Thank you. I appreciate your help."

The two continued to work their way around my dress without a word. When the entire dress was marked and pinned as Madame wished, she gestured for Tenni to help me out of it.

Once I dressed, I said, "Madame, may we speak privately?"

"Certainly." She gestured to Tenni, who left through the back curtain. "How may I help?"

"That was my question exactly," I said. "Clearly something is amiss. If I may help in some way —"

"You've done enough," Madame snapped.

I stared at her, shocked, hurt. "What happened?"

"It's what has not happened which distresses me."

"I don't understand."

She glanced away and spoke bitterly. "I'm a foolish, foolish woman. I have never before given my regard so poorly."

I felt perplexed. "Have I offended you?"

Her head drooped, and she gave it a small shake. "I know you don't share my feelings. But after all the years you have known me I thought you might have some instant of consideration for my injuries —" She shrugged. "— perhaps once write to inquire as to my health. Even if you saw me as a mere merchant ...."

It had completely slipped my mind. "I'm sorry."

She shook her head. "You're not. It's clear now. How could I have been so blind? You used me, my shop, my friendship, even my regard. And when I needed you — when your husband and his men stood threatening — your first impulse was to run away. Abandon us, who have given so much. Your loyalty is only to yourself." Madame turned away, hand to her forehead. "I can't stay here anymore. Once this is sold, I'm moving."

This shocked me. "Moving? Where?"

"If you must know, I have bought a shop in Clubb quadrant. But I hope you will not visit."

Madame wished never to see me again? How could this be? Then I remembered the eggshells in front of her shop the other day. "You no longer wish to be associated with me."

"That's not what this is about, and you know it." She sighed, her voice dropping to a whisper. "I must leave. Your men will pursue me, but they won't attack once I'm in Clubb quadrant."

"But they weren't our men! They were impostors, dressed in our livery. Our men won't hurt you. My husband's given orders."

She stared at me, mouth open. Then her expression hardened. "Even so. I will stay no longer."

"What'll happen to Tenni? Her little sisters?"

Madame shook her head. "I have secured a position for Tenni at a shop nearby. She's of age now and may do as she likes." She pointed at me. "But you must not embroil her in your schemes any longer. The girl has suffered enough."

I pondered Madame's words, and how much they echoed Vig's, the night he helped me question Morton's young "ace," Clover. His misery as he said: *You **used** me.*

Who is your loyalty to, Mrs. Spadros?

Your loyalty is only to yourself.

My heart crumbled. I used to know who I was. I used to know what to do. Spadros Manor had changed me. Being around these quadrant-folk had changed me. If I didn't get out of Bridges I feared it would destroy me. "You're not the first to tell me such things." Her eyes were as red as mine must have been. *I did love you, if not as you wished.* "I'll trouble you no further."

I retrieved the list and left, wondering not whether she would forgive me, but whether I was worth forgiving.

The Paper

When I returned to Spadros Manor, Doyle Pike sat on the parlor sofa. But Mr. Pike sat as if he owned the Manor and everything in it. His clothes were as costly, his hair as immaculate, as when I saw him at his law office in February. He didn't rise when I entered.

I took a few steps forward. "May I help you?"

"Come in, sit down," he said. "It's time we had a chat."

I sat in a chair across the coffee table from him. "Would you care for some tea?"

He surveyed me. "No, I don't think so." He leaned forward, putting his elbows on his knees. "I did work for you —"

I felt certain he hadn't lifted a finger: surely his grandson Thrace did every bit of it.

"— and yet I've not been paid."

I shrugged. "We had an agreement. It isn't my fault you were unable to collect from them."

At this, Mr. Pike began to laugh. It was more of a cackle than a laugh, being a man of advancing age, yet it was merry. "My dear, when a new man comes to apprentice, do you know the first thing I teach him?"

"I couldn't possibly."

He grinned his alligator grin. "That a thing not written is nothing at all." His grin faded. "You see, we do **not** have an agreement. We never had an agreement. What we have is your word against mine."

"You would fight Spadros Manor?"

"I'd wager your Mr. Spadros — pick either — knows nothing of our 'agreement'. Am I right?"

Fear gnawed at me. What could I say?

"So I believe now we can come to an agreement." He leaned forward. "This time, in writing."

"What sort of an agreement?"

"Now I know how much these men owed Dame Louis, I know what my fee would have been had they paid their debts. I'd like to have that money, but now she's dead, they have no incentive to pay."

"I still don't see how that's any of my concern. You get them to pay, you can have it all."

He frowned. "Because I sent them letters on behalf of Dame Anastasia Louis, the inquest has fixed its attention upon **me**. I testify tomorrow morning. Before your husband does, in fact. Who am I to say directed me to send these letters?"

I stared at him in horror.

His face became smugly amused. "You see, this matter is entirely your concern. If I say you directed me to send these letters, it would lend credence to the idea that Spadros Manor acted as Dame Anastasia's enforcer. Imagine that — Spadros Manor coercing its own merchants to pay one of their friends when the merchants suspected fraud. That in itself might be enough to turn the quadrant against you. But then the question would arise: did the Spadros Family **know** the gems were false, and coerce their merchants to take them anyway?"

Oh, gods, I thought. What have I done?

"If the Spadros Family was to do that to another quadrant, your people would cheer. But to turn against its own people ... ?"

I felt trapped. "What is it you want?"

"I testify that Dame Anastasia hired me directly. I never mention your name. In return, you pay me 1% of what they owed her as we agreed."

"How much did they owe?"

He handed over a paper, with a list, and a tally. The 1% was even calculated for me. It was ten times more than I'd handed over to Joe. "Where could I possibly get this kind of money?"

"That's none of my concern." He produced two papers for my signature. "Do we have a deal?"

The clock ticked. I heard a noise in the hall.

I had to keep Mr. Pike from speaking against me. So I signed them both. Mr. Pike slid one across the table, putting the other in his briefcase. I folded my copy, sliding it in my pocket.

The door opened; Tony walked in. He didn't so much as glance at Doyle Pike. "Mrs. Spadros, may I speak with you?"

I rose, heart pounding. "Why, certainly. Please excuse me, Mr. Pike." I followed Tony into the entryway.

Tony snapped, "Why is that man here?"

I could have told Tony about Dame Anastasia's case and my predicament. Looking back, I probably should have. But the way he spoke angered me. "I did tell you I had a lawyer."

Tony froze. "This is a mistake, Jacqui. Do not —" He bit his lower lip, then said, "You must not. I beg you, dismiss this man from your service at once."

A terrible thought came to me: Did either of them know about Thrace Pike's pamphlet? "Why?"

"The man is unprincipled. He's dangerous. I — I can't protect you from him, should it come to that." He gasped, eyes widening in horror, and he gripped my hands. "Have you signed anything?"

Should I tell him? "No, but —"

"Sign nothing until our lawyers see it. Please. Promise me?"

Tony didn't trust Doyle Pike. Would he agree to pay such a sum? Certainly not.

I smiled, relaxing. Joe and I would leave Bridges soon. No one would ever find us. If Tony didn't know about the agreement, and never became involved, no one would have to pay a thing. "I promise. Be at peace; you have nothing to worry about."

Tony let out a breath. "Thank the gods you see reason." He pulled me close, kissed my forehead. "You gave me a fright."

I hugged him, patted his arm. "All is well."

We went back into the parlor. I said, "Mr. Pike, send me what you have at your convenience, and I'll let you know what I decide." My eyes flickered in Tony's direction.

Mr. Pike stood, a small smile on his face. "A pleasure doing business with you, madam."

We escorted him out. Tony still appeared uneasy. "What did he mean, business?"

I shrugged. "Isn't that what all tradesmen say?"

"I suppose," Tony said. He glanced around, he voice dropping to a whisper. "But show me whatever he sends you. I must learn how much he knows. If news about Gardena and Roland were to surface —" he shook his head, "I could be sent to the Prison."

I gaped at him, imagining the horrors which must be in such a place, with Jack Diamond as its Keeper. "But why?"

Tony put his hand to his forehead. "Come with me."

We went to the gardens, then past them out to the meadow. When Rocket saw us, he followed, tail wagging. When we stopped, he lay down at our feet.

This seemed a good place to speak privately, as there were no bushes to hide a listening ear. But we stood silent for a long time.

"Thank the gods certificates of birth aren't public record," Tony said. "Did you wonder why my son's certificate was cut?"

"I did."

Tony let out a breath. "I almost don't know whether to be glad or afraid."

"What is it?"

He put his hand to his forehead, staring at the ground. "In Bridges, a child's certificate has three boxes in the corner. Before them is a question: how came this birth? Marriage, whoredom —" he paused, and his face was white, his jaw tight. "Or rape."

I gasped. "Gardena called it rape?"

He turned away, dropping his hand to his side. "She says her father snatched the paper from her, marking it over her protests." He ran his hands through his hair. "But I don't know what other outcome I would want. I couldn't marry her — I was betrothed to you, and my father would have it no other way."

Why did Roy insist on our marriage? I never had found the

answer to that. Did Tony even know?

"I couldn't let Gardena and Roland be sent to the Pot. What kind of life would that be? What torments would they endure?" He shook his head. "I'd already seen what growing up there did to you." He turned away. "I couldn't go to my father. He'd have killed her, or taken my son as hostage, or perhaps both. Whatever he thought would hurt me most." He paused for a long time, and when he spoke, he sounded desolate. "And I couldn't let her be sent to another city. I'd never see her again."

He still loves her, after everything that's happened.

I kissed Tony's hand. "You couldn't bear to see it written."

Tony shook his head, staring at the ground.

Moved at his suffering, I hugged him, eyes closed, trying not to weep. What would he do when I was gone?

The Promise

We walked for a while round the garden in silence, then Tony went inside. I sat on the veranda while a maid fetched my cigarettes. Once I had them, I went back to the garden to smoke.

Pip and his sisters ran across the meadow, Rocket bounding along behind them. As I lit my cigarette, Pip saw me, spoke with his sisters, then began to walk towards me. His older sister grabbed his arm, shouting, but they were too far away to make out what they said. His little sister stood still, face fearful.

Pip shook off his older sister's arm, but didn't come to me. So I went out to them. "Are you well?"

Both the girls had Amelia and Peter's straight brown hair and brown eyes. The older one, a girl of twelve, glanced away, cheeks coloring. "Yes, mum."

The little one was six. She didn't appear afraid, only confused.

I squatted in front of her. "How about you?"

Pip said, "She told me something. I was about to tell you."

"No!" The older one stomped her foot. "Mommy and Daddy said not to tell anyone! Especially not her!"

I looked up at the girl. "Especially not me? Perhaps I should go talk with them about this then."

She stepped back, face pale. "Please don't tell them."

"I won't, if you let your little sister tell me what she heard. This is my house. If you want to live here, I can't have secrets."

The girl bit her lip for a moment. "Okay."

Her little sister gave her a smug smile. "I heard Mommy yell at Daddy because he told Mr. Roy of things in the house here."

I was so surprised I could only stare for a moment. "He did?"

"She didn't actually yell," Pip said. "They whispered. But it was like yelling." He turned to his little sister. "Right?"

She nodded. "She was angry. And he was angry too, 'cause he said he was only trying to 'tect her and —"

"Pro-tect her," the older girl said.

Her little sister acted as if she hadn't heard. "— but I don't know what for."

Pip and I exchanged a glance, and I found the older girl peering at me.

She knows something's wrong.

How much had they told her? She would've been two when Pip was born — but if the servants had gossiped in front of her, she might already guess much. "Don't worry about that. This is a matter for adults." I smiled at them. "I'm glad you told me."

Her older sister said, "You're not angry?"

I considered this. "No, I should have expected it." I rose. "But let's not worry your Mommy and Daddy about it."

The oldest girl said, "May we go play now?"

"Yes, but I'd like to speak with Pip for a moment." I turned to him. "If you don't mind."

"No, mum," Pip said, "I like talking with you."

The girls ran off. Rocket followed them, tail wagging.

"Pip, I'm going to tell you something which nobody can know about, not even your sisters. Can you keep a secret?"

"Yes, mum."

"I'm going to go away."

Pip stopped, staring at me with his mouth open. "But why?"

I gazed at the sun, low and dim in the overcast sky. "Because I don't want to live here anymore." Should I ask? "If I find a place that's safe for us, do you want me to send for you?"

Pip shook his head. "No, mum. I like it here now that I'm in the kitchens. I like Mistress Anne, and Monsieur, and the maids. I like learning how to cook." He smiled. "I even like being with the men at night. They tuck me in and tell me stories." He grabbed my hand. "I promise I'll be good. I won't ask any more questions about Mommy. Just — please don't go away."

I hugged him. "Oh, Pip. It's not because of you." How could I explain it? "What if they made you stay in the stables with your Daddy? How would you feel then?"

He considered this for a moment. "Bad. I'd — I'd want to run away." His look of astonishment was so much like Roy's the day I asked him to teach me to shoot a moving target that I almost laughed. "But you're the lady. Why do they make you do things you don't want to?"

I smiled to myself. "That's an excellent question, my dear. You're quite smart for being only ten. But I don't know. And you mustn't ask anyone else. Promise?"

Pip nodded gravely. "I promise. When will you go?"

I shrugged. "Soon, I hope. My friend is getting tickets."

He smiled, placing my hand on his cheek. "I hope not soon. Will you tell me bye before you go?"

I squeezed his little hand. "I will."

So Peter Dewey reported to Roy Spadros. No wonder Amelia was angry with him. What might Amelia have passed along to the man who tried to destroy her, without even knowing of it?

The Discovery

We left for Market Center directly after breakfast the next day, leaving instructions for Pearson to run the morning meeting. While Tony was speaking to the inquest, I waited in a small room, an armed maid standing by. They offered me tea, yet I mostly sat thinking. What could they possibly have to speak to Tony about?

Tony never returned, yet they told me it was my turn.

I was ushered into the grand chamber, which was full. A raised stage sat to my right; nine men sat behind a table of dark wood. Bright lights shone on the entire section.

The maid directed me up three steps to a raised area just before the stage with railings round it. She opened a small gate on the side facing me. I sat in the chair provided. A row of men sat at the far wall beyond the stage in relative darkness, taking notes. A fierce-looking uniformed man stood next to the stage. Mr. Trevisane had described this man: the bailiff, who kept order.

Two long rectangular tables faced the stage. Mr. Trevisane sat at the closest table; I didn't recognize anyone else.

Tony sat in the balcony, along with many from the other Families. But Jonathan Diamond wasn't anywhere I could see. Why wouldn't he be here? Was he ill? Had something happened?

To my horror, Jack Diamond stood leaning on a door-post at the back of the hall, arms crossed, head shaven, dressed entirely in white. He nodded grimly as our eyes met.

Why was Jack here? What might he do? And where was Jon?

The man sitting in the center of the row on stage spoke, but as if he had said it too many times:

"May I remind the witness and the chamber that this is a coroner's inquest. The Coroner's Office and Traveler's Federation are here to determine whether the destruction of flight A26 was due to an accident or a deliberate act. If this board determines the destruction was due to a deliberate act, its goal is not to determine who caused that act. It merely transmits its factual findings and recommendations to the District Attorney. It does not determine innocence or guilt, nor does it prosecute criminal acts; that is for the District Attorney's office. Witnesses are under oath; falsity may be prosecuted." He turned to me. "Do you understand?"

Was this the judge? "Yes, sir."

The bailiff appeared. "Please stand and state your full name."

"Jacqueline Spadros."

"Do you swear to tell the entire truth or suffer the Fire?"

"I certainly wouldn't wish to suffer the Fire!"

Someone in the hall laughed.

"Answer the question, mum."

"Yes, of course."

"You may be seated."

The chair wasn't particularly comfortable, but I managed.

A tanned, white-haired man seated at the second table of attorneys stood. "How old are you?"

I didn't care for the man's manner. "I don't believe we've been introduced, sir."

Scattered laughter, and some applause.

The judge said, "Madam, this is the District Attorney of Bridges, Mr. Chase Freezout."

I nodded to Mr. Freezout. I couldn't in all honesty say it was a pleasure to meet him. "I'm twenty-two, sir."

"And your date of birth."

"Yuletide Center."

Mr. Freezout appeared confused, but gathered himself quickly. "Very well. Please tell us where you were born, mum."

"Bridges, so far as I know."

"Where in Bridges?"

"Spadros quadrant, sir."

"At home? In a hospital?"

Mr. Trevisane stood. "Objection. Of what relevance is this?"

The judge turned to Mr. Freezout. "This seems fair."

"I believe my questions will become clear in time, sir."

"We don't have all day."

Someone in the audience snickered.

The judge said, "Mrs. Spadros, please answer the question."

"What was the question again?"

Scattered laughter.

Mr. Freezout said, "Where exactly were you born?"

"I don't know, sir."

"I see. Where did you live as a child?"

"In the Spadros Pot."

Horrified gasps from the crowd.

"I beg your pardon?"

"In the Spadros Pot, sir. To be more precise, the Cathedral."

The audience murmured. The judge banged his small hammer, which quieted the room.

"And your birth name?"

"I don't recall."

Mr. Freezout blinked in confusion. "Madam?"

"I was quite small then."

Laughter filled the hall. Tony leaned his hand on his face.

Mr. Freezout turned red. "This is a serious business, Mrs. Spadros. Do you mock the board?

"Of course not! I don't wish to suffer the Fire, so I'm telling the entire truth. I simply don't recall these things."

He seemed put out. "Very well. What's your mother's name?"

"My mother's name," I almost said "is" but then I remembered Molly's warning, "was Fanny Kaplan."

"And your father?"

"Peedro Sluff claims this. But I don't know for certain."

"I see." It seemed he didn't approve of my answer. "Can you tell us exactly what happened the day of the zeppelin explosion?"

Make him draw information from you. "Certainly." I folded my hands in my lap.

He waited, then seemed impatient. "Would you, mum?"

"Oh! Of course. Well, first, after I rose, I had my tea and toast. If I remember correctly, I had the last of the blackberry jam. Then I read my mail, and the news. My maid and I discussed what I might wear to the Celebration. We decided on my new Spring gown. Then I took my bath, and —"

Mr. Freezout snapped, "Mrs. Spadros!" He paused as the outburst of laughter from the crowd died away. "Please limit your comments to what you saw at the zeppelin station."

Excellent. He had leapt over the exact part I didn't want to speak of. "Well, sir, the station was quite lovely. I arrived with one of my husband's men in order to see off a friend. But we encountered a great deal of traffic and bother on the way and arrived after the zeppelin left. You know the rest of the story."

"Actually, we don't, Mrs. Spadros, which is why you're here." He paused. "What was your friend's name?"

"Dame Anastasia Louis."

Murmurs throughout the chamber.

"I see. How long had you known Dame Louis?"

"Since my engagement dinner. We met there. I was seventeen, sir. Almost six years now."

"And what was the nature of your relationship?"

"Sir?"

"Were you friends?"

I felt a sudden melancholy. "Yes. She was one of the few friends I had in this city."

"I would imagine Mrs. Jacqueline Spadros has many friends."

I smiled, feeling bitter. "You would imagine."

"Your husband's man who accompanied you to the zeppelin station. Would you tell us more about him?"

I shrugged. "A man like any other. In his middle thirties. A bit taller than me, brown hair. The men called him Morton."

"And where is this ... Mr. Morton?"

"I don't keep track of my husband's men."

Mr. Freezout put his hand to his chin. "How came a woman of the Pot to marry Anthony Spadros?"

"I was brought to his home as a young girl of twelve."

More murmurs from the crowd.

"For what reason?"

"As a playmate, I suppose."

"And you stayed there from the age of twelve?"

"No, sir. I was only there during the day, and occasionally with his family on outings and vacations. I was sent back home to my people most nights until I came to be sixteen, then I was brought to stay permanently at Spadros Manor." More murmurs. "My husband and I were engaged to be married the year after."

"I see. And did you agree to this engagement?"

I didn't meet his eye. "Of course."

"So you lived in the Pot, and were brought to Spadros Manor every day? Or just some days?"

"Some days."

"Which days?"

"I never knew which day it would be, sir. Mr. Roy Spadros would send his men for me."

He went to his table, picked up a tan folder full of papers, each with a small yellow sheet stapled to it, and flipped through them. "What does your husband do, mum?"

"Do, sir?"

"How does he provide for you? Afford to hire men?"

I made my face all innocence. "Why, he's a gentleman, sir. We have extensive holdings, and live off the proceeds."

"Is your husband not the heir to the Spadros Family?"

"Well, he's their only son, so ..." I paused, as if in thought. "I never considered it that way."

"So you're saying you're unaware of the activities of the most powerful criminal organization in Bridges?"

The room erupted: shouts, gasps, applause.

"Objection!" Mr. Trevisane was on his feet. "Slander! **Foul** slander!"

The judge banged his hammer several times, with no effect.

The bailiff shouted, "Order! We shall have order!" He slammed a thick staff into the floor as he spoke, without any reduction in the noise. He then lifted a large pump-action shotgun, and racked it. At the sound, the crowd silenced at once.

The judge said, "Sustained. We're not here to cast aspersions on the character of either the witness or her husband. Keep your personal opinions to yourself or I'll charge you with contempt."

Mr. Freezout seemed at a momentary loss. "Very well. Mrs. Spadros, I wonder if you might explain something for the board."

"Certainly, sir."

He lifted the folder. "If it please the board, I wish to enter exhibits 234 through 275, letters exchanged between Dame Anastasia Louis and Mrs. Jacqueline Spadros."

Fear spiked through me. Anastasia didn't destroy my letters?

"Objection," Mr. Trevisane said. "Private correspondence of a gentlewoman and an aristocrat, even one deceased, should not be a matter of public discourse."

"Overruled," the judge said. "Mr. District Attorney, you are only to bring matters directly related to the disaster into the public record. Are each of these letters so related?"

"Yes, sir," Mr. Freezout said. "Every one."

The judge said, "So entered."

Mr. Freezout picked up a letter and said, "Now, Mrs. Spadros, I wish to discuss exhibit 234 ..."

He made me explain each letter. Of course, they were all coded, and appeared innocent, but he rightly asked about each. What dog did I refer to? We only owned one, as had been reported by our staff. What was this red dog I asked about?

At the end of the discussion, I felt fatigued. "I have trouble understanding how any of these relate to the zeppelin, sir." Spats of laughter here and there; I imagined many of the audience felt the same way. "But I'm just a simple woman from the Pot."

"I'm tending to agree," the judge said. "You will show reason these are related to the event or withdraw them."

"I wish to prove a pattern of deception and intrigue, focused on these two women." He turned to the audience. "Clearly —" He picked up a letter. "— this letter regarding the coal-man named Frank you wished to hire — living on Pagliacci street in Spadros quadrant — is not a real letter. There is no such street in Spadros quadrant, nor anywhere in Bridges. Therefore, this is some sort of code." He put the letter down as murmurs filled the hall.

The judge said, "Proceed."

"Were you aware, Madam, that Dame Anastasia Louis had an intimate personal relationship with a young man calling himself Frank Pagliacci?"

"I only became aware of this shortly before her death."

He lifted a letter up. "So this letter was not seeking a coal-man for hire, as you told the court earlier."

Murmurs from the crowd.

"I didn't know there was no such street, sir. A man brought a card with the address."

"Do you have the card to show us?"

"No, sir — I'm sorry, I must have thrown it away."

"Why were **you** seeking a coal-man for hire? Does Spadros Manor not have a housekeeper?"

"Not at the time, sir. I've since promoted our Keeper of the Kitchens to that role."

Mr. Freezout took up another paper. "I wish to enter exhibit 276, a letter found on the ground near Gate 19 after the disaster."

"Objection! We weren't informed of this," Mr. Trevisane said.

"May I remind you, sir, for the last time," the judge said, "that this is not a court of law. Mrs. Spadros is not on trial. The coroner's office has no obligation whatsoever to inform you of its evidence." He turned to Mr. Freezout. "So entered."

Mr. Freezout read, "I quote: 'Dear Anastasia, I wish you the best of success. Please accept this token of my esteem. Yours truly, Jacqui.'" He looked at me. "Did you send this letter?"

"No."

He returned to his table, took out a form. "I have here exhibit 277, an invoice for the movement of three tons of ammonium nitrate to a ..." He peered at the paper, "Bryce Cemetery —"

Hearing the name sent a shock through me, and I stared at him in disbelief.

" — in the city of Dickens, for shipment on March first, 1899 — the day of the disaster. This shipment was scheduled for flight A26, the exact flight which now lies destroyed."

Murmurs ran through the hall.

Placing the paper on the table, he said, "The scheduling of

this shipment was at special request and signed by your husband. Had you any knowledge of this?"

"No, sir."

"What if I told you an analysis of the handwriting suggests you wrote both this letter to Dame Anastasia and the invoice?"

Alarm struck me. "What?"

"Do you deny it?"

"Most certainly!"

"As you deny knowledge of the streets in your own quadrant? As you deny knowing your home doesn't use coal?"

Fear struck me. Of course our home didn't use coal; Spadros Manor sat on top of the Magma Steam Generator. How could I have been so foolish?

"Objection!" Mr. Trevisane howled. "Badgering the witness."

"Sustained," the judge said, but the damage had been done.

Why didn't Anastasia destroy my letters?

"I have no further questions for this witness," Freezout said.

"We will recess until tomorrow," said the judge.

I sat unmoving, feeling wobbly. Staring out at the crowd, I saw Jack staring back at me. I expected he might gloat, but he instead fixed me with a level, determined look then turned away, an attendant opening the door for him.

The maid led me back to the small chamber.

Tony came to me then, and with his men helped me to our carriage. "I'm sorry, Jacqui," he said, once the doors were shut.

"What did they ask you about?"

"Letters, invoices ... I told them about the letters your friends stole from you. Pearson told them the same."

"Pearson was there?"

"He went early on; we were still at the Country House. The house staff have already testified."

"Tony, why did Ottilie, Treysa, and Poignee steal the letters?"

"Your kitchen maids?" He shook his head. "I don't know."

"Did you not have them questioned?"

He put his head in his hands. "No."

"Why not?"

He raised his head. "They were your friends, Jacqui! You

wanted me to put them to the question?"

"I didn't want you to torture them, but ... if you would have tried to get answers from them before you had them killed, we might know more of who they were sending my letters to."

"I didn't know anything about the letters."

It was true; I only learned of them after Pearson had their rooms searched. "We are truly f —" I only stopped myself in time.

Tony nodded. "I know."

We sat there to the sound of hoofbeats. Tony took my hands. "No one has charged us with anything. But if they do, we can fight this. Don't lose heart." He kissed my fingers. "You did nothing wrong. Our lawyers can find a way through."

I didn't see how things could get any worse.

* * *

When we returned, I had a glass of bourbon while Amelia did my hair. After tea, Tony decided to go for a walk, taking several of his men with him. I sat in my study with a drink, the window open to let in the breeze. Amelia sat in the corner, mending.

I drained my glass, poured another. If Anastasia wanted to keep my letters, why didn't she take them with her?

Or did someone in her household steal them too?

"Mum," Pearson said, "Master Joseph Kerr here to see you."

Relief washed over me. Finally, something was going right today. "Please send him in."

Amelia focused on her mending, so I toasted Amelia and Pearson both, and drank to Joe's arrival.

I pretended to keep writing, but in truth, I felt all a-flutter at the thought of seeing him. When the door opened, I rose. "Joe! How good to see you!" I offered him a seat on the sofa, sitting across the low coffee table from him. "How can I help you?"

He glanced in Amelia's direction. "I need to speak with you on a matter of some delicacy."

Ah. "Amelia, would you excuse us for a few minutes?"

She stood, put her mending aside, and curtsied. "Yes, mum."

"Go to my room and take your mending. I'll be up shortly."

"Yes, mum."

When the door closed, we both stood. He came to me,

speaking in a whisper. We didn't touch, yet he stood so near I could feel the heat of his body. "Jacqui, I have terrible news. My cousin is a secretary for the coroner's board. He records all that's said, both in the grand chamber and in the back room. He told me a meeting just took place to finalize the board's report."

Joe looked so alarmed that I felt afraid. "What did they say?"

Joe took my hands. "They believe you bombed the zeppelin."

Joe covered my mouth. "No one must know, not even your maid. That was my cousin's price for telling me."

"But why? Why would they think that?"

"You have access to the Spadros Family fortune. A dozen people saw Dame Anastasia bring a package on the zeppelin. She said you gave it to her. They say the letter to her lying on the floor at the gate was in your handwriting. The package almost certainly contained a bomb, which ignited the tons of —" He shook his head. "— I can't remember the name. Something nitrite."

"Ammonium nitrate."

"Yes. Which they say you shipped by forging your husband's signature. And they have testimony from your own gardener: you asked if this ammonium might be used to bomb something."

I gasped, staring at him in horror. "An innocent question! My husband asked me to investigate what the scoundrels who stole our money bought with it."

Joe said, "They believe you have motive. Who else but a Pot rag would bomb the zeppelin on the anniversary of the Coup?"

I remembered Madame's file with the name Eunice Ogier.

This false Red Dog Gang didn't just want to frame the true Red Dogs for their crimes.

They wanted to frame **me** for them.

I turned to Joe. "But I didn't do it!"

"I know. But they plan to arrest you in the morning. And the District Attorney vowed death to anyone involved."

Death? How would anyone think I could do such a thing?

"Here, sit," Joe said, taking my arm and guiding me to a chair. "You look about to faint." He went to my desk, poured a drink and handed it to me. "This should help."

I took the glass from him and sipped at it.

Joe sat in the armchair beside me. He reached in his coat pocket, flashed three tickets edged in red. "One for each of us and one for your Ma. We can go tonight."

Ma never answered my message. But we could stop by the Cathedral and get her on the way. I finished my drink, set the glass on the table. "What about Josie?"

"Josie feels her place is with our grandfather." He shook his head. "After all he's done, she won't go, even to be free of him."

"Don't berate her, Joe; she's probably afraid. Once we're someplace safe, we'll send for her."

Joe nodded, his eyes never leaving mine. "We will." He touched the side of my face, eyes penetrating into my soul. "Oh, gods. You're so beautiful. I didn't dare hope this would really happen. I never thought we'd have the chance to be free."

All I could see was Joe. Thrusting my hands into his hair, I drew his face towards mine and kissed him with all my heart.

We rose, Joe pulling me to him, his hands on my buttocks, his cane thumping to the floor. His cock pressed hard against my body, and I wanted him right then and there. He kissed my cheek, my ear, my neck, and oh, it felt heavenly. "My coach is outside."

Our lips met. My hands went to his belt, but he clasped my face in his hands. "Oh, gods, I want you more than anything, but we have no time. We must leave now, before your husband —"

Tony said, "Before your husband comes home?"

The Gift

We jerked apart. Tony stood in the open doorway, staring at me, his face pale and stricken.

How long had he been standing there?

I turned towards Joe, but he had left through the open window, cane and all. Stunned, I turned back, letting out a squeak of fright: Tony stood right in front of me.

Tony placed one hand on each armchair, shoved them over, then grabbed my upper arms so tight they hurt. His face was red, his jaw clenched as he stood over me, eyes wild, shaking with rage. "How could you do this!?"

I shrank back in fear. I had never seen him like this.

Then he shoved me aside, but not far, and turned away. He said through gritted teeth, "I **refuse** to be my father."

I feared approaching him. "Please, Tony — let me explain."

Tony's knuckles were white. "Explain. How could you possibly explain this?"

This was what I most dreaded: telling Tony the truth. "It's a long story." I walked to the window, leaned my forehead against the cool pane, not sure where to begin.

In the dust on the ledge, it said, "10."

Ten. That must be when the zeppelin left.

The clock above the fireplace chimed half past six.

I had an idea.

I turned to Tony, who still faced away. "I'll tell you

everything. I swear it. But ... I feel unbearably distressed, and you must too. Plus I — I've had too much to drink. We shouldn't talk in such a mood; we might say hurtful things we'd later regret." Would he go along with this? "Please, would you allow me a half hour to collect my thoughts? Wait for me in your study. I'll tell you it all, I promise, and there will be no doubt as to the matter."

He let out a bitter laugh. "To collect your thoughts."

"Yes. I'll make a list, so I forget nothing." This was true, at any rate. "I swear to you, there will be no more lies. You of all people deserve the truth." But I had never meant for it to be revealed this way. "I'll tell you everything." At this, I felt sad. "Everything. And I think that when you know everything, you'll understand."

Tony's voice shook. "One half-hour."

"Yes."

He didn't move. "Did you **ever** love me, Jacqui?"

I remembered the night he told me he confronted Roy, when I gave myself to him gladly. I regretted that still. "Yes, once, I did."

He left the room, closed the door, and never looked back.

* * *

Pearson gave me a puzzled glance as I emerged but said nothing. I walked down the hall towards the veranda. The courtyard bell rang, and one of Tony's men hurried past going the other way.

Stepping out onto the veranda, I stood by my little bird's cage, alone in the darkness.

I placed my hands on the cold white wires. I could go to Tony right now, confess everything, and submit to whatever Tony and Roy devised for me. And if I survived, I could return to my life.

As Jon said, perhaps Tony and I could get through this. Maybe I could learn to love him. Or if not, maybe I could, like Molly — or Amelia — find some small happiness in captivity.

But I wasn't like them.

I would die if I remained at Spadros Manor. Perhaps not all at once, but like my poor houseplant, I would wither, and eventually I'd lose everything that made me ... me.

Air died trying to rescue me from the Spadros Family. Joe

might at this moment be fighting for his life to get to the zeppelin.

I couldn't turn back now that I had a chance at freedom.

I stared at my little bird, and it stared back.

I opened the door to its cage. "Be happy."

It hopped out and was gone.

* * *

"Amelia, I wish to take a walk before dinner."

She gave the clock a glance. "Right away, mum." She hurried in my closets and to the right, where she kept my walking dresses.

I went to the left, to my hiding place.

"I can get whatever it is you need, mum," Amelia said, her voice muffled by the racks of clothing.

I slid open the wall panel. "No need, I have it here." I retrieved my bundle: my blue dress, wrapped around Anastasia's makeup book and the envelope with the rest of my money.

I stared at Roy's note, the scrap from Marja's hand. I didn't dare burn the first real evidence of the Red Dog Gang's plot, yet the thought of taking them with me made me ill. And I couldn't give Roy's note to Tony — not on top of everything else.

So I left the notes there, where I hoped they'd remain until the Manor itself was destroyed. The panel slid back in place, and no clue to what lay behind it remained.

When I returned to my room, Amelia held a corset, dress, hat, and shawl, which she plopped onto the bed.

I set my bundle on the dresser, then unlocked the drawer.

The small envelopes with my evidence from the carriage David was transported in during his kidnapping. A lock of my mother's hair. The pressed daffodils Jon gave me on New Year's Eve. My magnification spyglass. I tucked these and the money in my handbag, set it on top of the dresser, and left the drawer unlocked, my loaded pistol inside.

My gaze went to the stationery-box, given from Tony's love for me. My gift to him — the truth — was long overdue. A cruel gift, but the only one I ever could offer.

I poured a glass of bourbon, sat at my tea-table, lit a cigarette, and opened my stationery-box. I took a long drink and a long drag on my cigarette before writing.

Tony —

I didn't tell you everything about the night Jack Diamond's friend died. That night, my best friend Nicholas Bryce was murdered trying to save me from being sold to the Spadros Family.

Joseph Kerr and I pledged our love at sixteen. Yet Roy Spadros ensured this marriage with a gun to my head as we waited to enter the hall. He threatened to kill me if I told you the truth. He threatened to kill my family if I tried to return home.

Someday Roy Spadros may find me. He may even kill me. But I can't live like this anymore.

I care for you, Tony, but as a sister does her brother. I neither wish to cause hurt nor scandal — but you deserve a wife who loves you.

Please make no true search for me. Take this chance: go to Gardena and win back her affection. Be with your son. You can persuade her father and brothers to accept you. It may help if you show them this letter.

Once a suitable time has passed, declare me dead and marry. Make a life of happiness and peace.

— Jacqui

I removed Tony's wedding ring and moonstone, folded them inside the letter and put it in the envelope, which I sealed. I then wrote a list, and placed both the list and envelope on my dresser.

It was done. Hopefully he could use my gift to buy his freedom. But that was up to him now.

Amelia was draping my dress onto the bed, where the other items lay arranged.

"There's no need for a corset or fixing my hair." I smiled at Amelia's questioning glance. "We'll only be out a short time."

She smiled back. "If you wish, mum."

She helped me into my dress, hat, and shoes, then returned to the bed for my shawl. I placed my handbag, the letter, and my list in my right pocket. Anastasia's makeup book went into my left pocket, then I removed my gun from the dresser drawer. "Turn round, Amelia, but do not scream."

Amelia flinched when she saw my gun, but she didn't scream. "Mum, why are you doing this?"

I picked up my favorite blue dress, the one Tony and I loved so well, and tossed it onto the fire. "We're leaving." I grabbed her arm and brought her through my closets. "Take a shawl." She hesitated, so I thrust one of mine in her arms.

I dragged her through Tony's room, into the hall, and down the stairs. I peered out. No one was around. I pulled her to the side gate and out to the street. No one was there either, which was odd. "We're on a stroll." I pushed the gun into her side. "If you call out or struggle, I will shoot you."

Amelia gasped. "Mum," she whispered as we walked. "I've always been good to you. Why do you threaten me?"

"Because I will not go back." I thought of how much she loved Tony. "And I fear you might try to stop me."

Amelia said nothing as we walked towards the taxi-station. I handed the carriage-driver a dollar and my list. Then I handed Amelia Tony's letter. "Mr. Spadros expects this letter from your hand at exactly seven. He may kill you if he doesn't receive it."

The clocks began to chime the hour, and her face went pale.

I leaned out the window and hit the side of the door. "Run!"

* * *

Men stood outside Bryce Fabrics, so I had the driver turn into the alley a block away. "If those men approach, leave me here."

The driver nodded. His goggles were on, his eyes distorted.

I crept down the alley through deepening twilight. The Red Dog mark on the wall appeared untouched.

Eleanora seemed astonished to see me at her back door.

We stood in the half-darkness of her back hall. Once the door closed behind us, I told her, "I'm leaving Bridges."

"You're leaving? Where?"

I shrugged. I'd forgotten to ask. "A friend got the tickets."

She said nothing.

"Do you remember the couple in the police station who told you about my investigator business?"

Mrs. Bryce nodded.

"Tell me about the woman. Was she an outsider?"

"Yes, I'm sorry, I forgot to say. I suppose it was because she said she was from Dickens too. It surprised me, her accent being so strong and all, but she said she was from some part of town I'd never been to called ... what was it? Oh, yes, 'Little Island' I believe is what she said. I could barely understand her."

This had to be Morton's "business partner," Zia. "Tell the men to beware of her. She's no friend; I have reason to believe she's a Fed, who's working with the men who took your son."

She might have even been the one who took him — a boy would be more likely to go with a pretty woman than a man.

"Why would the Feds take David?"

"I don't know. It's possible she abandoned the Feds to run with these men." I sighed. "Who knows what goes through the mind of an outsider?"

Mrs. Bryce snorted in amusement. "They're very different."

"May I ask one thing more?"

"Of course."

"Where's his body?"

"Herbert?"

"No ..." I was going to say, "Air," but she didn't know him by that name. "Nicholas."

Mrs. Bryce didn't speak for a moment. "Mr. Bryce took him home. He's buried in Bryce Cemetery."

And they had all that fertilizer sent there. "Who knew of it?"

She shrugged. Crickets chirped in the distance. "He's next to his father. That's the only thing which consoles me."

How could she stand losing him? Then to lose her other son as well. And David might as well be dead. I gazed at Eleanora with new respect. In spite of everything, she'd survived.

As if reading my mind, she put her hand on my arm. "You'll want to see him before you go."

I followed to her candle-lit back room, sat beside David. "I'm going to another city. I'll send for you when I can."

David lunged for me, crying out, "Don't go!" He wrapped his arms around my waist, clinging to me as if I were his only safety.

Mrs. Bryce gasped. "It's the first time he's talked."

I put my arm around David, kissed his hair. "I don't know if you remember your brother Nicholas." I glanced at Eleanora; I knew now what to give her. "He died for a reason." I struggled to get the words out. "I was sold to the Spadros Family. My own father sold me. But your brother died trying to get me free. And now I have a chance. I don't know what else to do. I don't want to leave you." I could hardly breathe. "But they'll kill me and my Ma if I don't."

David didn't move, his eyes tightly shut.

Eleanora's mouth hung open for several seconds, then she knelt before us. "Davey, she has to go. All the men in the neighborhood are outside watching over us. Come on. Let go."

David nodded, put his arms around his legs, and began to rock, but slower.

I felt as much a traitor as the first day I stood here, when Eleanora asked me to find him and I refused to go. "I'm so sorry."

David's eyes flickered to me, but he never stopped rocking.

The Subterfuge

I stepped into the alleyway and leaned against a wall. Leaving David had been more difficult than leaving Tony, and I felt drained by the effort.

To my surprise, the carriage hadn't moved. I got in the carriage, grateful for the chance to rest, and we set off.

A few blocks later, the carriage stopped.

I peered out of the window to my left. We sat in a cul-de-sac of abandoned buildings; the street was dark.

"You won't see much out there," the driver's voice from the other window startled me.

"What's wrong? Why have we stopped?"

"Frank told me to expect a woman, but I never thought it would be you." The man displayed my list, the goggles around his neck shifting as he did so. "Bryce Fabrics. Market Center. The zeppelin station. This sounds like a going-away list. Even sent a note with a servant." He shook his head. "What a way to leave a man." He frowned at me. "Just like a fucking Pot rag." Then his expression became calculating. "Trying to get away unseen, are you, Mrs. Spadros? It's going to take a lot more than a dollar to keep me quiet."

"How dare you?"

He opened the door, his hand resting on the top edge. "A young, pretty woman, all alone. Seems I can dare whatever I want. For starters, you can give me your ticket money."

I considered the ten dollars in my handbag. No, that was for the Pikes. "I don't have any money with me."

"Then your ticket."

"My ... friend bought the tickets. He awaits me at the station."

"Well, he'll just have to wait his turn." He leered at me, then a wicked grin spread across his face. "No, I don't think I'll share. After I'm done, you'll just disappear in the river. And I'll tell whoever asks you wanted out at ... that saloon you go to."

I stared at him, appalled. Were the drivers in the city talking with each other about their fares?

"You're all whores there in the Pot, aren't you?" He chuckled. "This is as good a place as any to get started."

He climbed into the carriage; I opened the door behind me. "Frank wants me? Why aren't you bringing me to him then?

He grabbed my right hand, but I pulled free, stumbled, and fell out of the carriage onto my back.

"I'm sick of being his butt-boy. I'm getting some of my own, and to hell with him." He lumbered round the back of the carriage, loosening his belt. "You're not getting away that easy."

I unfastened my holster right before he got to me, pulling my gun as he hauled me upright.

He stuck his face in my hair. "My, don't you smell nice."

I shoved the gun in his gut. "You can let go or you can die."

"Baby wanna play rough, does she?" He grabbed my hair with one hand, his zipper with the other.

I shot him, the sound muffled by his belly. The horses reared. He gripped my hair as he fell, pulling me on top of him.

I untangled my hair from his fist, then ran. My hands shook, my heart pounded.

Then I stopped. He still had the list.

The horses stomped about, but the street was empty, so I crept back and found the list in his pocket. He lay on his back, staring, eyes wide, mouth open.

The gods-damned driver tried to violate me!

I gave him a good kick in the head.

I also got my dollar back.

I shook out my clothes and hair as I walked, so I didn't smell of gunpowder. Plus it helped to be doing something; otherwise I thought I might start screaming.

As it was, my breath sounded much too loud. Fog lay on the streets, which made the night seem even darker. Any noise made me jump as I hurried along.

I got to where the streetlights worked. In the darkened storefront window, my hair was wild, my face streaked with tears.

I wiped off most of my makeup. Remembering instructions in Anastasia's book, I used some of my eye makeup to make my nose narrower, my cheekbones even more pronounced than they were, to add circles under my eyes and a cleft in my chin. I put my shawl over my head like a cape.

A block over, I found a liquor store. Unlike my father's, it had a bar and even a few tables. I needed a drink. "A double bourbon, neat," I told the girl, who was maybe fifteen.

She snorted. "I thought you Dealers didn't drink."

I laughed at the idea. "I'm not one of the Dealers."

But in the mirror behind the bar, with my shawl up over my head, I did look like one. This girl had probably never seen one of the Dealers in her life. "You got any cigarettes?"

"Sure."

The girl handed me my drink, my smokes, and my change, and even gave me a light. I glanced at the clock on the wall. Almost eight. I had plenty of time.

And Tony would never find me here.

I walked ten more blocks before I found a taxi-station, the fog deepening as I went. The driver squinted at me. "Blessed Lady, I would never take your money."

I lowered the pitch of my voice. "May the Dealer smile upon you, my son."

The man beamed.

I gave this driver the address from the letter Thrace Pike sent me, hoping it would at least be close to his home.

At the bridge, the guards stopped the carriage. "We're looking for Mrs. Spadros. Have you seen her?"

So Tony was searching for me after all. Or perhaps Roy was.

"No, sir. Got one of the Dealers bound for the Plaza here."

I held my breath as the guard glanced inside, but he waved us through.

The Escape

The home of Thrace and Gertie Pike lay on a dismal back alley full of narrow steps leading up to equally narrow doors.

Gertie appeared at my knock, baby on her hip, wearing an old-fashioned house dress with an empire waist. She appeared pregnant. "May I help you?"

I dropped my shawl around my shoulders. "I'm sorry." I glanced around. "It's Mrs. Spadros. I had to come here secretly." I leaned forward. "With your money."

She peered at me. Then recognition dawned on her face. "Oh! Mrs. Spadros! Please come in."

A windowless room stood before me. A row of wooden hooks lay to my right; a few coats hung there. To my left sat a small round table and chairs. Beyond that, a staircase went up. A pot-bellied steam-stove stood on the back wall, its flue going through the ceiling. A stew-pot sat on the stove; good smells filled the air. Baskets of potatoes and onions sat near the stove, and a large round loaf with a third neatly sliced away sat on the table.

The whole downstairs was smaller than my bedroom.

I glanced at her. "I see congratulations are in order."

She blushed. "Thank you." She seemed ill at ease. "Thrace said you disguise yourself at times. I'm sorry I didn't invite you in sooner. My husband's not home at present."

"Really?" It was almost half-past eight.

"He's a hard worker. He wants to learn all he can." Gertie

smiled proudly. "He'll have his own law firm someday."

Now this was surprising. "A high ambition."

"Not for himself, mum — he wants to make the city better."

Good luck with that, I thought. Bridges was a madhouse. I handed her the envelope. "I wish him all the best."

Gertie Pike peered inside it, then sighed. The baby laid its head on her shoulder. "I'm sorry, mum. I didn't believe you'd come through for us."

I smiled at her. It didn't matter what she thought. I had survived. I had done my duty. Now on to freedom! "Thank your husband for his help."

She gazed at me a long moment, then opened the door. "Mum, I hope you find what you're looking for."

* * *

Once the door shut behind me, I twisted my hair into a bun, put the shawl around my shoulders, and hurried the half mile to the train station.

At this point, I realized I had forgotten to give Eleanora the change I set aside for her.

I'll send it to her when Joe and I get wherever we're going, I thought. Besides, a bit more money might not hurt to have when we got there.

I wore no hat — I must have lost it at the carriage. I wore no corset, and I was more than a bit dirty. A few people waiting on the platform glanced at me when I arrived. But no one said anything and no one followed.

I glanced at the clock. A quarter to nine.

Across the tracks, several policemen walked along the platform. One looked my way — Paix Hanger, of all people.

Had he been demoted to walking station patrol? Or were the police here on some other matter?

He caught my eye, but seemed not to recognize me.

The train to Clubb quadrant arrived. Once we were towed free of the tunnels, I watched the landscape. Conductors strolled by, yet none took note of me.

I relaxed against the window. I had escaped.

At the time, I thought nothing of Joe's exit through the

window. He would be the natural target for Tony's wrath, and could do little to help if caught by Tony's men. I felt grateful he managed to hide long enough to leave me the message. Joe was crafty: if anyone could elude the Spadros Family, he could.

I changed trains at Riverfront station. Then we were off, chugging through fields of gold in the near-darkness.

The Aperture glinted from behind the fog as we traveled. Its gargantuan brass plates moved aside as an immense airship rose to greet it, then passed into the darkness beyond our dome.

The zeppelin station glowed from within, an enormous half-cylinder of stained glass laid on its side. Airships far taller than the station stood quiet, their vast balloons lit by the boiler-fires below as they prepared for their next journey.

My failure to learn who killed Marja grieved me. With the law after me, I didn't have much choice but to leave Bridges. Someday, when things were settled, I would return to Marja's case, to David's kidnapping, and make it all right.

* * *

Although canvas filled the damaged spaces, the zeppelin station was still grand and beautiful, with a high vaulted ceiling of stained glass, oak, and brass. Huge chandeliers hung overhead at intervals. Hundreds of dark wooden seats filled the station, people walking to and fro over the polished oak floor, which was littered with hundreds of ticket stubs edged in blue.

None of the Spadros men were in sight, so I sat in the center of the station, where Joe could see me plainly. It was half past nine. Joe would come for me soon.

The Descent

Every step, every movement might be Joe. As ten o'clock passed, I felt frantic. Where was Joe? What happened to him?

I remembered the courtyard bell. Had Tony decided even then to search for Joe? What if Tony's men found him?

Then another fear arose: Would Tony's men — or worse yet, Roy's — search here? Yet I saw none of Tony's men. Could Tony possibly not have realized I meant to leave the city?

I imagined Tony's face when he got my letter: the rage, the hurt. The terror when he learned I was gone. He'd stop at nothing to find me, if only to make sure I was safe.

Amelia had no idea where I might go. Tony would send men to Joe's house, or perhaps Madame's. And he had sent word to the bridge guards. After that, he wouldn't know where to look.

Roy might think of sending men to Vig's, but Blitz would probably think of the same thing. Hopefully, Blitz could keep Vig from becoming agitated about my safety — or fighting Roy's men.

But Sawbuck would be furious. Where would he look for me?

I mentioned Air in my letter, which would lead Sawbuck to the Bryce's house. It would take him some time to get there, and she wouldn't be able to tell them anything.

Or could she? I told her I was leaving the city!

What had I done? Why didn't I warn her?

Eleanora wouldn't tell. No one from the Pot would. Would they hurt her? Threaten David?

I was such a fool to involve others. I should have known Tony would pursue me. Hopefully, they'd never be able to connect the taxi-driver with me. That would whip Tony into a frenzy.

The incident reminded me too sharply of the night Vig and I met. I should've known better. I should've had my gun out when the carriage stopped. I would never trust a stranger again.

I felt no remorse for killing the man. To this day, I'm not sure I could have done anything else.

The entire day had been a disaster. But there was no going back, no fixing it. The matter was out of my hands now.

But where was Joe? Had he meant to leave at ten tomorrow?

No, he said we could leave tonight. So where was he? Could they have found him? What would they do to him if they did?

* * *

It was after midnight when a hand dropped on my shoulder, startling me so much I let out a cry.

Jonathan Diamond crouched beside me. "Hush, my love."

Morton — Morton! — stood next to him.

"What are you doing here? How —?" I was going to ask how they knew each other. But then I remembered what Gardena said the day of the explosion: *He's a friend of my father's.*

Morton chuckled. "I can't believe you actually did this."

"Come," Jon said. "We can't let the reporters find you here." He grabbed my hand, pulling me along. Morton took my other arm, hurrying beside me.

"Reporters? Why?"

Then I remembered Joe's words. If they believed I bombed the zeppelin, and learned I left home, and found me here ...

Morton opened the door. "We don't have time for this."

The streets were empty but for what appeared to be an ordinary dark brown taxi-carriage with its Hackney stallions. Yet the driver was the same dark-skinned, white-haired Diamond man who drove Gardena's white and silver carriage the day of the explosion. The old man smiled and nodded as we approached.

Jon glanced around, opened the carriage door and shoved me inside. Once we set off, Jon said, "Mrs. Regina Clubb has invited you to stay at the hotel since your incoming visitor's flight was delayed. All expenses paid by the Clubb Family, of course."

"But, Jon —"

Morton put his finger to his mouth. "Master Diamond isn't here. You haven't seen him in ages. You haven't seen me either. A porter brought you to your room. Do you understand?"

I glanced between the two of them, suddenly aware of the driver's listening tube. *They're trying to keep us all alive.* I smiled in spite of my distress, and took their hands. "Thank you."

Jon squeezed my hand, his dark eyes never leaving mine. How did Jon know I went to the zeppelin station? How did he and Morton get into Clubb quadrant in the middle of the night?

I dared not ask. I had never been so glad and grateful to see Jon in my life, and I didn't want to put him in any harm, ever.

Shortly, the carriage pulled up to a side door. Jon whispered, "Be careful what you say, Jacqui. Mrs. Clubb was a Memory Girl."

I frantically tried to recall what I'd said to the woman, then nodded. None of that mattered; I had to get out of the city alive.

Morton led me down a golden-carpeted hallway. We entered a brass- and oak-lined mechanical lift, ascending two floors.

I whispered, "What's your agreement with my husband?"

"I won't betray you, if that's what you mean."

"No, of course."

We exited, then he stopped in the middle of the hallway, glancing to the side.

I nodded. Clubb Hotel of all places was sure to have listeners.

"I told him who my employer was," he gave a wry grin, "and we came to an agreement." He glanced around. "Come on."

I put my hand on his arm. "Wait."

Joe said the Clubbs started the Red Dogs children's street gang. Morton told me his employer wanted to know who suborned the Red Dogs. "You work for the Clubbs."

Morton chuckled, glancing away. "I've done work for them all at one time or another. Let's get you inside." He took me to a door, using a brass key hung around his neck under his shirt to let me in. The room was luxurious in its decor. "Stay here," Morton said, returning the key under his shirt. "Lock the door. And don't open that door unless someone knocks."

I nodded.

"You have your pistol?"

"Yes."

"Good. I don't think you'll need it, but —"

I smiled at him. "Thanks."

I grabbed his arm. "I must get a message to Joseph Kerr."

Morton blinked. "Who?"

"Joseph Kerr. Jon — Master Diamond knows him. Please ask him to find Joe and tell him I'm here."

Morton shrugged. "I'll pass along the message."

A wave of relief washed over me. "Thank you."

Morton tipped his hat and was gone.

It was one in the morning. But I did not sleep.

* * *

Pacing my room, I heard men walk past, the clanking of keys, voices I didn't recognize. I couldn't make out what they said, and I felt frightened by Morton's warning. Where was Joe?

The sky lightened and birds began to sing. My cigarettes were soon gone. I drew back the curtain with trembling hands. Carriages went past. The streets filled with people.

A knock: I flew to the door. Morton's warning stopped me. "Who is it?"

A woman's voice. "Your breakfast, mum."

Breakfast? I could hardly breathe for worry, let alone eat. "Is there wine on the tray?"

"For breakfast, mum?"

"Never mind. Take it away."

Joseph Kerr would never leave Bridges without me.

Morton had no reason not to tell Jon of my request.

Jon would bring the message to Joe, I had no doubt of it.

If Joe were alive.

I paced, hands shaking, heart racing. I couldn't consider it.

If Jon left Morton at the hotel, Morton would have to get a taxi to Diamond Manor, which would be difficult that late at night. Jon might stop to have breakfast or take his medicine before traveling to Hart quadrant. Jon's father might forbid him to leave:

214

Jon would have to send men to find Joe.

If the Spadros men chased Joe from the zeppelin station or slowed him down, Joe might not know where I was yet.

The crowd grew outside. Travelers, yes, but also reporters. Were these the ones Jonathan feared would find me?

A woman began laughing in the hallway outside my door.

Lunch arrived. My stomach roiled at the smell: I sent it away.

Surely Jon knew I needed to see Joseph Kerr, or at least, to know he was well. Where was Jon? Why hadn't he sent word?

The shadows lengthened. The laughter in the hallway came and went, but I found nothing funny in my situation. Could this woman not find somewhere else to loiter?

The room seemed too hot, then freezing cold. I couldn't open a window and had nothing to light the fire with. So I huddled under my bedding, then cast it onto the floor with my shawl.

When the knock came a third time, I begged the woman outside the door to find Jon and ask him to come here at once.

Late that evening, a knock came. "Jon?"

A man's voice. "The Keeper of the Court is forbidden to speak with you at this time. Is there someone else I might call?"

"No," I said. "Thank you."

I sat, disheartened. Mocking laughter echoed down the hall.

An entire day had passed. Even if Morton never reached Jon, Jon would realize I'd want Joe to be contacted. Surely Jon could have gotten word to Joe — or at least someone who knew Joe — by now. Even if he sent a messenger boy, it would take at most a few hours to reach the Kerr's home. Where else would Joe go?

I knew Joe better than anyone other than Josie — he might appear relaxed, even lazy, yet nothing stopped him once he had a focus for his desires.

But he didn't come to me.

Why was that woman laughing?

My hands shook so badly I could barely hold the blankets around me. As hours went by without a knock on the door, and the sky began to lighten, I had to face the truth: Joe was dead.

Joe would have come for me by now if he still lived. Or sent a messenger to make sure I was safe. Even if the Spadros men had injured him, he'd send someone, perhaps his cousin, who could get past whatever rules they had here.

The Spadros Family must have caught him.

I imagined that beautiful man lying cold and silent, or in Roy's clutches suffering some horrible torture on my account.

The thought of Joe being tortured left me wracked with grief. We were so close to freedom!

What should I have done?

I'm not a religious person. But that night, I prayed to the Dealer, the Floorman, Lady Luck, even the Shuffler, who heeds no one. Perhaps Joe was hiding, or hurt. Maybe someone would help.

As time passed, even that hope faded. No one could help us, even if they wanted to.

My only hope was that Tony caught Joe, not Roy.

That Tony told his men to kill Joe quickly.

That Joe didn't suffer.

* * *

I did little but weep; I couldn't eat or sleep. I didn't dare open the door. Where would I go? All my money was gone. Roy would burn the Cathedral if I went back to the Spadros Pot. Anywhere else I might go would put my friends in terrible danger.

So I stayed. There was nothing but water to drink, and when I did drink, it came back up. My hands shook in fear, and guilt gnawed at the depths of my stomach. The laughter outside came and went, even when I screamed for her to stop.

I got Joe killed, just as I got Air killed. And Ottilie, Treysa, Poignee, Stephen, Herbert, Anastasia, and Marja. And now, possibly Eleanora, David, and my Ma.

Everyone who came near to me died!

Even when I cried myself into oblivion, every noise sent me into terror. Between Jack Diamond, Frank Pagliacci, Tony, Sawbuck, and Roy, I wasn't sure how long I had to live.

I wasn't sure I actually wanted to.

The Cruelty

A sharp rapping on the oak door.

Heart pounding, I crept towards the sound, pistol in hand.

Regina Clubb didn't so much as glance at my gun. "Wipe your face, Mrs. Spadros," she said. "You look frightful."

Stifling my embarrassment, I turned away. She followed, closing the door behind her. I holstered my revolver, gesturing to a chair across the low coffee table with a shaking hand.

I suppose I did look frightful, but I refused to give her the satisfaction of seeing me take her advice.

She displayed a flask. "I suspect you need a drink."

Yes. I lunged across the table, grabbing the full flask from her. My hands shook so bad I almost dropped it, but once I got it open I only spilled a little. I loved how it tasted, the burning in my chest, the way I felt afterwards. "You don't know how good this is," I said with a sigh. "Thank you."

I thought Mrs. Clubb would continue her mocking laughter, but she gazed at me soberly. "I suspected you'd visit us. But I never thought it would be so soon."

"What do you mean?"

Mrs. Clubb smiled. "Seeing you at my Women's Center in January puzzled me. But it wasn't until Gardena Diamond asked us to smuggle someone from the city that I took interest."

"I don't understand."

"Our meeting today was inevitable. You have no friends of standing but Jonathan and Gardena, yet it seems you've had a falling-out. You've dismissed your dressmaker, you're sending messages to the Pot, and you've called on no one but the Kerrs. And they — in particular, Master Kerr — are the only ones close to having any standing calling on you. Thank your mother-in-law for keeping **that** quiet."

Did Mrs. Clubb know everything?

She handed me my newspaper, a zeppelin price circled. "I didn't even need this to predict your actions."

She had spies even in Spadros Manor!

"I don't know what went on between you and your husband, nor do I wish to. But I believe we can help each other."

She sat for a long moment, gazing off to the side, and I wondered what she thought I could help her with. I snuck my handkerchief out for a quick wipe when she wasn't looking, because it seemed undignified to keep sniffling.

She smiled, leaning back. "You alone stand in the way of the most important thing to my Family: the happiness of our son."

I snorted, suddenly angry. She cared so little for Nina — now this pretense of caring about Lance? "You murderous bitch. Happy. Like what you did to Nina?"

Her face went white.

"As far as I can tell, you twist your children to be your shadows, crush them until they fit your mold. Control them until they become as conniving and power-hungry as you. Nina was good and beautiful, and you hounded her into her grave. Kitty escaped to the Dealers, but now you're doing it to Lance. The only reason you want Roland and Gardena is because Roland is Tony's son. Will you turn them into golden-haired puppets, too?"

Regina Clubb sat, face pale, mouth open.

The color returned to her face, and Mrs. Clubb's tone became bitter, dripping with sarcasm. "Why, yes. It's not because Lance loves her, or because she's beautiful, or fertile —" as if I might be jealous of that, "— or because she wanted children so desperately as to risk her life to have one. It must be because we're trying to steal your husband's bastard and turn him against you."

I shook my head. "Do you think I'm stupid? Perhaps I am. My husband saw through this nonsense with the boat, yet I did not. The Ace of Clubbs was never your son! Roland is your Ace in the hole. He's the Spadros heir! You don't need me, why, you don't even need Gardena — all Lance need do is raise the boy to love you and you have three quadrants in thrall. How could anyone oppose you? This so-called courtship is just a way to make Gardena and her son your hostages."

Although Roy wouldn't care, Tony must be in terror of how Gardena and Roland might be used. Why did Julius Diamond agree to it? What hold could they possibly have on him to make him sacrifice his own daughter?

I had a sudden thought: I had just traded one cage for another. "You may have me here, but I'll do everything I can to stop this farce, even if it means my death."

Regina Clubb surveyed me, her eyes narrowing. "Which may come sooner than you think. The District Attorney placed a warrant for your arrest, claiming your flight proof of guilt."

I stared at her in shock. "You really believe I set a bomb in the zeppelin carrying my dearest friend?"

"They'll believe whatever I tell them."

I felt trapped. "What is it you want?"

"I want you to stop this opposition to Lance's courtship of Gardena Diamond."

"Why? So you can have the wedding, after which time Gardena has an 'unfortunate accident'? Whatever Gardena may have done before she knew me, I will not see her used this way."

Mrs. Clubb's eyes and nose reddened. "You truly believe we would murder a girl our son loves just to claim her child? You must think we're as monstrous as Roy Spadros!"

I snorted in disgust. "All you ever said was 'Nina, stand straight,' or 'Nina, be quiet.' 'How will I find her a suitor?' was all you cared about. You hated everything about her, did everything you could to keep her from happiness. And now she's dead!"

She rested her face in her hands, and when she raised her head again, her eyes were full of tears. "Do you remember the high tea you and Molly Spadros came to? You were a young girl."

I was fourteen. Eight months had passed since that glorious summer afternoon, and I hadn't seen Nina since. Molly led me to a woman wearing the latest fashion who looked at least ten years my elder, perhaps twenty. "I'm sure you remember Nina Clubb."

Too thin, her lackluster hair crimped and bleached, her skin sallow. Dark circles lay under her eyes.

I stared at her in horror. Oh, Nina, what have they done to you?

"We left the next day for Azimoff."

"I don't understand."

"Her kidneys failed."

I stared at her in shock. Nina was sick, and I never knew?

"Azimoff has the best doctors in Merca," she said, as if I didn't already know. "The only hope was for her to be placed into a mechanism for eighteen hours a day to cleanse her blood." Mrs. Clubb shook her head. "Needles in her arms, legs ... poor girl, she had a horror of needles from the time she was a small child.

"At first, Nina screamed in terror every day, but gradually, she seemed to accept her lot. She grew stronger. But we couldn't stay there, and she couldn't return to Bridges. We tried everything. The Cultural Correctness Committee has overlooked Alex's arm, but they couldn't accept this ... machine-life. They said it was unnatural, threatened to expose us to the whole city." She put her face in her hands. "We wrote every day, visited the very next weekend. We thought she was improving. But one day Nina rose from the machine when her duty was done, told her nurse she was taking a walk, went to the roof, and flung herself from it."

I gasped.

Mrs. Clubb nodded, her face pensive. "We should have told you what happened. You were just a child — I didn't know you cared so much about her."

I did. I loved her more than anything.

I stared at my hands. "I'm sorry."

When she spoke again, her voice had softened. "I see now why Gardena Diamond no longer trusts us." She twisted her wedding ring, gazing at it. "I promise we mean Gardena no harm." She looked up at me. "What possible benefit could we get by throwing away an alliance with the Diamonds? They'd go to war if anything happened to her. We have much more to fear from this match than Gardena does."

I hadn't considered this aspect of the matter.

"Gardena will no longer see Lance, nor will she speak with us. Please, we must have your support. In return, the Clubb Family will support you during your trial." She smiled, amused. "After all, you did risk your life to warn us."

I wanted Tony to meet his son, have a happy life with Gardena. The last thing I wanted was for Gardena and her son to get mixed up with the Clubbs. "Why can't you just let me leave?"

Mrs. Clubb sighed. "We don't just let anyone leave, Mrs. Spadros. Everyone pays, one way or the other. Are you offering something in return?"

"Are you asking me to betray my Family?"

"I'm not asking you to do anything. I'm merely reminding you that the Clubb Family doesn't run a poorhouse. How will you pay for the privilege of getting on a zeppelin? What could you offer us to make it worth implicating ourselves? The District Attorney knows you're here. He believes you guilty for the murder of hundreds. He wants you hanged."

Why? How could Mr. Freezout dare to threaten the wife of the Spadros heir? Someone must be paying him an enormous amount to make the danger worthwhile.

My plan only worked if I disappeared, so Tony could make a show of searching for me. By now the entire city knew I was here.

Roy might choose to overlook this, if only to torture Tony more. But neither of them could be seen helping me. Sawbuck ... Tony's men ... the staff ... they would never forgive what I did. I publicly betrayed the Family; they would demand my death.

If Tony or Roy helped me now, their men would cut them down, the same as their father before them.

Other than Jon and Gardena, the Diamonds had little love for me. Except perhaps for their mother, Rachel — although in her condition, she could do little more than she had already. The Diamonds would hardly risk war with Spadros by supporting me.

And I suspected that going to the Harts would bring a new

assortment of problems. Since Joe was under Hart protection, Tony, if not Roy, had cause to demand reparations for Joe's "insult" from Hart quadrant — or even attack.

Mrs. Clubb's voice startled me. "Mrs. Spadros, I want to help you. We mean you no harm. We wish Gardena and Roland only the best. I'll even give a token of goodwill: the name of your Pot rag's murderer."

I sat up, focused on her. Perhaps I shouldn't have drunk the entire flask. "You know who killed Marja?"

"Indeed. We've found many names for this woman. Most call her Black Maria —"

Black Maria was another name for The Queen of Spades. So this woman claimed control of the quadrant? I wondered what Molly would think of that.

"Others call her The Little Bird, but it's by no means an endearment. Everyone fears her. She's taken over a gang in Spadros called The High-Low Split —"

A shock went through me. The children's street gang I belonged to when I lived in the Pot.

"— and killed many of those who opposed her. She consorts with a notorious rake calling himself Frank Pagliacci. But it's an alias; there's no one registered with that name. We think she's involved with a group he runs called the Red Dogs. This woman pulled the trigger on your friend; we have a witness to it."

I nodded, feeling melancholy. "Perhaps my age, with pale skin and black hair. I suspected as much."

Regina shrugged. "Ah, well."

My vision blurred. *Marja.*

And now, Joe.

Joe was dead. He had to be. Nothing would have kept him from my side once he learned I was here But he hadn't even sent a message. "Let this DA kill me, then. Why should I care whether I live or die? I have no Family. I have no home. I have no future."

"Oh, my dear girl," she said. "You're mistaken. You're talented, beautiful, and brave. You're a formidable enemy, but I'd prefer to be friends."

They don't as much as breathe without it being part of some intrigue, Tony had said at the Grand Ball.

Did I dare trust Regina Clubb?

I had bet everything ... and lost. If I wanted to avoid being torn by angry mobs or sent to the gallows, I needed them. "I only ask that my husband be allowed to see his son."

Startled, she gave me a long look, as if re-evaluating the situation, then strode to the door. "It's settled then." She faced me with a smile, but her smile made me uneasy. "It'll be a pleasure working together."

Settled? Working together? I rose. Even half drunk, I could tell something wasn't right. "Wait. What's to become of me?"

Still smiling, she crossed her arms, leaning against the door frame, regarded me with fondness. "The Floorman has truly blessed us. You're exactly what we need."

"I don't understand."

She uncrossed her arms, moving a step towards me. Her motions were graceful, serene. But a hint of sharp resentment lay under her words. "The Clubbs have always been seen as the dumb farmers, the quadrant of outsiders, the dirty greedy spies. Now **you're** here: Mrs. Jacqueline Spadros. The Spadros Family couldn't protect you — but we can! People will flock to Clubb quadrant, will open their doors to our influence, will even fight for our side, once they see how strong, how kind, how generous and merciful we are, even going so far as to defend a Pot rag —"

I flinched.

"— who the city believes destroyed our livelihood." She smiled gleefully, but it was unpleasant. "And not one of the Families will lift a finger against us!"

Me, the Clubb Family's winning card?

And I had just handed myself over to them.

I began to feel afraid. "Where are you taking me?"

"Not far: to Clubb Manor." She relaxed, her manner inviting. "You'll love it. You'll have your choice of rooms as our most beloved guest. You room next to our Inventor if you prefer. Lori's eager to know you better." She spoke as if our meeting had gone exactly the way she wanted it to. "You'll make a valuable addition to our intelligence service once you've been properly trained. It'll be much more rewarding work than finding cats and following philanderers." She tapped her temple with enthusiasm. "I believe that what's inside your head —"

Inventor Call's joy at my map of the Cathedral flashed through my mind. Was that what the Clubbs wanted? Access to the Cathedral's secrets?

"— is more valuable than you know —"

Wait, I thought. I do know something she doesn't.

"— This could save our city. And as long as you're with us, you'll never want for anything again."

Instead of no choice, I was suddenly presented with three. But I felt uneasy, hesitant. "If I told you what I know, would you let me leave?"

At this, Regina put her hand to her chin; her gaze turned inward. Then she nodded. "If what you told us was helpful. You could write a goodbye letter to Gardena, telling her you've reconsidered and wish her happiness with my son. We could tell the DA we interrogated you and found no evidence of crime."

I stared at my hands. The thought of betraying my people like this made me ill. I'd not only have to lie to Gardena, I'd be betraying Tony all over again. And the Clubbs could still broadcast to the city that they helped me.

I'd be free. But I would regret this the rest of my life.

I forced my face to reveal nothing. They were desperate. "What if what I knew wasn't enough?"

She shrugged. "My dear, competent farmers use everything they have on hand to their advantage. We'd like your knowledge, but if you hold something back, as I suspect you will, it doesn't matter. It wouldn't matter even if you chose not to tell us anything. Your friends in the Cathedral would give much, I think, not to see you harmed." She gave a dismissive wave of her hand. "You've agreed to help us with Gardena. As long as you hold up your end of the bargain, my offer of aid at your trial still stands."

Outrage surged through me. I was one of the Dealers' Daughters! Did she think I would open the Cathedral to blackmail? Use me as a knife at their throats — forever? I pictured myself — in a golden cage this time — being combed and dressed like a mannequin until my death.

I would die before I let this happen.

I stalked over, grabbed Mrs. Clubb by the arms and shook her. "The ONLY man I EVER loved is DEAD!"

She recoiled, face pale, eyes wide.

Mrs. Clubb was afraid of me!

Three men burst into the room, guns drawn.

The whole world went silent.

I remembered Tony's words: *The servants love you.*

The people love you.

Not the Family.

Me.

They'll believe whatever I tell them.

Not three choices. Four.

I could play this game too.

"Mrs. Clubb, I may be a Pot rag, but by the gods, I'm from the **Spadros** Pot." I dragged her to the window, opened the curtain, and showed her the mass of reporters below. "The only way you'll take me to Clubb Manor is bound and gagged. Or I'll scream for help everywhere we go. Flock to you? They'll flock to Clubb quadrant, all right. When my people hear you're 'holding me against my will,' you'll have war."

I gripped her arms, enjoying the pain in her eyes. "You want me to trust you? You terrorized and abandoned your own daughter, just —" I barely stopped myself. *Just like Ma did.* "I'll see Bridges burn before I become your puppet."

I shoved her aside. "I don't care if you, this DA, or anyone else murders me."

Mrs. Clubb glanced at the three men, shook her head. They retreated, shut the door. When she next spoke, she sounded weary. "It's house arrest or the Prison. Where will you go? Spadros Manor?" She handed over a letter:

Do what you wish.

Anthony Spadros

Seeing the name he hated so much written in his handwriting

cut my heart. Did he know she would show this to me?

I can't always be your Tony. These days, I must be Anthony, heir to the Spadros Family. And that man must be cruel if we're to survive.

No less than I deserve, I thought. My sweet Tony ... I was cruel to you as well.

"From your husband's note —" For a moment, Mrs. Clubb faltered. "— I'm not certain he wants you back."

*Did you **ever** love me, Jacqui?*

I must steel my heart, I thought. I can't weaken now.

The Spadros Family killed Joe, and I must never forgive them. I took a deep breath. "Good, because I'm not going back." I stared out at the mass of reporters. This was the only way I could keep my people safe and still give Tony a chance at happiness. "I have a property. I can go there."

"Spadros quadrant? You're not worried about your safety?"

I shrugged. "You're the one who needs me alive."

She peered at me. "And you won't oppose the courtship."

I began to laugh. "No, I won't oppose your precious courtship."

She didn't look convinced.

I held up my hands. "May the Dealer burn my cards if I speak another word against it."

That situation was in Tony's hands now. If he didn't take this chance to win back Gardena and Roland, he didn't deserve them.

Mrs. Clubb nodded warily. "Very well, then. I'll see if your property will be acceptable. And I'll speak with Mr. Diamond about your husband's son."

I snorted. "So you had no power to promise anything."

Mrs. Clubb left, closing the door behind her.

One of the reporters pointed up at me, and I posed for their cameras, waving from my window with a smile I didn't feel.

The Resolve

Eventually maids came in and out, cleaning, bringing food and more blessed drink. They drew my bath and got me ready to travel. A doctor examined me without even introducing himself, then spoke to Mrs. Clubb. What he found, I never knew.

I didn't care.

The Spadros Family had trapped me, enslaved me, and killed the only man I'd ever loved. I could never forgive any of it.

I pictured David Bryce forever rocking; his brothers Air and Herbert, both dead. And I thought of Josie, Eleanora, Madame Biltcliffe, and Vig Vikenti, who had each suffered so much — because of me.

* * *

That afternoon, the Clubbs — with tremendous fanfare — took me to my apartments through throngs of shouting men. Amelia was there with food and wine. My tenants and housekeeper had fled, so after Amelia went home to her family, I sat alone.

I'd chosen a furnished room facing the street, which had yet to be leased. I opened the window, drew back the curtains, and sat, feet on the windowsill, drinking wine in the darkness.

Trash littered the narrow street. The barricades stood silent. Past them, armed men wearing the dark blue uniforms of the

Court stood guard. One by one, the lights in the other houses went out as crickets sang.

The moon rose.

The whole city knew I was here. If Joe were alive, he would come to me now. He'd find a way to sneak past, or failing that, demand entry loudly enough for me to hear. Joe wasn't the most intelligent man, but he was cunning: if there was any possible way to reach me, he'd devise it.

He never arrived.

* * *

The next day, Honor brought my large white bird cage and its stand. My little bird lay bound with bandages, its eyes closed, its small chest heaving. "Mr. Anthony found it on the veranda, mum," he said. "Clawed by a cat. Dr. Salmon bound its wings so it could heal. We thought you might want to tend it."

I nodded, and he stood the too-large cage in the corner of my room. After he left, I opened the cage door to stroke its head, dribble water into its little mouth. It drank greedily.

I rested my forehead on the white wires. No matter what I did to help, it made things worse. "You didn't know how to live outside. All I wanted was for you to be free."

I was as free as I could be under house arrest in Spadros quadrant. But would someone kill me, or would I find this Black Maria first?

My talk with Mrs. Clubb had gained much. I knew where to look: the Spadros Pot. I knew many members of the High-Low Split. Someone would help me locate this false Queen of Spades who killed Marja. Morton could identify her. And when I found Black Maria, she would die.

If Roy Spadros or Jack Diamond or anyone else killed me first, then Joe and I would be together. Either way, I was free.

At this thought, my fear vanished.

That night, I resolved that whatever happened, I would never step back into Spadros Manor again.

~ This ends Chapter 3 of the Red Dog Conspiracy ~

Appendix

The Four Families

(Those members named)
Spadros

Motto: We never changed our name
The Spadros family has been in Bridges since the raising of the dome, being among the original laborers brought in to work on the project.

Patriarch: Roy Spadros (wife: Molly, daughter: Katherine)
Heir: Anthony (Tony) Spadros (wife: Jacqueline)

Other Son: Roy Acevedo Spadros (deceased)

Inventor: Maxim Call
Monte, his Apprentice

Retainers:
John Pearson, butler (wife: Jane, daughter: Mary)
Peter Dewey, stable-man (wife: Amelia, son: Pip)
Skip Honor, day footman
Blitz Spadros, night footman
Jacob Michaels, manservant
Dr. Salmon, private surgeon
Anne, Mistress of Kitchens
Monsieur, chef
Rocket, a bomb-sniffer dog
Poignee, kitchen maid (deceased)
Ottilie, kitchen maid (deceased)
Treysa, kitchen maid (deceased)

Business:
Sawbuck (Ten Hogan), Tony's right hand man
Duck, Associate (deceased)

Diamond

Motto: Diamonds protect their own

A large group of immigrant workers from the South African diamond mines settled in Bridges in the early 1500s AC. Proud of their unique identity, this disparate group of families began to call themselves "Diamonds" and exclusively intermarry.

Patriarch: Julius Diamond (wife: Rachel)
Heir: Cesare Diamond

Other Sons:
Jack Roland Diamond III (Black Jack, Mad Jack)
Jonathan Courtenay Diamond, his twin brother

Daughter:
Gardena Diamond

Retainer:
Daniel, manservant (deceased)

Others:
Octavia Diamond, a nanny
Roland, a small boy

Hart

Motto: Ready for anything

Descended from Appalachian and Chinese workers, Crispin Hartmann led one of the early street gangs of the 1700's. This gang called themselves the Harts and were a major player in the looting and other unpleasant acts seen during the Coup.

Patriarch: Charles Hart (wife: Judith)
Heir (and Inventor): Etienne Hart (wife: Helen)

Under protection:
Joseph Kerr
Josephine Kerr, his twin sister
Polansky Kerr IV, their grandfather
Marja, their housekeeper (deceased)
Daisy, a maid

Clubb

Motto: A golden harvest

Clover Banditerna was a worker on a farm near the zeppelin station until the Alcatraz Coup. Seeing an opportunity, he and his fellow workers called themselves the Clubbs Of Justice and seized the station, along with the controls to the Aperture.

Realizing no one could go in or out of the city without going through them, the group charged exorbitant rates and became extremely rich.

After the Coup, Clover Banditerna changed his name, calling himself Johnny Clubb.

Patriarch: Alexander Clubb (wife: Regina)
Heir: Lancelot Clubb

Inventor: Lori Cuarenta

Daughters:
Nina Clubb (deceased)
Kitty Clubb

Other players

Spadros quadrant

Dame Anastasia Louis, aristocrat and gemologist (deceased)
Eleanora Bryce, a widow
Nicholas (Nick, Air), her son (deceased)
Herbert Bryce, her son (deceased)
David Bryce, her son
Madame Marie Biltcliffe, a dress shop owner
Tenni, her shop maid
Vig Vikenti, a saloon owner
Peedro Sluff, a liquor store owner

Market Center

Bridges Daily, a newspaper
Acol Durak, the former editor (deceased)
Paul Blackberry, the current editor
Doyle Pike, a lawyer
Thrace Pike, a law clerk, Doyle's grandson
Paix Hanger, a policeman

Other/Unknown

Fanny Kaplan (Ma), a brothel owner
The Masked Man, her patron
The Travelers' Federation, an organization
The Red Dogs, a children's street gang
Stephen Rivers, a Red Dogs "chip" (deceased)
Clover, a Red Dogs "ace"
Master Blaze Rainbow (Morton), a gentleman
Zia Cashout, a rogue Federal Agent
Golden Bridges, a tabloid
Frank Pagliacci, a scoundrel
Birdie, a black-haired woman

Acknowledgments

Many people have helped me with this book, and I'd like to thank them. I appreciate the beta reader input from Tasha Reese, Corwin Loofbourrow, and Lenka Trnkova. I'd also like to thank Erin Hartshorn for her meticulous proofreading and Anita Carroll for her gorgeous cover design.

My street team, The Commission, helped get this book series into your hands! If you'd like to join The Commission, visit my website at JacqOfSpades.com and sign up to the newsletter.

Special thanks to my Patrons:

Dave Kobrenski

Cristina

Nancy

Phoebe Darqueling

Eirlys Evans

Rachel Heslin

Julian White

Melissa Williams

Follow the Red Dog Conspiracy on Patreon

patreon.com/red_dog_conspiracy

About the Author

Patricia Loofbourrow is a writer, gardener, artist, musician, poet, wildcrafter, and married mother of three who loves power tools, dancing, genetics, and anything to do with outer space. She also has an MD. Heinlein would be proud.

You can follow her at:
- Her website JacqOfSpades.com
- Twitter @Jacq_Of_Spades
- Tumblr red-dog-conspiracy.tumblr.com
- The Red Dog Conspiracy Facebook page.

Note from the Author

Thanks so much for reading *The Ace of Clubs*. If you liked the book, please contact me, or leave a review where you bought this!

The King of Hearts

Now Available

**What if the person who hated you most
was the only one who could save you?**

Thousands of gentlemen have gone bankrupt across the city of Bridges and trouble brews between the Diamond and Spadros crime families. Yet the city is united in its desire to exact vengeance for those murdered in the zeppelin bombing.

Penniless and alone, private eye Jacqueline Spadros confronts the lowest point of her life. Seen as an accomplice in the financial crisis and accused of a crime she didn't commit, Jacqui faces trial in front of a hostile jury — and could receive the death penalty.

Jacqui knows she's been framed for the bombing by the illusive Red Dog Gang. But will the jury believe her?

Part 4 of the Red Dog Conspiracy

Learn more at

JacqOfSpades.com

www.ingramcontent.com/pod-product-compliance
Lightning Source LLC
Chambersburg PA
CBHW050514190726